"I am Rajan."

A deep voice, edged with a soft, husky tone, and an accent that was English and exotic all at the same time. She took another step forward, and the glare of the sun moved into shadow, revealing him to her.

Long, dark hair curling to just below his shoulders framed a face that was all chiseled planes, softened by the lush curve of his mouth as he smiled at her. Teeth so white and perfect. Dazzling. His eyes were dark, nearly black. Skin the color of dark honey, and so smooth. Touchable. She flexed her fingers.

He rose to his feet, every motion graceful, and towered over her five-foot-four frame. She felt small, delicate in his presence. He moved toward her, one hand outstretched. "You must be Lillian."

"Lilli, please." Why was her throat so dry? He was only a man.

But no, that was a lie. He was the most spectacularly beautiful man she had ever seen. Far too perfect for her. But her skin was alive, tingly, simply looking at him.

In a moment he was in front of her, that smile making her light-headed as her blood rushed through her veins. She had to look beyond him for a moment, to the view of the rugged, dusky gray mountains like paper cutouts against the backdrop of stark blue sky. She had to catch her breath.

Her breath went right out of her when he touched her hand. Like fire. Like electricity on her skin. Was it only her nerves that were making her react like this?

"Come and sit by the water with me. It's cool out here."

His fingers folded around hers and her skin went hot beneath his touch as she followed him across the terrace. She couldn't speak, could barely think. She'd never been so stunned by the mere presence of another person in her life.

Calm down.

EXOTICA

Seven Days of Kama Sutra,

Nine Days of Arabian Nights

Eden Bradley

DELTA TRADE PAPERBACKS

EXOTICA
A Delta Trade Paperback / January 2008

Published by Bantam Dell
A Division of Random House, Inc.
New York, New York

Book design by Glen Edelstein

Delta is a registered trademark of Random House, Inc., and the
colophon is a trademark of Random House, Inc.

Library of Congress Cataloging in Publication Data
Bradley, Eden.
Exotica: seven days of Kama Sutra, nine days of Arabian nights /
Eden Bradley.
p. cm.
ISBN-13: 978-0-553-38510-6 (trade pbk.: alk. paper)
I. Title.
PS3602.R34266E96 2008
813'.6—dc22
2007034797

Printed in the United States of America
Published simultaneously in Canada

www.bantamdell.com

BVG   10 9 8 7 6 5 4 3 2 1

To B., with all my love

Acknowledgments

Exotica could not have been written without the sturdy and endless support of my divas, especially the chat-room-challenge divas, who helped me through a very rough time during the writing of this book, in particular: Miranda Heart, Sela Carsen, Nonny Morgan, Haven Rich, Emily Ryan-Davis, Kate Willoughby, and everyone who came in on the tail end of this and cheered me on.

Special thanks to my dear friends Crystal Jordan and Lillian Feisty, who listened to me whine, brainstormed with me, and read various bits and pieces as I went. Very special thanks to my darling R. G. Alexander, who was with me every step of the way, who was as in love with my heroes as I was, and who read draft after draft of this book. To my critique partner, Gemma Halliday—I'm still pretty sure the heavens would come crashing down if I sent a manuscript out without you looking at it first. And finally to my editor, Shauna Summers, whose amazing insights guided me in making this book everything it needed to be. Thank you!

EXOTICA

PART ONE

Seven Days of Kama Sutra

11.

Live the Fantasy

EXOTICA

**An exclusive fantasy resort set in the sultry warmth of
Palm Springs. The place for a woman to experience her
most secret desires in a safe, discreet environment,
surrounded by sheer luxury.
Choose your dream theme from among our five
Ultimate Fantasy worlds:**

- *Casablanca:* Live the glamorous and seductive era of the
  1940s.
- *Wild, Wild West:* Guaranteed to be the wild experience of a
  lifetime.
- *The Castle:* The romance of medieval times brought to life.
- *Pirate's Cove:* A pirate adventure you'll never forget.
- *Kama Sutra:* The ultimate in exotic fantasy.

**And coming soon: *Arabian Nights:*
The sensual luxury of a sultan's palace.
Relax in absolute privacy at one of the world's
finest luxury resorts.**

Come to EXOTICA, and live the fantasy. . . .

THE LIMOUSINE SPED THROUGH the desert, the sleek length of it gliding like a snake across the hot sand. Heat shimmered on the highway, the glare of the sun warming the darkened windows of the car, even though the air-conditioning kept the limo at a comfortable seventy-five degrees inside. Still, Lilli's hands were damp as, for the tenth time that morning, she looked over the brochure her friend Caroline Winter had sent her.

They'd hardly spoken the last several years, but they'd found each other through their college alumni association last year, just as Lilli was going through her divorce. They'd talked a bit through e-mail, and then by phone. Lilli could hardly believe it when Caroline had admitted what it was she did for a living, managing Exotica. But the idea had become more and more intriguing, until finally, Lilli hadn't been able to resist Caroline's repeated invitations.

Was she really going to this place? Was she actually daring to do this?

She shifted on the leather seat, the smooth surface sticking to her bare legs beneath the linen skirt she wore. She felt naked, somehow, just reading about Exotica, imagining what might happen to her there. Gloriously, yet shamefully, naked. But then, her life was full of contradictions lately, wasn't it? Had been since she'd found out what a sham her marriage was all these years. But that was behind her now, and coming here was a step toward making her new beginning. From now on, her life would be of her own creation, her own choices.

Still, she had to stop and wonder if she'd been completely insane when she'd signed on for this adventure.

Or maybe it was simply old habit, one instilled by Evan, to question herself, to worry.

Stop it.

She tapped her fingers on the armrest, her pulse racing as she stared out the window. Long stretches of sand dunes swept past, punctuated by tall, stately date palms clustered around the entrances to beautifully landscaped homes. She'd always loved Palm Springs; she found the desert soothing, serene. Why did she have a feeling after this adventure, she'd never see the desert in quite the same way again?

The driver's voice came over the intercom. "We're here, Madame."

A pair of enormous iron gates rolled back in front of the car. Imposing. Beautiful. Her stomach gave one hard twist. There was no sign here. The resort was far too exclusive, too discreet for that. Nothing more than those big gates closing it off from the rest of the world. Almost another world in itself.

They drove past sweeping lawns with peacocks wandering beneath the palm trees. Gorgeous hedges of blooming bougainvillea in shades of red and pink climbed the high stone walls on either side. As they pulled up in front of a long, low building, done in the same stone that seemed to blend naturally with the jagged mountain peaks in the distance, she rubbed her damp palms together.

This is it.

The car came to a stop and the brochure fluttered to the floor as the driver opened the door and helped her out. She was breathless, suddenly, standing in the heat and the brilliant sunlight. Dazed.

"Lillian DeForrest! You're here at last."

"Caroline." Lilli looked up to see her approaching,

an attractive woman with long brown hair pulled back into a sleek ponytail. She was dressed in a chic summer dress of white linen. The same beautiful, sculpted face and striking blue eyes she remembered. Caroline had hardly changed at all since they'd met in college.

Her friend leaned in and gave her a hug, enveloping her in warm, spicy scent. She stood back, and Caroline smiled at her. "Welcome to Exotica."

"It's so good to see you. You look wonderful."

"So do you. All that curly strawberry hair of yours; I've always loved it, and you still look like you're nineteen years old. How many years has it been since we've seen each other? But come inside. It's too warm today to stand out here in the sun."

She followed Caroline up a wide, shallow staircase and into the cool interior of the building. Inside, it was all sparse, calm elegance. High ceilings made the space feel airy. Polished tile floors led to a high, curved reception desk made of some light-colored wood.

An attractive young woman greeted Lilli from behind it. "Welcome, Ms. DeForrest."

"Samantha, please see that Ms. DeForrest's luggage is sent to the Kama Sutra suite."

"Yes, Caroline. Right away."

"Would you like to see a little of the grounds before I take you to your suite?"

"I'd love to. This place is . . . intriguing."

Caroline smiled at her. "Come with me, then."

She led her across the cool expanse of tiled floor, beyond the reception desk, down a wide hallway, and through a pair of French doors at the back of the building.

Dazzled by sunlight, Lilli pulled her sunglasses from

her purse and slid them onto her face. In front of her was the brilliant green of a wide, sweeping lawn with meandering pathways twisting beneath the towering palms. Bordering the lawn were high walls, punctuated by gates in various styles. And in the center an enormous rectangular pool of calm water sparkled in the sunlight. Bronze statues of male nudes done in classical Greek style stood sentry at each corner. They were graceful. Erotic. A faint pulse of heat beat deep in Lilli's body, just looking at these statues, thinking about what she was doing here.

Caroline made a sweeping gesture. "Exotica is very much like an adult Disneyland. Each of our fantasy suites are like tiny cities done in different themes, with servants' quarters, background players, the appropriate architectural details. See there? You can see the tower of the Medieval Castle over the wall. That's our largest section, where guests share the main castle with each other, so there's an entire royal court going on all the time. It's very popular."

Lilli followed Caroline's gesture and saw what appeared to be ancient stone parapets that could have belonged to King Arthur, with colorful flags flying in the slight breeze.

"It's beautiful. Amazing really."

"We do everything we can to make the fantasy as real as possible, to make it all come alive. We want you to immerse yourself. That's why our companions work on bimonthly rotations, with thorough medical checks in between. Condoms break the fantasy far too easily. All of the men here are clean, so our clients never have to worry."

Lilli shook her head, her pulse fluttering. "You seem

to have thought of everything. It's so ... strange that you can talk about such things so matter-of-factly. And I can hardly believe I'm here. That a place like this exists." She laughed. "That you work here, run this place."

"Sometimes I can hardly believe it myself." Caroline shrugged. "But it's just my life now. And after your first night here, you'll hardly be able to remember your life anywhere else."

A small shiver went through her at Caroline's words. What was she so afraid of?

Caroline put a hand on her arm. "Don't worry, Lilli. He won't do anything you don't want him to do."

"Oh God. That word. 'Him.' That makes it seem all the more real, for some reason." A small trickle of perspiration ran down the back of her neck.

"Why don't you come back inside and relax, maybe have some iced tea before you meet him?"

"Yes, I'd like that. I feel like I need to ... to catch my breath. Do you have time to sit with me? Talk with me?"

"Of course. We can get caught up. And I'll answer any questions I can. Come."

Caroline led her back into the artificially chilled interior of the reception building, but this time she took her into her private office. It was as open and airy as the reception area had been, with tall banks of tinted windows overlooking the lawns. Caroline gestured to a pair of creamy leather couches, but Lilli paced the floor instead, gazing out the window, as Caroline went to the intercom on her sleek glass-topped desk to ring for drinks.

"Lilli, you're as wound up as a clock. Come sit down with me on the sofa and tell me what I can do to make you more comfortable."

"I ... I'm not sure. This sounded so wonderful when

you first told me about it. Okay, a little...fantastical, maybe." She settled on the plush sofa, sinking into the soft leather. "After you explained it to me, after I thought about it, I realized it was exactly what I've needed. But now that I'm here it's a bit intimidating, the idea of being with a man." She let out a small, harsh laugh. "I'll be forty in a few weeks. No one but my husband has seen me naked for years. My ex-husband. And Evan was never... very kind in his evaluation of the way I looked."

"You didn't deserve that," Caroline said, her voice low, a small edge of anger there.

"No, maybe not. But here I am, nonetheless, about to face my fortieth birthday and not feeling great about myself. Part of what I'd like to accomplish this week is to feel more confident. Less hard on myself. More feminine, if that makes sense. But the hardest part for me is the idea of just...letting go, you know?"

Caroline nodded and said quietly, "I think I do."

"Do you...have you ever become involved with any of the men here?"

"What? No, of course not."

"Why 'of course not'?"

Caroline shifted in her seat. "I have to maintain a certain professional distance. It helps me to do my job with a clear head."

"I guess that makes sense." Lilli paused. How could anyone work in such a place and remain so unaffected by what went on here? "Is it because...of what happened with Jeff? That ability to distance yourself?"

Caroline blinked, looked away.

"I'm sorry, Caroline. It's not my place to bring that up."

"No. It's fine. There's no one else anymore who even

knows about that part of my life, other than you. It's been five years. It's long behind me." She paused, smoothed a hand over her already perfectly sleek hair. "I think I get that ability to detach from my mother. You met her when we were in college. You know how cold she was."

Lilli could see the belying flush on her friend's cheeks. "I'm sorry," she said again. "Yes, I know how your mother was. It's just that, after that . . . episode with Jeff, and even more, what happened with Sarah, you really shut down, distanced yourself from everyone for a long time. Not that you didn't have every right to. I know it's none of my business . . ."

"No, it's alright. There isn't anyone else I can talk to about it. And it's been so good talking with you this last year, reconnecting. I've needed a friend."

"So have I." Lilli smiled.

"Go on then," Caroline urged her, even as her fingers twisted together in her lap.

"It just seems to me that maybe your detachment from what goes on here generates from that experience. Because I know I couldn't be so cool, so removed, working here. I don't know how anyone could be, surrounded by all of this. By the men, frankly."

Caroline gave her a wan smile. "Well, maybe that just makes me the perfect person for the job."

"Maybe." But Lilli wasn't so sure of that.

A soft knock at the door and a uniformed maid brought in a tray with two tall glasses of iced tea, a small bowl of sugar, and another full of lemon slices.

"Thank you, Marcy." Caroline held a glass out to Lilli, then took one for herself and squeezed a lemon wedge into it.

Lilli sipped her tea. "I just wish I could calm down and relax."

"It's natural to be a little nervous. This isn't the sort of thing most people do every day."

"It's definitely not an everyday occurrence in my life. I haven't even dated since I left Evan. How do I do this? How do I let go and just . . . experience whatever's offered?"

"Rajan will help you. He's one of our best."

"Rajan?" Lilli's stomach knotted, hot and tight. "Is that his name? The man who will be my . . . companion?"

"Your Kama Sutra lover."

Lilli took a long drink from her glass, trying to cool the blood racing fast and furious through her veins. "Oh God. I'm really doing this, aren't I?"

Caroline nodded, smiling at her. "Are you ready to see your suite? To meet him?"

"I think so." Lilli pulled in a long breath, blew it out. "Yes. I'm ready."

Caroline stood, offered Lilli a hand. "Good. I'll take you to the Kama Sutra suite. To your fantasy."

Back out in the bright sunlight, they climbed into a white golf cart and followed one of the paths across the lawn. When they reached a pair of heavy iron scroll-work gates, a guard nodded them through. Instantly the air felt different. More moist, sultry. Dense, tropical foliage crowded the edges of the narrow, pebbled path and the scent of flowers was heavy in the air.

The cart rounded a turn in the path and Lilli caught her breath as a structure came into view. A long, narrow pool of pure blue water led to what appeared to be a small reproduction of the Taj Mahal, complete with graceful minarets and domes, and walls inlaid with calligraphy and flowering patterns of colored stones.

"I've never seen such a beautiful place."

Caroline stopped the golf cart at the front entrance. "The designers really outdid themselves, didn't they? I'll take you inside."

They got out and walked up a short tiled path to an open archway. Lilli put her hand out to touch the carved stone of a pillar, then pulled back. "I'm sorry. It's just that everything is so unbelievably gorgeous. Like something out of a dream."

"A fantasy, Lilli." Caroline smiled at her. "And it's alright. You can touch it. You can touch anything you like here."

Lilli turned back to the column, laid her fingers against the surface. She was surprised at how soft it was, almost like soapstone. And the jewels set into the carving looked like real jasper, rubies, sapphires.

"Incredible," she whispered.

"There's more." Caroline parted the dark red silk curtains hanging like a sheer mist across the entrance and they walked through.

Inside was a private garden courtyard, surrounded on all four sides by the walls of the building. Clusters of date palms stood here and there, glorious flowering vines climbed everywhere, and bird cages stood on pedestals amidst the lush vegetation. Greens in every shade, splashes of red, pink, gold, and the sweet perfume of exotic flowers surrounded her. The delicate strains of sitar music floated on the air.

Caroline guided her along the path, up a shallow flight

of steps and into what appeared to be an enormous bedroom.

Yes, exactly like a dream.

There were few solid walls, just the silk-curtained
archways. The floors were gorgeous, interlocking tiles in
a complicated pattern. In the middle of the room stood
an enormous bed on a high, carved teak platform. The
four intricately carved posts were draped with lengths of
embroidered silk, the bed piled high with pillows in
every shade of the sunset and sunrise: pinks, oranges,
reds, ambers. On a low table inlaid with mother-of-pearl
stood a silver burner full of incense; the smoke smelled
like pure sex to her.

She turned to Caroline. "This is too lovely."

Caroline nodded. "I knew you'd like it. I should go
now. Rajan is waiting for you on the terrace. Will you be
alright?"

Lilli nodded, her neck tight as piano wire, her palms
damp. She felt like some shy schoolgirl. She was being
ridiculous, but she couldn't seem to calm down.

"Thank you, Caroline."

Her friend gave her a quick hug. "Call me if you need
anything."

Lilli nodded, watched as Caroline left. Then she
turned to face the open archway leading to the outer
terrace.

He was on the other side.

She set her purse down on a small table, smoothed
out her linen skirt, which suddenly felt too heavy on her
skin. She tucked a strand of her curling hair behind one
ear. And went to meet her Kama Sutra lover.

Pulling the curtain aside, Lilli stepped through, onto

the tiled mosaic floor. The sun was softer here, filtered by the silk drapes fluttering at the edges of the terrace. The sun shone through the silk, casting shadows in red and gold everywhere.

At first all she could see was his silhouette against the sun, the shifting colors of the silk playing over his skin. He was long and lean, resting on the raised edge of a pool of water, a tiered fountain making music from the center of the pool. He was shirtless, and she could make out the rounded curve of wide shoulders, strong, muscular arms.

She swallowed hard.

"I am Rajan."

A deep voice, edged with a soft husky tone, and an accent that was English and exotic all at the same time. She took another step forward, and the glare of the sun moved into shadow, revealing him to her.

Long dark hair curling to just below his shoulders framed a face that was all chiseled planes, softened by the lush curve of his mouth as he smiled at her. Teeth so white and perfect. Dazzling. His eyes were dark, nearly black. Skin the color of dark honey, and so smooth. Touchable. She flexed her fingers.

He rose to his feet, every motion graceful, and towered over her five-foot-four frame. She felt small, delicate in his presence. He moved toward her, one hand outstretched. "You must be Lillian."

"Lilli, please." Why was her throat so dry? He was only a man.

But no, that was a lie. He was the most spectacularly beautiful man she had ever seen. Far too perfect for her. But her skin was alive, tingling, simply looking at him.

In a moment he was in front of her, that smile making her light-headed as her blood rushed through her veins. She had to look beyond him for a moment, to the view of the rugged, dusky gray mountains like paper cutouts against the backdrop of stark blue sky. She had to catch her breath.

Her breath went right out of her when he touched her hand. Like fire. Like electricity on her skin. Was it only her nerves that were making her react like this?

"Come and sit by the water with me. It's cool out here."

His fingers folded around hers and her skin went hot beneath his touch as she followed him across the terrace. She couldn't speak, could barely think. She'd never been so stunned by the mere presence of another person in her life.

Calm down.

He led her to the edge of the marble pool. The water was blue, sparkling. She watched the play of it in the fountain in the center. Someone had placed handfuls of flower petals there, and they danced as the water moved.

Then his hand was on her chin, lifting her face so she was forced to look into those glittering black eyes.

"Don't look away, Lilli. I want to see you. And you need to see me, to know me. We're going to become very close during our time together. You musn't be afraid."

She blinked up at him. "I'm not. I'm just...you're a little larger than life."

He smiled at her, the corners of that lush mouth lifting a little. His mouth was too beautiful when he smiled. And she was going to touch it. To kiss him.

God.

Too good to contemplate, really. But she needed to calm herself, to let go of her fear, her tension, if she was

going to enjoy this. And he was far too good not to enjoy. She pushed away those old doubts about him not
finding her pretty enough, sexy enough. This was for
her. And he was a hired professional. What he thought
shouldn't matter.

"You're very thoughtful, aren't you, Lilli? I'm not
speaking of being considerate, although I have a feeling
you're that, too. But your mind is working. I can feel it."

"Yes." Heat crept into her cheeks.

"I believe I may have the perfect cure for that."

He moved around behind her, slid his hands over her
shoulders. He was so close she could feel the heat of him
against her back. When he leaned in his breath was
warm in her hair. His voice was low, soft. "Give yourself
over to this, Lilli. To me. I will take care of your every
need, I promise you. And if I don't anticipate something,
all you have to do is ask. But I'll try not to make you
ask. I'll do my best to read you, to know what it is you
desire before you can put it into words."

A shiver ran through her, making gooseflesh rise on
her skin. Yet at the same time, in her mind was the
thought that he said these same words to all of his
clients.

He went on. "You must learn to relax. To let go all of
those thoughts running through your mind, holding you
back from the pleasure of the moment. I'll help you."

His hands slid down her bare arms. His palms warm,
reassuring, and lighting tiny fires of need everywhere he
touched that arrowed down, deep in her belly.

"Will you allow me to do this for you, Lilli?"

God, right now she wanted to allow him to do anything, this total stranger. This beautiful stranger. *Her*
stranger.

Even as her pulse hammered with fear, the word came out on a whisper. "Yes."

"Ah, I knew you could do it." His hands moved back up, and his fingers threaded through her hair. "Such glorious curls," he said. "Like satin. And the sun lights it up in red and gold. Like something precious."

Another long shiver went through her system. She could not believe this was really happening.

He went on, his voice that same low, soothing murmur. "We'll talk later. But for now, I want you to become comfortable with me. To know me. Do you like the water, Lilli?"

"Yes. I love the water."

"Then swim with me."

She nodded. "Just let me get my suit."

"There's no need. It's only the two of us here."

He moved away from her, and she turned just in time to see him untie the strings on his loose linen pants. And nearly gasped aloud when he let them drop to the floor, revealing his naked flesh in all its golden glory.

2.

HE WAS MAGNIFICENT. Her body went warm all over at the sight of him, all of that beautiful honey-dark skin, and his thick, semi-erect cock jutting from a nest of black curls between slim, tapering hips.

Jesus.

Her mouth was actually watering. She swallowed hard.

"Come, join me in the water." He held a hand out to her.

She couldn't move, couldn't think. There was nothing her body wanted more right now than to be naked with him. And the idea of being in the water was sensual, exciting. But could she do this? Could she reveal her body, her self, to a man she'd met only moments ago?

This is what you're here for.

He laid gentle fingertips on the front of her blouse. Even though she could barely feel the weight of his flesh against the fabric, her nipples went hard.

"May I?"

She nodded, and he unbuttoned her blouse, slowly, watching her burning face. She had to look away.

Who was this man she knew nothing about? But it didn't matter, did it? He was here for her. For her pleasure. And he was too beautiful, his touch exquisitely tender.

She looked back at him, into his black eyes. "I've never been handled this way by a man before. As though I were . . . fragile." Why did that make her want to cry?

"Not fragile," he said. "Delicate. There is an intrinsic delicacy about a woman, despite how strong she may be. It is my duty as a man to recognize that, to cherish that which is different between men and women. And if I may say so, Lilli, it is about time someone did that for you."

Every inch of her skin went hot as he spoke, as he slipped the buttons loose one at a time, then slid her blouse from her shoulders. He set it on a padded lounge chair next to them. Then, with almost reverent hands, he unzipped her skirt. She gripped the waistband with her fingers, her body a confused jumble of nerves and desire.

He stopped what he was doing, silently looked at her for permission to continue. It wouldn't have worked nearly so well if he'd pleaded, cajoled. But he simply gave her the time to make it her decision. She took a deep breath and, after a moment, nodded, her fingers loosening their grip on the fabric. He knelt and drew the skirt down over her legs while she tried not to let him see her trembling.

When he stood again before her, he traced his fingertips across her bare shoulder, moved them over her collarbone. She tried to ignore the awareness of her own nearly naked body, revealed to him, with all its imperfections. Imperfections her ex had never failed to point out to her. Never mind that she was almost forty; he'd always expected perfection from her. And she had never, ever managed to deliver.

No, don't think about that now.

"Your skin is so soft," Rajan murmured. "Lovely. Shall we take this off, too?" He touched her bra strap, slid his hand down to the catch at the front of the lacy cups.

She paused as her breath caught in a tight tangle in her chest. Her nipples were hard, wanting.

Yes, just do it.

She nodded, and he smiled as he undid the clasp with one quick motion. The bra fell away. She closed her eyes, the sensation of being so bare before him almost too much. Too exciting, too nerve-wracking. Her sex was damp and aching.

Don't think. Just feel. That's what you're here for, finally.

"Beautiful," he whispered. "So beautiful. Come into the water with me. I need to swim with you."

He took her by the hand, helped her into the pool, which was deeper than it had appeared. She slipped into the water. It was exactly the right temperature, just warm enough to be comfortable on the skin, soothing. He slid in beside her and they floated, watching each other, surrounded by the scattered rose petals spilling from the fountain.

How strange, to be almost naked in the water with this man. This beautiful man. Surreal. She could not believe how badly she wanted him. Yet every muscle in her body was so tightly corded she could barely breathe.

He took her hand under the water and raised it to his lips. They were wet, cool, and so soft against her skin as he kissed her fingers. Her breasts ached.

Yes, to have him touch her, to kiss her there!

He drew her closer. "Anything you want, it shall be yours. Anything. Do you understand, Lilli?"

Her ex-husband had never asked her such a thing. Had she even asked herself? "Yes. I understand. But honestly, I hardly know what it is I want," she admitted. "It's been such a long time since I've had a chance to think about it."

"A woman like you should have whatever you desire. And you will. This is what I am here for. For you. I can see that you're nervous. You don't need to be, truly. Nothing will happen here unless you want it to."

He moved around behind her in the water and whispered almost into her ear, "May I touch you, Lilli? Hold you?"

Her breath hitched, but before she had time to think about what he was asking, she said, "Yes."

He pressed his body against her back. She could feel every hard plane of him. Wanted to feel more. His arm slid around her waist, holding her up, moving a little deeper into the water. He held her there quietly, while she mentally forced her thrumming pulse to calm.

"Just lean into me, Lilli. Let me do it all."

"I'm trying," she murmured.

"Yes. I can see that you are. Try to relax now. Tell me, Lilli, may I touch you?" He paused. "I want to touch you, your lovely skin. But I will do it only with your permission."

"Yes."

The breath really went out of her then. Had she just told this stranger he could put his hands on her? But she wanted him to. She was dying for him to touch her, frankly. She didn't want to fight her need for him, wanted to allow the desire to take over her body, to let her mind go quiet. And she did her best to, as he began to move his hands over her.

He felt like the water itself against her bare flesh, but warmer, more solid. Yet that fluid, as his palms smoothed over her skin: her sides, her stomach, down over the curve of her hips. She was coming alive beneath his hands, and the sense of weightlessness itself was sensual, amplifying his every touch. Her sex ached, clenched with need.

She focused on the solid wall of his muscular frame behind her, the heavy arc of his erection pressing against the small of her back. And when he feathered his fingertips over her breasts, she let out a small gasp.

"Yes, let it happen, Lilli," he murmured. "This is what I am here for; to please you." His fingers grazed the taut peaks of her nipples. "Let me please you. Let me pleasure you."

"Yes..."

Was that her voice, so soft with surrender? But she didn't want to question herself. She wanted—needed—to have this experience with him. And her body was burning, begging for his touch already.

He cupped her breasts in his wide palms. The sensation beneath the water was incredible, so soft, slippery. Desire rippled over her skin. She focused her gaze on the distant mountains as he squeezed gently, kneading her flesh. Sighed when he took her nipples in his fingers and rolled them.

Oh God.

Her stomach tensed as he slid one hand down. She had to fight not to arch her hips into his touch.

What is happening to me?

He paused at the edge of the lace panties he'd left on her. "Tell me you want this, Lilli."

Her sex gave one sharp squeeze, went hot, flooded with need. And at that moment, she gave her body over to the experience, to him. There would be plenty of time to question it all later. "Yes. I want this. Touch me, please, Rajan."

"Your wish is my command."

He moved his hand lower, beneath the lace, and down to the cleft between her thighs. Pleasure shafted through her; the need for release was immediate, overpowering. His fingers played over her flesh, and she pressed her hips into his hand.

"Rajan," she gasped.

"Yes, I know. You need it quickly now, the first time. I will take more time later, I promise. I will teach you the art of the Kama. But for now . . ."

He pressed two fingers inside her and she moaned, pleasure lancing through her body. With his thumb he circled her clitoris. She couldn't stifle her moans.

"It's good, yes?" His voice was still that exotic, husky whisper, his breath warm in her hair. She pressed her body back against his, needing to feel him.

He circled faster, pumped his fingers, angling until he hit her G-spot.

"Oh!" The sharp stab of pleasure was almost shocking; it was that intense, that keen. A wave washed through her, the first wave of orgasm.

"Please," she muttered, not caring that she was begging.

"As you wish, my Lilli."

He moved his hand faster, burying his fingers inside her, pressing against her clit. And she came in a crushing wave, the agonizing ache of desire too long unsated. The water seemed to move around her, to fill her as his hand did. And even as she came, she recognized the sensuality of the water, of his naked flesh against her back, of his hands on her body.

When she stopped trembling he turned her in his arms and she let her head drop against his chest. She felt grateful. Humbled.

And she still wanted him. Needed him inside her.

She looked up at him and blinked. He was smiling down at her. Then he leaned in and brushed her lips with his.

Her voice shook with desire. "Rajan, will you make love to me?"

"It will be my greatest pleasure."

Rajan pulled her from the water, wrapped her in a towel, and lifted her small frame in his arms.

Lord, to have her ask him like this! He was nearly out of his head. He would have to calm down in order to give her what she needed. Something about this woman...

He shouldn't have kissed her. Not that it wasn't al-

lowed. But it was dangerous with Lilli. Powerful. Overwhelming. When had that ever happened before?

He'd found all of his clients attractive in some way.
Until recently. But before this restlessness had set in, he'd
always found something special in each woman, something unique, something to be appreciated. Several he had
even found beautiful. But never had he met a woman
who threatened the utter control he was so proud of.

She weighed nothing. He loved the size of her, the
enormous hazel eyes fringed in dark lashes that made
her seem doll-like. That plush, pink mouth of hers. The
sweet purity of that mouth made him want to do all
sorts of things to it. Push his cock between those baby
lips . . .

He leaned in and kissed her again as he carried her
inside. Impossible not to kiss her. Moving the fragile silk
curtains aside, he laid her on the bed. He immediately
pulled her innocent, pink lace panties off her, dropped
the scrap of wet fabric on the tile floor, laid her naked
body out on the bed. Almost too much for him. His cock
was about to burst.

Breathe.

He took in a deep, gulping breath, commanded himself to calm. Reminded himself to just do his job.

The way the mere scent of this woman hit him, like a
blow to the gut, went far beyond the duties of his job.
He wanted her. *Her.*

She is a client. A woman, the same as so many others.

But no, he'd known she was different the moment
he'd laid eyes on her. Especially after these last difficult
months, when he'd begun to resent his work here, his
clients. His response to her confused him. Stunned him.

He lowered his body over hers. She was almost tiny

beneath him. So luscious, with her lovely pale skin. Her breasts were almost too large for her small, finely toned frame. Her nipples were growing harder and darker by the second as he gazed down at her, making his groin tighten, fill. When he glanced at her luminous eyes, he saw her nerves returning. She'd had a few too many minutes in which to think. But he would take care of that.

He leaned over the soft mounds of her breasts and took one luscious pink tip into his mouth, felt her shiver in response. So sweet on his tongue, that swelling nub. He sucked gently and she moaned. His cock twitched, hardened even more. But he had to explore her, to discover the secrets held within her fine flesh.

He slid downward, swept his lips across her stomach, her skin still a bit damp from the pool. Her hands went into his hair and she tried to sit up, but he pushed her back down with a gentle hand.

"Shh, lie back, Lilli. Enjoy."

He could feel her tensing as he moved his mouth lower, dipped his tongue into her navel. She squirmed gently. Then he moved lower still, to the triangle of curls between her thighs. He could only stare for a moment. The Gates of Heaven. He had heard a woman's sex referred to that way a long time ago. He had always believed it. But never more than at this moment. He inhaled the scent of the water on her skin, the musk of her arousal.

Ah gods . . .

He had to command himself to calm, not to press his aching cock into the silk bedcovers. He took a moment, then bent to his task.

He brushed at the dark blonde curls with his lips, a light, teasing touch, and smiled when he heard a soft "oh" from her. He did it again, heard her draw in a sharp breath. Then he used his fingers to part the damp folds to reveal her pink clitoris, swollen and shining with her desire already. Irresistible. He flicked the tip of his tongue, tasting her. She sighed. He flicked again, and again, until she arched her hips.

He drew back a few inches. "Did you know that in the Kama, there are ten steps to pleasuring a woman in this way? I will show you everything eventually."

She moaned softly in answer.

Oh yes, he wanted to bring her pleasure. He wanted to make her squirm, come once more before he had her. He moved in and took that sensitive nub of flesh into his mouth and sucked.

"Oh!"

Her hands gripped his hair, pulling tight. He sucked harder. And he moved his fingers down and buried them inside her.

Inside, she was all tight, damp heat. Unbearable that it wasn't his cock enfolded in that velvet sheath.

Not yet.

He sucked at her clit, plunged his fingers deeper, and she came hard, her thighs tensing, her sex clenching around his fingers. She tasted like heaven.

When the shivering stopped, he raised his body over hers once more. Her cheeks were gorgeously flushed, her eyes glowing. Beautiful, this woman. He needed to be inside her.

He rolled onto his back, sat upright, pulling her with him. Her hands went to cover her breasts, but he gently pulled them away. "There is no need to hide, Lilli. You're so beautiful. Your body is beautiful."

"I'm . . . I'm not beautiful." Her cheeks were hot, flushed.

He caught her gaze, held it. "You are exquisite." He paused, watched a myriad of emotions cross her features, leaned in and brushed a kiss across her lips. He whispered, "Let this happen."

When he felt her muscles loosen again he helped her to straddle his lap, his legs crossed in lotus position, his hands clasped around her narrow waist. "Wrap your legs around me, Lilli, so that your feet come together behind me. Yes. This is what we call *Kirtibandha,* the Knot of Fame."

He lifted her body so that she was poised above him, tilted his hips until his cock rested at that warm, wet opening. He watched her face, the languid post-orgasm gaze, her lips full and pink.

He kissed her then, kissed her and kissed her, just her lush little mouth beneath his. Lord, he had never been so hard. But he couldn't stop kissing her. Soon she was panting into his mouth, her tongue pressing between his lips. Her wet opening against the tip of his cock was pure torture. He pulled her down onto his swollen shaft and pushed into her.

Pleasure, hot and pure, lanced into his body. He heard her gasping breath. Her legs tightened around his waist, and she tilted her hips, opening herself even more to him. Pulling back, he looked into her eyes, glowing with flecks of gold and green, like precious gems. She bit her lip, her teeth coming down on that soft pink flesh. He felt another stab of pure lust at the thought of that pink flesh at every opening to her body. Using his thighs for leverage, he thrust up into her, hard.

"Ah!"

Pure rapture coursed through him, from his cock to his stomach, spreading outward. His mind was going blank, all control slipping away. What was this woman doing to him? But it was too good to stop.

He moved his hips, grinding into her, and she took all of him, took him deep. Her fingers dug into his shoulders, her nails biting hard into his skin. It thrilled him in a way he couldn't explain to see her like this, open to him, wanton. And her face above him was too lovely, too sweet.

"More," she panted.

He pumped into her in long, even strokes. Her hips moved to meet his with every thrust. The tension built in her body, her breath an uneven panting rasp. And as the keen edge of desire took him over, making his limbs shudder, her velvet sex clenched around his cock, pulling him deeper still.

As the first clutching waves of climax shook him, he caught the fire of her gaze and held it. They came together, eyes locked, shivering.

"Lilli..."

But what did he want to say to her? He didn't know. He couldn't speak. Couldn't think. His head was coming off.

He held himself inside her body, his cock still throbbing with ebbing sensation. And still, neither of them looked away.

There was power in her gaze. The power of desire. But there was more. He didn't want to think about it.

But he couldn't escape it, either. This woman, this Lilli, was the very embodiment of Shakti, the essence of Bliss.

He had been touched by a goddess. And he would never be the same again.

Lilli lay beneath Rajan's body, both of them damp, their skin sticking everywhere it touched: her breasts to his chest, their stomachs together, her thighs to his hips. He had somehow managed to roll over on top of her, their bodies still joined at that pulsing apex. He had her wrists pinned above her head, but she loved the way it made her feel: a sense of yielding, of opening.

He smelled better than any man she had ever met. Sweet and a little spicy. Or was she only imagining that? His scent seemed to go perfectly with his dark exotic male beauty. With the faint notes of sitar and flute playing in the background.

She had never felt so gloriously used in her life. Her legs ached, her sex ached, the weight of him crushed her breasts. She wanted him again already. She was trying hard to ignore the questions nagging at the back of her mind.

Am I pretty enough? Sexy enough? Good enough?

His warm breath hit her cheek before he kissed her there, softly. He whispered, "How are you? Are you alright?"

"Yes. I'm fine. I'm wonderful." She pulled in a deep breath, stretched a bit beneath him, willing it to be true. She *was* wonderful, physically. What had she just done with this man?

"Ah, I am too heavy for you." He began to move, but she pressed her legs tight around him.

"Don't go." What was that wrenching sensation in her chest? God, she was confused.

He was still inside her. Soft, yet filling her.

He settled in again, his muscles loosening. He released her hands and suddenly she didn't know what to do with them. She left them on the pillows over her head. Why this sense of discomfort now?

Rajan pushed himself up on his elbows and gazed into her eyes. "What is it, Lilli? You can tell me."

She pulled her arms down to cross them over her breasts, started to shake her head. "I don't know. I don't understand what's happening to me. I just . . . need some time to get used to this, I guess."

"To being with a man?" He bent and laid a gentle kiss on the hollow of her throat and her body responded with a soft, clenching squeeze between her thighs. "Ah, your body knows what to do. Give me fifteen minutes and I will be ready again."

That made her smile. "Really?"

"For you, I may be able to make it five. Why do you look so surprised? Do you doubt my ability?" He gave her hair a playful tug.

"No. I mean . . . truthfully, it's been a long time since I've been with a man who was that interested. Interested enough for a second round."

God, she sounded pathetic! She squeezed her eyes shut.

He lowered his head and kissed his way down her neck, making her shiver. "That is a terrible shame." He moved lower, pushing her arms out of the way to brush his lips over the swell of her breasts. "I cannot imagine any man having you in his bed and not making full use of you."

He was very good at his job, wasn't he? But he couldn't mean it. Her stomach knotted up. She grabbed his head, held it between her hands, lifting his face. "Please. Don't say things like that to me because you're supposed to. Please don't."

His dark eyes latched onto hers. "I swear to you, every word is true. What has happened to you to make you doubt that a man could mean such things?"

She turned her head away. "I didn't come here to talk about any of this."

"No. But I think you need to."

She was quiet, thinking.

"Lilli," he went on. "I am here not only to serve the needs of your body. I can be confidant as well as lover. I don't know you. I don't know your friends, your family. You can speak to me and your words will never leave this place. And I... I want to know you. I want to do whatever I can to make you feel good. Not because this is my job. But because I simply *want* to."

It seemed odd to open herself up to this virtual stranger. A stranger who already apparently knew her body better than her husband had ever bothered to. They were still entwined, his cock still resting inside her. This was as intimate as she'd been with any man in years. And he was right; it didn't matter what she told him, did it? Maybe talking about it, saying the words aloud, would help to get it out of her system.

"My ex-husband had very...concrete ideas as to what sex was about. I was young when we married. Too young to know better. I'd only ever had a few lovers before I met him. He was so in charge. Never passionate in bed but...I thought I could sacrifice passion for the sense of safety he offered me. Stupid of me, I know now."

Yes, stupid, stupid.

She paused, drew in a breath, and went on. "I thought his lack of passion was my fault for a long time. It's only been in the last year that I realized it wasn't about me. I left him a year ago. But I still haven't been able to shake the damage he did to my sense of self. Does that make sense?"

"He took your power from you."

"Yes. That's it exactly."

Her insides loosened up, just knowing someone understood.

Rajan's dark brows drew together. "Your visit to Exotica, then, is about finding your strength again."

"Yes."

"You will find it, Lilli. I see it in you. It may have been buried, but it's still there. I'll help you."

She nodded, her throat too tight to speak. She couldn't help the tears that sprang to her eyes.

He leaned in and kissed her eyelids, one at a time, then whispered, "It has been too long since someone has cared for you. Cared for you, treasured you. Your soul needs to be fed by that kind of attention. I will give you that. And you will leave here a stronger person. I promise you."

When had any man ever spoken to her this way, touched her this way? She couldn't get over it.

"Do you trust me, Lilli?"

"I'm trying. I know Caroline would never hand me over to anyone I couldn't trust. And I don't mean to sound melodramatic. It's just such a strange situation, and yet . . . I feel like this is the best chance I have to reclaim myself."

"Then give yourself over to me." He stroked her hair from her face, his glossy black eyes intense on hers. "I will teach you the sacred Kama, the art of love. The act of sex can be healing. I will help you heal."

He swept a kiss across her lips, making her shiver with heat once more, her shoulders loosening. His hands on her face were gentle, feathering over her cheeks, her lips, down her neck. Her body was lighting up with need again.

He was quiet then, kissing her, touching her, while she let her mind shut down and her body take over. He grew hard inside her, his cock swelling and pulsing.

Yes, she had a feeling he would help her, could heal her body, heal her mind. And maybe, in finding herself with him, she could finally heal her heart.

3.

SHE WOKE LATE in the night; she could sense the stillness, that aura of slumber which came at the center point between midnight and dawn.

She slipped from the bed, then paused in the dim light of the moon shining through the sheer curtains to look at him.

Rajan.

He was fast asleep, lying on his stomach. She could make out the strong curve of his buttocks, the planes and shadows of muscle across his wide back. His hair was a midnight tumble on the pillows.

She pulled her gaze away and walked, naked, through the archway leading to the terrace. Outside, the gentle drone of crickets kept accompaniment to the splash of water in the fountain in the center of the pool. Such a serene place. Everything so luxurious, so lovely, so calm.

She still could not believe the afternoon and night she'd had with him. They'd made love again in the big bed, Rajan moving her body, whispering the Sanskrit names for the positions, for the ways he touched her, before falling asleep. And she could swear he was as passionate about it as she was, every bit as turned on. Was it possible?

She'd never met a man like him. Certainly not her ex-husband. She nearly laughed aloud, stifling herself with a hand on her mouth. The two men couldn't be more different. Evan had never been imaginative in bed. He'd have had a heart attack, knowing what she'd done with Rajan in less than twenty-four hours. Evan had never been a man of passion when it came to anything but making money. She'd long since come to understand that he was simply born cold. Why did a small part of her continue to feel it was her fault somehow?

But no, she shouldn't think of it now. Not here. The idea of Evan and his aloofness, his betrayal, poisoned this place and all that was happening here. This was just for *her*.

How sad that even that idea seemed alien to her.

She shivered and realized the night air had grown cool. But the view was too pretty, with the quarter moon hanging in the soft indigo sky, and the top ridge of the mountains like a paper cutout against the glow of starlight. She wrapped her arms around her body, thinking she should get back into bed, try to sleep, when she heard a small sound behind her and knew it was him.

Rajan.

Her pulse fluttered with pleasure, was interrupted for

a moment by a wash of insecurity at being found naked, open to scrutiny. But then he slipped his arms around her, pulling her close. His body was big and warm. Comforting. Arousing. He was as naked as she was.

His voice was husky with sleep. "Why are you up, Lilli? Are you thinking? Dreaming?"

"A little of both, maybe. And looking at the sky, the mountains."

"Would you rather be left alone with your thoughts?"

"No. I'm glad you're here. I need to stop thinking so much. What time do you think it is?"

"Does it matter?"

His bare stomach was pressed against her back. He stood quietly with her while she melted into him a little, her muscles loosening. Thinking was impossible with him so near, her lovely stranger. But suddenly she found herself wanting to know about him, to know something of who he was aside from what he did here at Exotica.

"Rajan . . ."

"Yes?"

"May I ask you something?"

"You may ask anything you wish."

"Are you . . . I mean, is it alright for you to talk with me about your personal life? Or does your job require that you remain a stranger, a mystery?"

"My job requires that I do whatever will most please you. But *I* would talk to you willingly, about anything. What would you like to know?"

She was quiet a moment. "I want to know who you are, where you come from. Something. Anything."

"Ah." It was his turn to be silent for a while, then, "I was born in London. My parents are Indian, but my father was raised in England. He has a successful import business there. I am the youngest of seven. My brother, the firstborn, helps my father run the business. There are five girls, but I'm closest to my next oldest sister, Teja."

"Teja," she repeated. "What a beautiful name."

"It means 'radiant.' It suits her. She was a model in New York when she was younger, but now she runs a booking agency."

"Younger? She must still be young enough to model, even if she's a little older than you are." She was quiet a moment, thinking. Did she even want to know the answer to the question pulling at her mind? "How old are you, Rajan?"

"I am thirty-three."

"Ah. I'll be forty in a month." Why did the age difference seem a little wicked to her? Yet deliciously so.

"My auntie in Mumbai often told me women only improve with the years, and I've always believed her. My sister is thirty-five. Old for a model in New York. But she finds her work now more exciting than she did modeling."

"Do you talk to her often?"

"As often as possible. Once each week, at least."

"You're lucky, to be close to your sister, to have that kind of support. I'm an only child. And my parents mean well, I suppose, but we're not really close. They're sort of . . . ineffectual. They're both college professors, very much the absentminded professor types. In a world of their own, those two. They taught me the importance of academics, but not much else."

"My family taught me to love women." He ran a finger down the length of her arm as he spoke, causing goose bumps to rise on her flesh. "My sisters, my mother, my aunts, and my grandmother. We spent weeks, sometimes months, with my family in India, in Mumbai. I was surrounded always by women. It was there I came to know the value of the female spirit, to know women as vessels for the Divine."

"Is that where you learned about the Kama Sutra?"

"I learned the basic principles, yes. But later, as an adult, I became a student of the Kama." His voice lowered, pure smoke over honey. "A most devoted student."

He leaned in and laid a soft kiss on her shoulder. It went through her like heat lightning. She shuddered.

"So . . . mm, that feels nice . . ."

"Then I won't stop," he whispered, trailing his lips up the side of her neck.

She tried to concentrate as long shivers of pleasure raced over her skin. "So, why are you here, instead of in England with your family? In business with your father?"

He stopped kissing her, and his arms went lax around her. His muscles against her back went hard and taut. She turned to face him. His mouth was a tight line. "Rajan, I'm sorry. I shouldn't have asked you something so personal."

"No. It's fine. This is simply a sore spot with my family. I have . . . different goals than those they would like me to pursue."

"I'm sorry," she said again. "You don't have to tell me anything else."

He watched her for a moment. "Let's talk of more pleasant matters."

"Of course."

He smiled a little then, his features softening. "You haven't eaten. Shall I call for a meal?"

"At this time of night?"

"This is your fantasy, Lilli. You are free to make it anything you desire. There is a full staff waiting to attend your every need."

"But I don't even know what to ask for."

"I will take care of it. Come, back to bed. It's cool out here."

He led her back inside, handed her into the enormous bed, then turned and slipped through a small door. She was already under the sheet before she realized she hadn't even thought about the way her body looked as he'd led her across the room. She smiled to herself.

He returned quickly, and lit a trio of candles on the carved bedside table before coming to sit on the bed with her, still naked, lounging against the pile of pillows. It must be wonderful to be so utterly confident, so unself-conscious. Rajan's hand wandered lazily over her arm, his fingers stroking her skin.

"Lilli."

"Yes?"

"You seem to be more relaxed with me now. Are you?"

"Yes, I think I am."

"This is good."

"And you?" she asked him.

"Me?" He paused, his brows drawn together for a moment. "I am far more relaxed with you than I have been in a long time. Even this job, which would seem to be any man's dream, can get old after a time. You have made me love my work again."

"Rajan, please—"

"It's true." He pushed himself up on one elbow. "In these last months, six months, perhaps more, the pleasure in my work has worn thin. I've become jaded, maybe. Too used to it. I'm not sure. But every moment with you has been pure pleasure." He reached out and touched her heated cheek with his fingertips.

"I . . . I don't know what to say."

"You don't have to say anything. Simply accept that I am being honest when I tell you how beautiful I find you. How utterly desirable. How difficult it is for me to keep my hands off you. Wait until I've had some food and a chance to recharge and I'll show you."

He smiled at her and she smiled back, trying to absorb what he'd told her. He got under the sheets with her and pulled her close to him, and together they lay back on the pillows.

She could smell the scent of their sex on the silk sheets and, faintly, the amber incense that had burned in the room earlier. These scents seemed blatantly erotic to her. That, and the glow of candlelight, the way it played on his bare skin.

The quiet of the night surrounded them, as though they were in a cocoon. Separate from reality. She needed it, that sense of separation. Needed to pretend so she could be here, doing these things, having sex with a man she'd just met. And even though her stomach had begun to rumble, the arrival of a maid with their meal seemed an intrusion to her.

A lovely young Indian girl, dressed in a bright, saffron-colored sari. She went to an intricately woodworked table close to the archway leading to the terrace and silently set the large silver tray down. Rajan nodded his head, and the girl bowed, hands together in prayer position, and backed out of the room, the jeweled *bindi* on her forehead catching the candlelight.

Rajan rose and pulled a pair of robes in deep red silk from a hook on one of the bedposts, then took Lilli's hand. He helped her from the bed and slipped the silk around her shoulders, put the other robe on himself. Then he seated her in one of the pair of padded and inlaid chairs that flanked the small table before he seated himself.

"I ordered a bit of everything. I wasn't sure what you might like. Here, try these first. They are a favorite of mine."

He picked up a stuffed date from the colorful, heavily laden tray and held it out to her.

"What's in it?"

He leaned in and raised his hand to her lips. "Taste. Then you tell me."

She felt shy suddenly, with Rajan trying to feed her. But something about his whole persona was as in control, as commanding, as he was gentle. She nodded and opened her mouth.

He slipped the date between her lips and she took a small bite. Sweetness suffused her mouth, and a lovely, varied texture.

"Oh, that's good. Is it honey? And some kind of nuts."

"Pistachios. You have a good palate. Here, try some of this now. Mango ice cream. It will ready your tongue for whatever comes next."

He spooned some of the cold concoction into her mouth and she savored the fresh, sweet flavor. Rajan licked the spoon before scooping a mouthful for himself, a completely unself-conscious act that nevertheless seemed intimate to her, that he ate from the same spoon.

"Have you ever had *samosas*?" he asked her. "You

won't find better than the chefs make here, not even in India itself, although I would never say so to my aunties. You must try this."

Again he fed her, holding the small triangle of meat and vegetable-filled pastry to her mouth, letting her take a bite, then biting into it himself before feeding the rest to her. And all the while he smiled at her, as though he were pleased with himself, delighted with the pleasure the food brought her.

They washed their meal down with a strong chai tea, smoky and exotic. She felt utterly sated, in every possible way. Her stomach was pleasantly full, her body well-used. How odd to sit here like this in the middle of the night, with this overwhelming sense of contentment. The only thing that could make it better would be to feel his body next to hers again. How lovely, how luxurious, that she would in the next few minutes.

"Are you tired?" he asked her. "You must be. Come, let's go back to bed and be warm together."

He stood and took her hand, guiding her back to the bed, slipping the robe from his shoulders, then hers. Her arms went automatically to cover her bare body, but he stopped her with gentle hands.

"There is no need to cover yourself. You have the soft curves of a woman, as a woman is meant to be. I will keep telling you so until you believe it, Lilli."

She let her arms fall away, her cheeks burning, embarrassed as much at her own self-consciousness as by her nude body.

"It's alright," he assured her, his voice quiet, soothing.

He laid her down and slid in beside her, pulling her up against him as though he instinctively knew she needed to feel the solid warmth of his body. He settled her head on his shoulder, and she felt the bunch and ripple of muscles beneath her as he moved.

They were both quiet for a while. She was tired, yet utterly content to lie there and enjoy him. She was full and lazy. Too lazy to think anymore.

He said softly, "Shall I tell you a story while you fall asleep?"

"What kind of story?"

"I will tell you about Shakti. She is the Divine Mother and the dynamic principles of feminine power, consort of Shiva in the form of the Tantric Goddess, Devi. These gods originated the sacred sex of the Kama Sutra."

Lilli curled into his heat, the ease of sleep beginning to overtake her already. "Tell me more about Shakti."

Rajan stroked the side of her face with his fingers, gently, and she let herself be soothed by the rhythmic rise and fall of his chest beneath her cheek, by the low tone of his voice. "Her name translates as 'cosmic energy.' She is the Universal Creator. Tantric doctrine tells us that the female is life itself, because women embody the principle of Shakti. So you see, as a woman, you have a power which man can never know, other than by joining with you. Man is incomplete without woman. Even the god Shiva is powerless without the feminine energy of Shakti. Together, they create the balance and the Divine Power in the universe with which everything else is created. This is why the sexual union is sacred, profound."

"Mm...like the idea of sacred sex." A small quiver of desire ran through her, despite her sleepiness.

"I will teach you the art of sacred sex, Lilli. It is the Kama. It is Tantra."

"I think there is a lot you can teach me, Rajan."

Perhaps more than simply sexual techniques. She felt different with him, when she allowed herself to. Looser, more open, less inclined to dissect everything, to worry that her thighs were too plump, that her stomach wasn't as flat as it had been in her twenties.

That she wasn't good enough.

He laid a soft kiss on her forehead, but he was quiet. Was that a shiver she felt run through his body? But she was too tired to think about it. In moments, sleep claimed her.

That night she dreamed of brightly colored silks rippling over her naked skin on a soft, sandalwood-scented breeze. Sitar music played against a backdrop of singing birds. Rajan was there with her, whispering ancient prayers in her ear, his strong yet gentle hands roaming her body, bringing her pleasures she had never known before, as the dividing line between dreams and reality faded until she could no longer tell what was real and what was fantasy.

Morning came in the form of a pale light glowing behind her closed lids. Without opening her eyes, she knew at once where she was. She knew by the feel of the silk sheets against her bare skin, by the scent of flowers in the air, by the warm breath of her Kama Sutra lover beside her.

If she opened her eyes, would it all disappear?

She stretched and reveled in the satin of his skin against her side. Finally, she dared to let her lashes flutter open.

He was still there. Her heart gave a sharp beat of

gratitude, of yearning. But how was that possible? No, it was only his body she needed, nothing more. His beautiful body, his seeking hands, his clever mouth.

It was then she realized he was already awake and smiling at her.

"Good morning, Lilli."

"Good morning."

"I've already called for your bath attendants."

"Bath attendants?"

"Yes. To bathe you, as an Indian princess would be bathed."

"Oh. I don't know . . . I don't know if I want anyone else here. I don't know if I can . . . Do I have to?"

"You don't have to do anything unless you wish it. I thought you might enjoy being bathed."

"Not by a stranger."

He was silent a moment. "Would you like for me to bathe you, Lilli?"

She would like for him to do anything that included him touching her. "I think I would like that."

From the way her body was responding, heat flooding into her sex, her breasts aching, she was sure of it.

He smiled, raised her hand to his lips and kissed it, sending a small thrill through her. "Give me one moment to cancel the order, and then to draw your bath."

He rose, gloriously naked as he went through the small door next to the bed. He returned a few moments later.

"What's behind the door, Rajan?"

"That is like the curtain which hides the wizard in *The Wizard of Oz*. Behind it is a telephone which will never ring so that you are not disturbed. This is how we order food, maid service, anything else you desire. It is kept hidden away so you don't have to think about these things. So that you needn't ever be pulled out of the fantasy. Did I ruin it for you just now, telling you?"

"No, and I was the one who asked. They plan for everything here, don't they? Every small detail."

"Ah, wait until you see your bath. It is like no other. A masterpiece. I will go and fill it now."

She lazed in bed, relaxing to the muted sound of running water as Rajan filled the bath in another room. She'd used a small, beautifully tiled water closet, complete with a bidet, last night, but the tub must be elsewhere.

She stretched again, hardly able to believe she was here, that these things were happening to her.

Rajan stepped back into the room, still naked, entirely comfortable in his own skin. She envied him that, wished it for herself. He came to the bed and offered her his hand. "Your bath awaits, my princess."

She got up, let him slip the red silk robe around her once more and lead her across the cool tiles. As they stepped through another curtained archway, the air shifted, becoming damp and sultry and filled with the scent of roses.

The room was unlike any she had ever seen. The walls and columns were carved and inlaid with jewels. Mosaics of elephants, tigers, and exotic birds done in exquisite detail adorned the walls, bordered with a design of flowering vines. In the center of the room was an enormous pool of water, tiled in intricate patterns of glittering gold and indigo, and scattered with floating rose petals and creamy white lotus blossoms. Steam wafted from the pool into the air, making the room seem insubstantial, dreamlike.

On one side of the impossibly luxurious bathtub was a polished bronze statue of Shiva standing five feet tall. Balanced in a dance-like pose on one leg, his six arms fanned out against the backdrop of an intricately carved *mandala*. In one of his hands he held a small drum, in another, a flame sprouted from his palm. Golden bracelets circled his wrists, and around his hips hung a swath of embroidered silk. A necklace of fresh gold and white chrysanthemums hung from the statue's neck.

On the other side of the tub was a golden figure which she took to be Shakti. The goddess sat on a heavily carved and inlaid throne of gold; at her feet was a small tiger. Embroidered and jeweled silk in sunset shades of red and orange hung about her shoulders. In her eight hands she held fresh pink hibiscus flowers in full bloom.

"It's so beautiful. I've never seen anything like it."

"I'm glad this place pleases you. Come, before the water cools."

Rajan pulled her robe from her shoulders, then slipped off his linen pants. "It is a little easier for you, this morning, to be naked with me, yes?"

She nodded as he held out a hand and helped her step into the bath, and the scented heat slid over her skin as he followed her into the water. "I'm getting used to it. We seem always to be naked in this place."

"The human body is sacred in itself, Lilli. Beautiful, always. And I find your body to be especially beautiful. You should feel no shame. Perhaps being naked here is what you need to help you understand this. Nothing happens in this universe without reason. Not even you and I being naked together." His voice lowered and a grin crooked one corner of his lush mouth. "Although I can think of many reasons for us to be naked together."

She had to smile at his words. "I am getting used to being naked with you. But I'm also beginning to accept that I'm...more a sexual being than I've ever realized before. And that sexuality is a part of who I am as a woman. That must seem silly to you...."

"Not at all. We will both discover more as we go, I think. But for now, I want you to enjoy the pleasures of the bath."

Rajan showed her a curved bench built into the tub, and had her recline there, her body just beneath the surface of the water. She noticed then a basket filled with white towels at the edge of the bath, a tray which held a variety of bar soaps, colored bottles, brushes, and sea sponges.

"The luxury of this place is almost too much to take in all at once," she told him. "I really do feel like a princess."

"Then lie back, my princess, and let me serve you." He pulled a towel from the basket, rolled it up tightly, and tucked it behind her head as a pillow. Then he took a silver pitcher from the tray, dipped it into the water. "Just close your eyes, lean back. Yes, that's it."

She did as he asked, relaxing in the soothing embrace of the water. She felt his hands on her face, smoothing her hair back, then the warm sluicing of the water as he poured it over her hair. Nice. Lovely, really, to feel so utterly spoiled.

"Just ease into the heat for a while, Lilli. Let it soak into your muscles."

She kept her eyes closed, basking in the warmth, the scented air, Rajan's silent nearness. She'd never met a man before with that ability of stillness. Patience.

"I'm going to leave you for a moment to bathe myself," he whispered, his mouth near enough that she could feel his warm breath on her hair.

Lazing in the soothing heat of the water, she watched through half-closed lids as he went to stand in the center of the bath, poured water over his body from the silver pitcher. It ran over his muscled shoulders, the brown planes of his chest, the narrow path of dark hair low on his taut belly. He was graceful, silent, as he moved a sea sponge over his skin, more beautiful than the bronze statue of Shiva, who stood sentry over them at the edge of the pool.

God, she was getting turned on just watching him, his big hands gliding over the hard-packed muscles of his abdomen. She wanted to touch him in the same way, his skin slippery with soap beneath her hands. When he tipped his head back to wash his hair, she was fascinated by the sight of his long throat, wanted to put her lips there, to kiss, to suck on that lovely golden flesh. And his dark nipples were every bit as inviting, glistening and wet. She had to suppress a groan.

He finished lathering his skin and dipped beneath the water to rinse off, coming up and pushing his wet hair from his face. Then, moving through the weight of the water, he came back to stand over her, his voice soft, his eyes glistening as his wet skin was. "Are you ready to begin your bath, Lilli?"

"Hmm...yes."

He took a fresh sponge from the tray and squeezed

some of the fragrant soap onto it. "We will begin at your feet."

He cradled her ankle and lifted her foot. He was so beautiful, standing there with the water pooling around his waist, droplets gleaming on his brown skin, from the tips of his black curls. Beautiful and noble-looking, like some Indian prince. She'd never seen a man with such a perfect body before, such flawless bone structure. So completely male. And yet, his mouth was soft and plush. Luxurious, somehow.

He smiled at her as he smoothed his soapy hands over her ankle. "According to the Kama Sutra, preparing yourself for your lover is a crucial part of the process. But it is also something which can be done together. We are meant to enjoy this part of the ritual."

The slip and slide of his hands on her skin as he massaged her arch, her toes, was lovely. Her nipples went hard the moment he touched her, her system buzzing with lambent desire. He worked his way up her calf to her knee, then gently lowered her leg into the water and began on the other foot. As always, he was concentrated on his task, focused, and this in itself seemed impossibly erotic to her.

When he was done he moved up to her arms, taking long minutes to massage the palms of her hands.

"Ah, that feels wonderful," she murmured. "I've never had anyone touch my hands this way."

He looked at her then; there was a sensual gleam in his eye, in the soft set of his mouth. "This is the way a woman's body is meant to be touched. With reverence. With care."

He moved his way up to her shoulders, using the

sponge to smooth the soap over her neck, her collar-bone. Her nipples were hard and aching for his touch. He was watching her now, his gaze on hers, and she felt the intensity of his look like a soft, warm blow. Her body throbbed with need.

"Rajan," she whispered as the sponge slid between her breasts.

"Shh...let me serve you, Lilli. There is no need to rush."

He rinsed her shoulders and arms with the pitcher, then moved the sponge over her breasts, one at a time, and even the gentle texture of it over her sensitive nipples made her sex squeeze hungrily. He moved lower, over her rib cage, her belly. She moaned, her thighs spreading, inviting him to touch her there.

And then his arms were around her as he lifted her from the water, moved to a shallower part of the bath. He set her down and they were standing, face-to-face, the water pooling around her hips. With one hand on the small of her back, he slipped the sponge between her thighs.

Ah!

She had to catch her breath at the sensation, her body blazing with need. And his gaze on hers was focused, intense, as though she were the only thing in the world that mattered. He moved the sponge, slippery and soft over her hungry cleft.

"Oh..." Her eyes fluttered shut as sensation rocked through her, her entire body clenching.

"You are so beautiful like this." His voice was a smoky whisper. "Lost in sensation, your lovely skin flushed. You make me need you. I need to touch you. Taste you."

"Yes," she murmured, the sponge moving over her

sex, his words making her shudder, desire sharp and pure lancing into her. She felt desperate suddenly, needed him, all of him: his hands, his mouth, his lovely, hard cock.

"God, what you do to me, Lilli." His tone was strangled as he dropped the sponge into the water and pulled her close, crushing her breasts against the hard plane of his chest. His cock was a rigid shaft against her belly. The energy between them shifted, intensified, a deep, primal lust burning. And all she wanted was him inside her body.

"Now, now, now," he murmured, as he picked her up, and she heard an edge of near panic in his voice, felt it herself, her heart racing.

She wrapped her legs around his waist, her body doing what it needed so desperately. His desperation drove her own until she couldn't think. All she knew was the animal need that hammered through her veins, hot and driving.

He backed her up until the wall of the tub was behind her, pressing into her back, helping to hold her up. She was trembling all over.

"Rajan, now!"

"Yes. Now," he gasped. And then he plunged home.

4.

HE WAS SHAKING all over. Not with weakness. No, it was easy enough to hold up Lilli's lithe body, wrapped around him. But his need for her was overwhelming. His cock inside her tight little sheath wanted to explode. Pleasure raced through his system. Nearly unendurable.

Control, Raj.

Eyes squeezed shut, he didn't dare to look at her. That would be the end of him, her innocent, lovely face. He pulled in a breath through his nose, holding perfectly still as he held the air in his lungs. Concentrating, he tried to move his focus to the *Sahasrara chakra* at the top of his head, to release some of the sexual energy from his system, then slowly exhaled. But still, his body throbbed with wanting.

It was a full minute before he dared to move, a

minute in which all he heard was her panting breath, and his own. When was the last time a woman had shattered his control this way? It hadn't happened with a client in . . . it had never happened with a client. Perhaps that was part of the reason why his work had become so empty for him. The women now a stream of nameless faces he didn't truly know, and never would . . . until this woman.

Focus.

One small thrust of his hips and she was sighing, her breath warm on his shoulder. Lord, this was going to be over all too quickly, just hearing her pleasure. He pulled another breath deeply into his lungs, gave in to the inevitable, and began to move.

She was tight, hot velvet clamped around his aching cock. Deeper. He moved into her, heard her soft sighs, and pleasure raced through him: his cock, his belly, his arms and legs, spreading outward, heating him to the core.

Even her hands on him were burning hot, branding his skin. He shook with the effort to hold his climax back. One more move and he would explode inside her.

Ah, even thinking about it was too good.

Lord, he had to slow down.

Too much, too much.

He moved quickly, pulling her from his body and setting her on the edge of the pool.

"Rajan? What are you—?"

"If I don't stop now, I won't be able to."

She reached for him, slid her soft hands over his shoulders, his chest. His nipples hardened as she brushed them with her fingertips. He covered her hands with his own, urging her, whispered, "Yes," showed her how to squeeze and pull on the taut nubs of flesh. Her small fingers worked gently at first, then more roughly. Sensation gathered in his chest, shot down to his groin. When she pinched his nipples hard between her fingers, he groaned, pulled back, his cock throbbing, begging for release. But he would serve her first.

He spread her thighs with his hands, and the sight of her pink nether lips was almost too much for him. He looked up at her face, saw her flushed cheeks, the softness of her mouth, her glazed, half-lidded eyes glowing like jewels. So beautiful, this woman. He wanted only to please her.

He moved his hands over her body, her ribs, the lush curve of her breasts. Her nipples were hard and dusky pink. So very tempting. He gathered her breasts together in his hands, bent, and took one hard tip into his mouth.

Ah, her skin was sweet, her flesh swelling as he swept his tongue over the rigid nub, then began to suck. Her hands went into his hair, held him close. Even the ripe flesh of her breasts brought pleasure to his hands as he kneaded them in his palms. He moved to the other nipple, sucked it into his mouth as she whispered his name on a sighing breath.

"Please, Rajan. Please, please, please . . ."

He could feel the heat coming off her. His cock was still rock hard, just from touching her, from the flavor of her skin. But it wasn't enough. There were sweeter places to feast on.

He moved his head lower, and her thighs spread farther apart as she opened to him.

He moved in with his hands first, plumping those lovely pink lips between his fingers, then leaned in to scatter kisses over her slick and fragrant cleft. She moaned and her thighs went absolutely loose, falling wide open.

Her voice was a breathy whisper. "Ah, Rajan...what are you doing to me?"

"This is called *Adhara-sphuritam,* the Quivering Kiss." He used his fingers to spread her wide. "And this is the *Jihva-mardita,* to rest my tongue here until you are swollen and wet, ready for more."

He bent closer and licked the slick folds of her sex, pushed just the tip of his tongue into her opening, and shuddered at her moan of pleasure. His cock pulsed, a hard drumming beat.

He pulled back to murmur, "And this is called *Chushita.* This is where I taste you deeply, drink you in." He lowered his mouth once more, spread her lips apart with his fingers until her clitoris was exposed to him. Taking it slowly into his mouth, he swirled his tongue over it, then began to suck.

Her hands were buried in his hair, holding on tight, as she groaned and panted. His cock was every bit as hard as the tight little nub in his mouth, her soft cries driving him on until he thought he might come just from this, from his mouth between her sweet thighs, from the taste of her on his tongue, from the harsh sound of her breath, from feeling her squirm beneath his hands.

He almost came when she did. He felt it, the hard clenching of her sex, her thighs tensing, then her wild cries. Pushing his tongue deep inside her, he used his lips to press on her clit. He pressed his cock into the hard tiles on the side of the tub.

Torture, not to be inside her.

She was still shaking when he pulled her back into

the pool with him. Her legs went around his waist and her arms around his neck as he slipped inside, impaling her. Suddenly he was the one shaking. Pure animal need raged in his system, taking over. All he wanted, needed, was to pound into her small body. Nothing else mattered.

"Rajan..."

"I need to be deeper, Lilli," he gasped, thrusting hard. "It's not enough, not enough."

He had to get some measure of control, damn it!

He pressed her hard up against the wall of the pool, lifted one leg until he cradled her foot in his hand, moving it out to the side until his arm was fully extended, opening her wider. "Twine your other leg around mine. Yes, exactly like that. This is the *Kirti* position," he murmured. "But this will be even better for you." He reached down between them with the other hand and pressed his thumb onto her clitoris, circling. "This is the *Tala*," he said between panting breaths, "my hand on you, opening you like a flower. Making you come. I want you to come again, Lilli."

He plunged, stabbing into her. Lord, she was so hot he could barely stand it. She was locked onto his shaft, that tight velvet clutch, and the last spasms of her climax squeezed him, pleasure lashing through his cock, his entire body. He pumped into her, doing his best to hold back while sensation built on sensation until, with one last thrust, his climax slammed into him. Fire burned behind his eyes, in his head, exploding. His limbs shook with the force of it, heat and pleasure rocking him, leaving him dazed.

And yet it wasn't enough, his cock somehow still hard and wanting. He kept pumping into her, holding her open to him, even as the last of his climax shuddered through him.

"Come for me, Lilli," he whispered.

"Yes..."

Her hands gripped the back of his neck as he thrust into her, pushed her hard up against the edge of the pool.

"Oh..." Her body tensed, shuddered, and this time he felt her orgasm rip through her, her sex tightening, clenching his softening cock. It didn't matter that he'd already climaxed. His body shivered along with hers.

They kept moving, her hips meeting his, until they were simply rocking, bodies joined. He let her foot go and her leg wrapped around his waist, their arms twined in a lovely tangle of flesh. Finally, her head fell onto his shoulder and she sighed.

He moved deeper into the warm water, dipped down until it pooled around their shoulders. His heart was beating hard, hammering against the wall of his chest.

Keep things in perspective, as always.

Why was that so damn difficult suddenly?

Lilli clung to him, her body still vibrating with the fading waves of climax. Her heart beat in time with his, chest to chest. Why was she so exquisitely aware of these subtleties? She took in a long, luxurious breath, loving the sensation of his cock still warm inside her, their twined limbs. And yet, she wanted to cry.

She didn't understand what was happening to her. She couldn't figure it out. Not now. Not with her head still reeling, her body humming with pleasure.

Later, later...

Now she only wanted to focus on his smooth skin

against hers, the solidity of his muscles, the exotic scent of him.

She pulled back to look at his face. His expression was dreamy, his dark eyes hooded and sleepy, his lush mouth soft. She wanted him to kiss her.

"Rajan..."

He smiled, making her melt a little all over. And then, as though he could read her mind, he bent and pressed his lips to hers, soft and sweet. And even now, her nipples went hard, her body lit up with need.

"Come, let's wash you again."

"No, I don't need it. I'm clean enough."

She didn't want to lose the scent of him on her skin.

God, she was losing her mind.

"As you wish." He looked down at her, his dark, glittering gaze on her mouth, then moving to her eyes.

"Lilli..."

"Yes?"

He was quiet, just watching her face. She couldn't read what was going on behind those jet-black eyes, but there was something... Then he shook his head, smiled at her again. "Shall we get out, then? Our breakfast should be waiting on the terrace."

She felt the loss of him with a small pang as he slipped his flesh from her body. Rajan stood dripping on the edge of the pool while he dried her with a thick white towel. Too sated and languid after what they'd done together to bother feeling self-conscious, she let him do it, let him wait on her. She had to admit she loved it, seeing him kneel before her while he rubbed her calves, her thighs, with the towel. And she realized that no matter how he waited on her, how gentle he was, she never saw him as anything but strong, powerful, in control.

Funny how her ex had always exerted his control by being domineering, demanding, harsh. He'd needed to put her down in order to feed his own sense of power. There would never be any going back, to that sort of man, to that sort of life.

When they got back to the suite, music was playing faintly. Someone had made the bed and scattered it with rose petals, lit incense, and left a small bowl of fruit and a pitcher of water on the bedside table. A swath of richly embroidered turquoise silk was laid out on the bed. She reached out to feel the soft fabric with her fingertips. She still couldn't get over this place.

"A sari for you, Lilli. They are perfect for the warm weather. I think you'll like wearing it. And this color will light up your eyes like the sky."

"It's lovely. But I'm not quite sure what to do with it."

"I will show you," he said as he slid into a pair of the white linen pants, tied the drawstring around his hips. "I will be your handmaiden, since you prefer not to have the servants here."

She laughed. "As pretty as any I've ever seen, in your own way, Rajan."

"I am pleased you think so." He grinned and moved up behind her, pulling the towel from her body.

"You're very good at this undressing-me thing."

"I like to see you naked. What can I say? I am a man of excellent tastes. But now I'll show you that I can dress you, as well."

He slipped the silk sari around her. It felt lovely against her skin, light and cool.

"The perfect Indian princess, just as I've said before." He paused, took her hand and turned it faceup, laid a kiss in her palm. "But these are naked, your beautiful hands." He paused once more, something she didn't understand shifting across his features. "Do you know what *Mehndi* is? Have you ever seen it?"

"Those red tattoos?"

"Yes. It is the ancient body art of India, more than five thousand years old, made of a powder from the henna plant. It stays on the skin for several weeks. I was taught by my cousins in Mumbai. It is a gift, of sorts, to paint someone's hands." He stroked her palm with a fingertip, making her shiver with delight. "I would paint your hands for you, if you like."

"Oh... I love the idea of it. And I'd love to do it, but I don't know... After I leave here, I have to go to a family wedding." She paused, her stomach tightening. "But I don't want to think about my life after I leave here, the luxury of this place." And the safety she felt there, with Rajan. But she wasn't ready to say that to him. She could barely admit it to herself.

"I understand." Was that disappointment she saw on his face? "Why don't we have our breakfast?"

He turned her hand over, brushed another kiss across her knuckles, and led her outside.

This morning a peacock joined them on the terrace, strutting around the pool, its feathers glowing blue and green in the sunlight. The air was warm; a soft breeze sent small ripples across the surface of the water, made the silk curtains hanging in the archways flutter gently. The tranquil strains of sitar music floated from inside the suite.

They sat on the padded chairs on the terrace, and

Rajan poured her tea from a silver pot, piled a small plate with fruit and pastries for her before serving himself.

Lilli watched him, the surge of muscle in his shoulders and arms as he moved, and a small, pleasant ache started between her thighs. God, she was acting like some infatuated schoolgirl, unable to take her eyes off him. Rajan smiled at her before biting into a pastry. His tongue darted out, licking a crumb from his lip. Too kissable, that mouth. Hard to think of anything else, watching him eat. Her body hummed with desire once more, simply looking at him. She really had to get herself under control. She could barely think of anything but touching him, kissing him, his hands on her. His cock inside her. And yet, she felt an odd sense of contentment simply sitting there with him.

What was that about? She hardly knew him. She would leave this place before she really had a chance to.

She turned to gaze out at the mountains. The air was clear, the mountain peaks one-dimensional against the stark blue of the desert sky. She took in the view, breathed in the soft, warm air, trying to clear her head, to calm her body.

"Are you always so quiet in the morning, Lilli?"

She saw Rajan wipe his mouth with a linen napkin as she turned back to him. "I'm trying not to think, I suppose."

"Sometimes trying not to think makes it that much harder."

"Yes." She smiled at him. He always seemed to know what to say, knew exactly how she was feeling.

"Do you want to tell me what you're trying not to think about?"

"That would defeat the purpose, wouldn't it?" But maybe he was right. She blew out a long breath. "I'm thinking of when I have to leave this place. I know I said earlier I didn't want to think about it, but I can't help it."

"You've only just arrived."

"I know. But when I leave, I'll have to go directly to this wedding."

"You're expecting it to be an unpleasant event, then?"

"Yes. I mean...I want to go. My niece is getting married. Well, my ex-husband's niece. But I saw this girl grow up, and we're close. I have to go. I wouldn't miss it. But he'll be there. My ex. And as much as I'd like to think I'm past what happened with us, I know seeing him will put all those old issues in my face."

"Ah. That can make for an uncomfortable situation."

"You have no idea."

"Then tell me, Lilli."

His eyes were on her, those dark, soulful eyes.

"It's such a classic story, the American divorcée." She stopped, her stomach clenching. She hated that feeling of being nothing more than another cliché, another statistic. "I caught him cheating on me. I wasn't too surprised, really. I'd suspected for a while. And he...well, he'd made it clear for some time that he wasn't entirely happy with me. But she was so...so damn young!"

"The worst kind of insult for a woman."

"Yes. That's it exactly. But it gets worse." She stopped again as a knot of old pain formed in her chest.

Doesn't matter anymore. It's too late.

She'd told herself that dozens of times, but this part still hurt. "The thing is, I'd always wanted to have children. But being so young when I married Evan, I didn't think to discuss it with him. I just assumed...Anyway, soon after we married he made it clear to me that he never wanted kids. So I gave that up for him. Stupid of me. And then, as the years passed, I got used to the idea, came to accept it. But now, this woman, this *girl* he married...she's pregnant."

"And you have to see them together, see her swollen belly." Rajan put a warm hand on her arm and said quietly, "I'm sorry, Lilli."

She shrugged, trying to swallow the pain that clogged her throat. "It doesn't matter anymore. At least, it shouldn't."

"If it matters to you, then it simply does. No one else can dictate your pain."

She leaned back into the cushions of her chair, her shoulders going loose. "You were right. I do feel better having told you."

"Good." He smiled, his dark eyes glowing.

"Have you ever been through anything like this?"

"No. I've never given my heart to one woman, not in a true sense. Infatuations as a young man, of course, but never anything more serious."

"Why do you think that is?"

He picked up his cup and drank. His eyes went soft, lost their focus. Then he said quietly, almost as if to himself, "I've never questioned it before. But perhaps it's time I did."

"I'm sorry. I shouldn't have asked you something so personal."

"You may ask me anything you wish; I told you so earlier, and I meant it. But this is a question for which I have no ready answer." He paused, sipped his tea once more. "I love women, in all their endless variety. I have always been surrounded by women: my family, friends, lovers. It has been . . . forgive me for saying so, but it has been such an easy thing for me. I haven't had to think about it, haven't had to put a lot of effort into it. This is very tempting to a man such as myself. I've sampled as many women as any man needs to in one lifetime. I must admit to that finally." He shrugged. "I'm not sure where that leaves me."

"Where do you want it to leave you? I mean, there are men who are perfectly happy spending their lives going from one woman to the next."

Doesn't matter. It's his business.

"Yes. Many men are happy with nothing more than the physical experience. For me, it has always gone deeper. I see the spiritual side of sex. This is something I've always explored. And I've had this idea in my head that this exploration would be eternal. That sex would be a world without end in itself. And it is. It has been. Except . . ." He shook his head, his dark brows drawing together.

"Except that you said you've been disenchanted with it all recently," she finished for him.

"Yes. Exactly. I've had to question what I'm doing, and even more, why I'm doing it." He smiled at her, took her hand. "I meant what I said, Lilli. That I'm rediscovering it with you. I'm finding my purpose here again. I know you may find it hard to believe, and I can't blame you. But please know that it's true."

She almost wished he wouldn't tell her these things.

"It *is* hard for me, Rajan. And not only because you work in this place, because this is the life you've chosen for yourself. And I'm not judging you for it. After all,

I'm here as one of your clients, aren't I? But also because of my own issues. You're helping me to become more accepting of myself. Of my body. A little, anyway. But I understand now how much more work I have to do. It's not easy for me to accept compliments. Especially from a man like you."

He leaned toward her, caught her gaze with his. "I hope you will learn to, Lilli. I hope we both are able to learn what we need to from each other. I believe certain people are put into our lives for a reason. Do you believe that? That our universe operates this way?"

"Yes, I do. I think even my ex, as awful as my experience with him was, came into my life to teach me to stand up for myself. Not to be so passive. I'm still learning."

He nodded. "Life is a constant learning process. I've always known that. But perhaps I've forgotten these last few years."

"Rajan..."

"Yes?"

"I want to do it. The *Mehndi*."

"Are you certain?"

"Yes. I want to do it. Why should I care what anyone else thinks? And I'll have..." She trailed off, stopping herself from saying that she would have a piece of Rajan to take with her. She didn't even know why that felt so important. "I just want to do it. For me."

"Then we will do it today." He smiled at her, brilliantly, and she went warm and weak all over. A lovely feeling. One she knew better than to get used to.

She would never in her life meet another man like Rajan. She understood that already. But he was a fantasy creature, wasn't he? She couldn't expect anyone in the real world to be like him. This place, her time here, was time outside of the realm of real life. It was fine to pretend while she was here, at Exotica. To live this fantasy with him for a week.

One week.

Not enough. Oh no, not nearly. But it was all she had. It would have to do.

They lazed in the sun and swam most of the morning, her body soaking up the heat and the water, relaxing her. Lunch was on the terrace: *samosas,* those wonderful pastries filled with meat and vegetables again, soft *naan* bread and cool *raita* made from yogurt and cucumbers, washed down with icy mango tea. And the whole time they touched each other: in the pool, lying side-by-side on the padded lounge chairs. She couldn't get enough of his skin beneath her hands.

After lunch it grew too hot to stay outside any longer. Rajan stood, pulling her to her feet. "Let's go inside and I will paint your hands for you, my princess."

Laughing, she followed him into the cool interior of the suite. A large wooden tray inlaid with mother-of-pearl had been set at the foot of the bed. And on it was a small bowl, a silver flask, a pitcher of water, and several brushes and narrow sticks.

"What do you want me to do?" she asked. "How do we begin?"

"Sit in the chair here, and rest your hands on the arms."

She moved to the chair by the arched window and settled the folds of her sari around her while Rajan picked up the tray and set it on the floor before her. He knelt at her feet, bent over the tray.

"I'm mixing the henna to the right consistency. It should be a firm paste, but not too tight to work with. And it should be fresh." She watched him measure and stir for several minutes. "There, we are ready to begin. I'll start with your left hand."

He took her hand in his and turned it faceup on the wooden arm of the chair, smoothed his hand over her wrist, her palm, her fingers. "Just relax."

She nodded, watching him as he dipped a brush with a tiny, tapered tip into the bowl and began to draw on her skin.

It tickled at first. A fine tickle that sent shivers of desire up her arm, through her body, making her need him to touch her. But she was fascinated, watching his steady hand outline a pattern on her palm. His head was bent, so that all she could see was his curtain of curling jet-black hair brushing his naked brown shoulders. His hands seemed so large against hers, yet he moved with precision, delicacy. And at the same time, the touch of the brush on the sensitive flesh of her palm was incredibly, unexpectedly sensual. She had to fight not to squirm, to close her thighs over the sharp ache between them.

Was it because it was *him* doing this to her? It didn't matter. All she knew was that it felt good. The sensation itself, but also to have him focused on her like this felt intimate. Sexual.

She watched as an intricate pattern began to emerge. "I didn't know you were an artist, Rajan."

"I have many talents." He paused in his work to smile up at her, to give her a wink.

She laughed. "I'm sure you do. You've shown me a few already."

"It helps that I love what I do."

Why did that make her stomach ache? Maybe because it reminded her that what he did with her, the way he made her feel, was just a job to him. But she was a paying client. Why should it matter?

It just does.

She didn't want to think about it.

She only wanted to focus on the exquisite stroke of the tiny brush on her hand, on the flex of his brown forearm as he worked. And when she sat back and allowed herself to relax, to focus on the sensations, her body started to buzz all over with the sheer pleasure of it.

He looked up at her. "This one is done. You will be able to see the true beauty of the pattern later, after we wash the paste off. Now give me your other hand."

She did. He took her hand in his, kissed the bare palm, leaving his warm lips on her skin for endless moments. A shiver ran through her. Heat and desire and something more. When he caught her gaze, her breath hitched in her throat. His fingers tightened on her hand. Something so intense there, in his face, in his gleaming black eyes, in his clasping fingers.

"Rajan..."

"Lilli. Do you feel it?" he asked, his tone almost a whisper. "The gift of it?"

She nodded, gooseflesh rising on the back of her neck, her body humming with desire, with the electricity running between them. For long moments they simply stared at each other, yet she swore she could feel his dark gaze as an almost physical sensation.

His voice so low she could barely hear it, he said, "It has been a very long time since I've done this for anyone."

She nodded once more, still unable to speak, a chill running over her skin. She was feeling too much to put it into words. She didn't dare.

Again that light stroking of her wrist, her palm, her fingers before he broke his gaze, bent his head, and started to work. And once more the sensual caress of the brush on her skin, more intense than ever, sent heat racing through her system until her breasts, the cleft between her thighs ached for those clever hands.

She watched him work, the way he held the little brush, the care with which he moved. She could watch him forever if it didn't make her want to touch him so badly, his smooth dark flesh, those muscles bunching and moving beneath his skin.

"There, I'm done."

A sinking sensation in her stomach. She didn't want to break this sense of quiet, burning connection between them.

"You must keep your hands in this position without touching anything for three hours," he told her, "until it dries."

"Are you joking? I can't move for three hours?"

Rajan sat back on his heels, desire raw in his glittering eyes. "I suppose that leaves you helpless, doesn't it? But I'm sure we can find some way to entertain you, my Lilli."

5.

RAJAN PUSHED THE TRAY away and wiped his hands on a cloth. Still kneeling before her he bent his head and laid a soft kiss on one wrist. "Oh yes, I can find many ways to keep you busy for a few hours."

She almost groaned aloud, simply thinking about what he was implying. Seeing him on his knees before her, the muscles in his thighs taut and strong.

He moved his mouth up the inside of her arm, trailing hot kisses over the sensitive skin there. She was shivering immediately. He placed his hands on her thighs, lightly, and caressed her through the delicate silk. Looking up at her from beneath a haze of heavy, dark lashes, he said, "I think I like having you at my mercy."

A crooked grin tilted one corner of his mouth, one

dimple flashing, as he moved his hands up her rib cage, until they were just below her breasts.

Yes, touch me...

He slipped his hands up to cup the full, aching flesh in his wide palms and a sigh escaped her lips. "Yes, I think we will both enjoy this very much."

His grin faded away and his features went soft and serious as he gently pinched her hardening nipples between his fingers, the sensation a little rough through the silk of her sari. Pleasure shot through her, swift and hard, and she almost came right up off the chair. Then he was untying the sari and letting it slip from her body; it pooled around her waist.

God, she wanted to touch him.

Rajan pulled the silk down over her thighs, the fabric brushing against her skin like water as he slipped it out from beneath her, drew it down her legs, over her ankles. She sat naked in the chair. Naked and helpless, with her hands full of the damp henna. Every inch of her skin was on fire with lust. She didn't care what she looked like for once, truly did not care about anything but what this man was doing to her. And that strange sensation of utter helplessness that made it all better, hotter.

"Beautiful," he murmured, before leaning in to lay a soft kiss, then another, on her stomach, his open mouth wet and warm. Then he was using his teeth, a gentle nip in between the kisses, which gradually became real bites. His teeth sinking into her flesh, hurting but lovely all at the same time.

She moaned.

He moved lower, his lips brushing the top of her thigh, his hair falling all over her skin. She wanted to bury her hands in his dark hair, to guide him to press his lips to that lovely ache between her thighs. Too awful that she couldn't do it. Too awful and too delicious at the same time.

His hands and his mouth were everywhere, gliding over her body in smooth, sweeping strokes, biting into the flesh of her thighs. His mouth was hot and damp, leaving a trail of scorching need everywhere he touched until she was squirming in her chair. She could hardly stand it.

"What do you want, Lilli?" he asked her, his voice a quiet murmur.

Even better that he was making her say it.

"I need you to touch me. To kiss me. Please."

He looked up at her, his eyes brilliant, glossy, his mouth lush and beautiful. "I am touching you, kissing you. But you need more, don't you?" He paused, laid a soft kiss on her thigh, then looked up at her again. "You need me to touch you here, don't you?"

He smoothed his palms over her breasts, and her already rock-hard nipples swelled under his hands.

"Yes . . ."

"And even more, to touch you here."

He slipped one hand between her thighs, brushed his fingertips over her slick cleft.

"Yes!"

"But you need me to kiss you even more, don't you, my Lilli?"

With his hands he parted her thighs and bent his head to lay a soft kiss on the curls there.

"Oh God . . ."

He blew on the damp curls, his breath warm, stunning. "Yes, this is what you need most of all, isn't it?"

"Yes, Rajan. Please."

"Anything for you, Lilli. My princess."

He moved in and just breathed on her for a moment, inhaling deeply, then exhaling, his breath hot and moist, making her open even more to him.

"Yes, that's it, Lilli . . ."

With his fingers he caressed her swollen folds, a fine shock of heat and need. She was drenched, shaking.

"You're so pink, so wet. So lovely, like some rare orchid. I can hardly bear to look and not touch. Not taste." He leaned in and flicked his tongue at her clit. "Like honey," he whispered. "Like heaven."

"Oh . . ."

He massaged the lips of her sex with his fingers, spread them apart, swept his tongue across her opening, making her moan and writhe. And she remembered the name for what he was doing to her: *Jihva-bhramanaka*, the Circling Tongue. Desire reverberated through her body in trembling waves. The waves turned into a jolt of pure pleasure when he began to suck on her clit.

Chushita. Yes. And then, more intensely, *Bahuchushita*, Sucked Hard.

"Oh, oh, oh . . ."

She was trembling all over, as much with the fierce need to touch him as she was with the pleasure burning through her body. An absolutely overwhelming yearning to get her hands on him.

"Rajan," she panted, "how much longer until I can wash my hands off?"

He lifted his face to look at her, his eyes were burning darkly, his smile a little wicked. "Nearly two hours."

He was massaging her quivering thighs with his hands. She could see his erection pressing against his linen pants.

Her mouth began to water, her insides clenching, wanting to be filled.

"I can't wait. I swear I can't wait."

He placed a soft kiss on her mouth, and she could taste herself on his lips, salty and sweet at the same time. It seemed utterly erotic to her, intimate.

"I have to touch you," she murmured against his mouth.

"Ah, but that you cannot do." He kissed her again, nipping her lower lip.

She groaned.

"But I can, Lilli."

"You can... what?"

"I can... touch me. For you."

She smiled, her pulse quickening. "Do you mean...?"

"Yes."

"Oh God."

He bit her lip again, gently, then kissed her hard before pulling away. "Does that mean you would like me to do this for you, my princess?"

"Oh yes."

Her body was on fire simply thinking about it.

He moved away from her and with quick fingers he untied his linen pants and stepped out of them. Then he went down on his knees on the floor in front of her again. His body was so beautiful, every strong line and ripple of muscle, the soft black hair on his arms. And his cock was absolutely rigid, a solid staff of golden brown flesh. Her sex gave a hard squeeze.

Rajan locked eyes with her, his dark, intense. "Is this what you want?" He brushed the tip of his cock with his fingertips.

Lilli nodded, unable to speak, trembling with lust. She had never seen anything like this before in her life.

"The human form is divine, is it not, Lilli? No matter the shape, the age of a person, there is art in the naked body in its natural state. There is something elemental about it. The great sculptors of the world know this. In motion..." He paused to give his cock a stroke, then another. "Or when perfectly still." He stopped, letting his hand rest around the thick shaft.

Lilli licked her lips. "Yes. Like some erotic statue."

"Yes." He began to feather his fingertips across the head of his cock. "There can be beauty in everything about the human body. But nothing is more beautiful than pleasure itself." He wrapped his hand around the shaft and squeezed. He drew in a short, gasping breath, held it for a moment. "Nothing is more beautiful to behold than the way in which pleasure manifests in the human body."

He squeezed his cock, slid his hand up to just below the head, squeezed again. The head turned a darker shade, a lovely, deep gold.

"Yes...beautiful." She clenched her thighs together, trying to ease the sharp ache there. She was soaking wet.

"I love to see how you respond, your breasts, your skin flushing. Your pupils dilating." He was stroking his cock in rhythm now, his gaze on her face. His voice was low, ragged, breathless. "Your mouth...ah, so difficult not to lean in and kiss you. To take your mouth..."

She watched, fascinated, as his hand moved up and down the heavy shaft, the tip of his cock glistening. And she was shaking all over, pleasure traveling through her body, a steady pulse of thrumming, raw desire.

"Rajan..."

"Yes. I need you, too, Lilli." His voice was rough with pleasure, as rough as his hand was now on his cock. "I need you to touch me. I need to be inside your lovely body. But at this moment, I can only imagine this is your hand on me." He stroked faster, harder. His eyes fluttered closed and he drew in another deep breath before he opened them again. They were dark, glowing. But she had to look back to his cock, his hand pumping, stroking the rigid shaft. She was too fascinated. Her desire for him at this moment was almost unfathomable.

"Lilli..." His voice was a panting rasp. "Put your thighs together. Yes, that's it. Since you cannot use your hands. Now squeeze them tight."

She did as he asked, sensation searing through her, driven by the sight of him touching himself, by the pained look of rapture on his face.

"Now rock your body. Match your rhythm to mine. Yes..."

She rocked, the motion and her tightly clenched thighs causing friction on her clitoris, on the lips of her sex. Small frissons of pleasure shafted deep into her body. The friction, the image of him, was making her crazy. She needed to come already.

And as she watched him, his gaze was on her face, his hand fisted over his cock, which was glistening at the tip with pre-come. Her mouth watered, wanting to taste him. She licked her lips, and even the wetness of her own tongue was erotic to her.

"Rajan..."

"Yes, I'm nearly there. Ah..."

He pumped himself harder, his hips thrusting to meet his fist. She rocked harder, faster, and watched as he began to tremble all over. A shiver started inside her, her sex burning, clenching. And as she hovered at that keen edge, he cried out, his body going rigid as he came, the pearly white come shooting onto his stomach. His gaze, locked on hers, made her feel his climax, deep in her own body, somehow. Her muscles tensed, pleasure swarming over her, seizing her deep inside as her own climax roared through her.

He called her name, over and over as her body shivered with surge after surge of orgasm, and a million stars shattered behind her eyes. A million points of blinding light in a dark velvet sky that burned into her body. And although he hadn't even touched her just now, that burning ache reached some deep place within her no one had ever touched before.

By the time Rajan woke, the sun was already beginning to set in a sky blazing with orange and pink. The colors filtered through the flowing silk curtains, casting rosy shadows across the tile floor.

He'd carried her to bed, her body limp and weighing almost nothing in his arms. So precious. She was still asleep; he could tell from the slow rhythmic rise and fall of her breasts beneath the sheet. Her hands rested outside, the henna a dark clay on her fair skin. He'd have to clean her hands when she woke up. But for now, he simply wanted to watch her breathe, to study the long lashes resting against her cheeks. Her hair was a riotous tumble of strawberry curls on the pillows. He had the urge to touch it, to lift the silky strands to his lips.

What was she dreaming of? Or was she simply floating in the arms of sweet, quiet sleep?

His dreams had taken a new direction. One which included Lilli.

Impossible.

Still, he couldn't turn his mind away from the fleeting images that passed through. He was having a hard time separating them suddenly from the dreams he'd been hanging on to for so long, the dreams for building his future. For the first time, he considered the possibility of a woman being part of that future. How much better would it be to attain his dream, and to have someone to share it with?

He was never supposed to think this way about a client. He had never thought this way about any woman.

So why her? Why now?

Despite his claim that sex was a spiritual matter to him, that there was something sacred and profound about the act itself, regardless of who he was with, he had begun to realize he'd been missing something in his life. Perhaps he'd been wrong all this time.

Sex with Lilli was more intense, more profound, than it had ever been for him before. And it had to be about *her*.

Yes, he'd been missing the point, hadn't he? He'd been so busy looking for his spirituality through the act of sex that he'd failed to see how much more meaningful it could be with someone he truly cared for. Someone he saw as an individual, rather than simply as a woman, one drawn from the endless pool of female humanity.

He drew in a deep breath, pulling in the scent of her hair, her skin, the scent of sex. The incense in the background only seemed to enhance everything else. To make him want her even more.

Lord, he had to get things in perspective. He had no

right to expect anything from her once she left here. She would never accept from him anything more than what he could give her in this fantasy place. She was a client, a wealthy and lovely woman. And he was... he was a man who had made love to too many women without ever having truly loved any of them.

If only she weren't so beautiful, so utterly sweet, so open, so insightful. Even her suffering was lovely to him. Yet at the same time, all he wanted was to take that pain away. But how perverse did that make him? And who was he to do that? She was a grown woman, and so much stronger than she realized. If he could do nothing more than help her see that, then he could let her go.

Let her go.

He didn't want to. His chest knotted up just thinking about it. And the idea that he cared this much was a little shocking to him, something it would take some time to get used to.

A soft moan and her lashes fluttered open, her green- and gold-flecked eyes sleepy, glowing. She saw him looking at her, smiled. And something inside him broke apart in a warm rush.

Oh yes, he was in deep trouble. But he couldn't find it within himself to care. Not with her smiling at him, with her body warm and naked in the bed next to his. And his cock growing hard just looking at the glorious color of her eyes.

Lord help me.

"Mmm... I slept so hard. Did you sleep, Rajan?"

"Yes. I've only been awake a few minutes." He stroked her hair from her face, then picked up her hand, turned it over and kissed it. "We should wash the henna off now."

"Oh. I'd forgotten all about it. I hate to have to get up now."

"Then stay right here."

He slipped from the bed, went to the bathing room, and returned with a pitcher of warm water, a soft washcloth, a hand towel, and a small bowl. Carrying it all to the bed, he set everything on the nightstand and poured water into the bowl. Dipping the washcloth in, he wrung it out and began to clean the dried clay-like substance from her skin.

She sat quietly while he worked, her whole body in an attitude of yielding. He loved to see her like this, when she stopped struggling and gave herself over to him.

He patted her hands dry, then held them up to show her the intricate design.

"Oh! It's so beautiful." She held her hands closer to her face, turned them over and over. "I can hardly believe this is on my skin, for some reason. The detail is amazing."

"I'm glad you like it."

"I do. I love it. Thank you." She reached up, curved her hand around the back of his neck, and pulled him in for a kiss.

Her touch went through him like wildfire. She was normally so passive with him. Just the fact that she'd instigated the kiss seemed significant. And her lips were almost unbearably sweet pressed to his.

She pulled back, but her warm hand still rested at the back of his neck. "Rajan...? I have a question. Would you mind...I mean, would it be odd if I...took a little break to go talk with Caroline tonight?"

"Of course I don't mind." A small lie. "I understand

you and Caroline are longtime friends. But would you prefer she come here? I can leave you two alone, go back to the lodge for as long as you wish."

"The lodge?"

"That's where we all live—the staff."

"Oh. I suppose I never thought about that."

"Which is exactly as it should be. There's no need for you to concern yourself with mundane details while you're here."

She bit her lip and her hand slipped from his neck. "No, I suppose not. But it still seems strange to me, all of this. And things have been so intense between us, Rajan. There's so much for me to absorb, to sort out in my head. I just need to . . . center myself a bit, I think."

"I'll call her office now."

"Thank you."

He started to get up from his seat on the side of the bed, but she stopped him, her voice quiet. "Kiss me again before you go."

"Gladly."

He moved in, pressing his mouth to hers. She opened for him, her lips soft and pliant, her tongue as it swept into his mouth as sweet as honey, making his groin tighten and fill. He held her cheek, her skin like satin beneath his palm. He couldn't get enough of this woman.

When they pulled apart her cheeks were flushed, her pupils dilated. "I'll go to call her, then I'll leave for a while. Caroline will know how to reach me when you are ready for me to return to you."

"Thank you, Rajan," she said again.

His heart was hammering away in his chest. He could barely stand the idea of leaving her, even for a few short hours. But he had some thinking to do, as well. He had to get his head on straight. Because right now, he couldn't seem to think about anything but Lilli.

Lilli had dressed in the turquoise silk sari, and had even managed to figure out how to put it on by herself. She sat at the table on the terrace, watching the dying glow from the sun reflect in the pool, the colors spreading across the water.

She could smell that faint scent of chlorine from the pool, but the acrid edge was tempered by the scent of flowers in the air. The only sounds were the crickets singing, the splashing of the fountain and her own blood pounding inside her head. So peaceful, so lovely, as it always was here, and yet she couldn't seem to sit still. Her fingers twisted in the silk covering her lap, rubbed over the textured embroidery. Her mind was racing.

"Hi, Lilli."

She turned to find Caroline stepping out onto the patio. She was dressed in white linen slacks and a sleeveless top, her sleek brown hair in a tightly coiled bun at the back of her long neck. She looked cool, beautiful, and infinitely calmer than Lilli felt at this moment. Caroline slipped into another of the padded chairs and toed off her white sandals.

"Thanks for coming to see me, Caroline. I would have come up to your office..."

"Oh, don't worry about it. I was glad to get out for a while. I've been cooped up in there all day. It's much prettier here."

"This is the loveliest place I've ever seen."

They sat quietly for a few minutes, as though Caroline

instinctively knew she was trying to work things out in her mind.

"Caroline, I just needed to talk to you."

"We can talk about whatever you'd like. Are you unhappy with Rajan?"

"What? No. Definitely not unhappy. But I am confused. I can't seem to figure out if what I'm feeling is ... normal under these circumstances."

"What are you feeling?" Caroline asked gently.

Lilli shifted in her chair. "I'm not sure I know. I'm feeling so much at once. So much more than I thought I would." She paused, twisting the silk of her sari tighter around her finger. "You know, I expected this to be an adventure. I expected some fairly spectacular sex. To find a sense of freedom."

"And have you found that?"

"Yes. God, have I found it. The sex is ... I'm sure you don't want to hear this."

"No, it's fine. I run this place, remember?" Caroline smiled at her. "I'm hardly shockable."

Lilli shook her head. "The sex is frankly the most incredible physical experience of my life. But it's more than that. Rajan is ... he's the most amazing man. The most amazing human being. He's so gentle and so instinctive. He knows what I want even before I do."

"I'm glad he pleases you."

Lilli shook her head again, harder this time. "That's not what I mean. No, it is ... God, I can't even talk about it."

"Just take your time."

Lilli sat quietly for a moment, trying to force her thoughts into some reasonable order. Now that it was coming out, it was a tangled mess. But she needed this, needed to talk to someone, to figure it out. To ground her.

"I don't know where to start." She held her hands up in a gesture of helplessness.

Caroline leaned forward and grabbed one of them, turning it over and asking, "He painted your hands?"

Lilli stared for a moment at the lovely, intricate designs covering her palms. "Yes. Is he . . . did you know he could do this?"

"Yes, of course." Caroline let go of Lilli's hand and sat back. "We keep a profile on all of our companions, a list of their talents. Many of them can sing, play an instrument, ride a horse. Rajan's also a talented massage therapist. That's how he came to work here, initially. It's just that he's never actually done a henna tattoo on any of our clients. I'm . . . a little surprised."

Lilli stared at her hands again. "Do you think this means something?"

"I don't know. Maybe it does. What are you thinking, Lilli?"

She shifted in her chair again, ideas filtering through her head at a hundred miles an hour. "Do your clients ever feel as though . . . they may have feelings for the companions here?"

"Of course. Women aren't as good at separating sex from emotions as men are."

"I suppose not," Lilli said quietly. "But I think it's more than that. I know that sounds crazy. I started out understanding he was just doing his job. But there have been moments when I'm not so certain that's all it is." She stopped, staring into her lap and twisting the fabric of the sari between her fingers once more.

Caroline was quiet for a while. Then, "Tell me what makes you think so. I don't mean to doubt you. I just want to understand."

"I'm doubting myself. Doubting him. I know I'm a natural worrier. God, my ex hated that about me, even though he did everything he could to make it worse. And I hate it about myself. But Rajan does get paid to . . . do this. To work here."

"Yes, but he's human, too."

"He's said a few things. He's insinuated several times that I'm more than just another client to him. He's come out and told me as much. But I don't really know what to believe. What to trust. It's all so strange, and so fast. It's crazy! I've been here for two days. And it's so intense, I don't know if I'm making it all up as I go along. If I'm just reacting to the sex, this sense of intimacy that may be nothing more than a part of the fantasy."

"Lilli, normally I wouldn't encourage a client to become involved with one of our companions. But I'm definitely getting the sense that there's more going on here. The things he's said to you. The fact that he painted your hands. If you two have something real, well, I wouldn't stand in your way.

"I can't get inside your head, or his," Caroline went on. "But if you're feeling so strongly, then it's certainly something to explore. And I think you can talk to Rajan. He's worked here for as long as I have. I don't know him well, but well enough to know that he's a good man, Lilli, which is why I sent him to you. He wouldn't tell you anything that's not absolutely true. He's not one of those men who manipulates words, who manipulates people."

"No, he doesn't seem to be that kind of person. He's far too spiritual for that, unless *that* whole thing, the spirituality, all that stuff about sacred sex, is a lie...."

"It's not."

"But I don't know if I'm brave enough to confront him with this." Lilli pulled on the fragile silk of her sari. "I don't even know if I should. I don't quite trust myself, I guess."

"Well, I'm probably the last person in the world to give relationship advice, but I'd talk to him, if it's making you so uncomfortable not to know."

"Maybe I will. I just have to decide first if I really want to hear the answers."

She wasn't sure she was ready to hear this was just a part of his job, making her feel good. Because no matter how bizarre the idea was, she wanted this to mean something.

Bizarre, yes, but she was beginning to crave him, to feel a sense of loss at even thinking of leaving Exotica, leaving him behind. It didn't make sense. But maybe it was better that way. Better, maybe, not to look at things too closely, to dissect everything, as she always did. Because if she really took this apart, piece by piece, she was a little afraid of what she might find.

6.

RAJAN STALKED the length of the living room in his apartment in the lodge, where all of Exotica's companions lived. He stopped to look out the window as though he could see through the dark, all the way to where Lilli sat in the Kama Sutra suite. Ridiculous. But he couldn't stop himself.

Why was he so agitated? He was behaving like some lovesick teenager.

He ran a hand through his hair, the pull as his fingers caught in a tangle momentarily distracting.

The pale walls of the apartment suddenly felt as though they were closing in on him. The place was large and airy, beautifully furnished. Nothing but the best at Exotica, even for employees. He'd always appreciated it, since he often spent a month or two at a time there, whenever it was another Kama Sutra companion's turn to serve in the suite, while he got his medical checks. He was one of four Kama Sutra companions. They switched off, three of them taking breaks while the other worked.

Work. It was hardly work this week, was it? No, he enjoyed every moment he had with Lilli. He hadn't even had to go through his usual ritual, the mental exercises he did in his head to see the beauty in each of his clients, to prepare himself to adore them in the way they deserved. That ritual which had become so much more necessary, so much more difficult in recent months. And even then, with his last handful of clients, he'd had to work so hard at being gentle, nurturing, sexual; all of the things he was supposed to be for them. In truth, there was a constant, underlying, ever-growing sense of resentment. He almost hated himself for it. He certainly felt guilty. But he hadn't been able to find a way out. He'd kept at it, his prayers and meditations, asking for— begging for—that old ability to do his job so effortlessly.

But none of that concentrated effort had been necessary with Lilli. He'd known his experience with her would be different from the first moment he'd seen her.

And now...now he didn't know what to do. He'd spent his life in a state of comfortable confidence. Perhaps too much so, his ego fed by his doting sisters, his aunties and cousins. He truly had never expected to be brought to his knees by a woman.

But he'd known her for two days. Two days! This was impossible. He wanted nothing more than to please her, to be with her, to touch her, to breathe in the scent of her skin. But what, in the end, could she possibly want from him?

Looking around the apartment, he searched vaguely for some point of comfort, some place to settle in. But the cool, modern furnishings simply looked cold to him, the angular brown suede sofa, the big easy chair he sat in on those rare occasions when he watched television. Even the Indian artwork he'd hung on the walls, that taste of home, brought him no comfort.

He realized with sudden, aching clarity that he truly had no idea how to handle this situation. Giving in, he picked up the phone and went back to stand at the window as he dialed his sister in New York.

"Hello?"

"Teja."

"Raj! What are you up to?" His sister's voice held that edge of New York mixed with her English and Indian accent. So American.

"I'm glad you're there." The clear tone of relief in his own voice was shocking, even to himself.

"Is everything alright?"

"Yes. No." He jammed his fingers into his hair. "Lord, I don't know. Everything is not alright. I don't know what's wrong with me."

"Ah."

"Why do you say it like that? As though you know something I don't?"

"I'm a woman, Raj. When will you understand that we have talents you men simply don't possess?"

"You're teasing me."

"Yes, but only because you're my brother and it's impossible to resist. But also because I do know what your problem is."

"Do you?" He was getting angry. He wished she would just get to the point.

"It's a woman, isn't it?"

He was momentarily stunned. "What makes you think so?"

"I can hear it in your voice, little brother. That halting breath. The confusion, the near panic. It has to be a woman."

"It's nothing I can't handle, Teja."

"Then why call me?"

"Who else would I call?"

"Then I'm right?"

"Fuck. Yes, I suppose you are."

"Tell me about her."

He had to take a moment, to think, to figure out what to say. The right words just didn't exist. "She is unlike any woman I have ever come across. She is stunning. But with this quiet, innocent beauty. Fresh. But there is so much more than mere beauty there. Something about her . . . touches me. I can't explain it to you. Is it possible, to feel this way, after knowing someone only a few days?"

"I think so. The hard part is hanging on to that for any length of time." He heard the pang in her voice, knew she was thinking of her own broken engagement only a year ago. "So, tell me, did you meet her at work?"

"Yes."

"Is she a massage therapist? A maid?"

He was quiet for a moment. "Lilli is a client."

"Tell me you're joking, Raj."

He began to pace again, nerves stringing his muscles tight. "I know. It's a terrible idea. But truly, she is not one of the pampered prima donnas we sometimes have here. She's a real person."

"Rajan, there are too many complications in this situation. You know these women are there to live out a fantasy. Once that fantasy is over, how can you expect to have any sort of future?"

He stopped to stare out the window at the rounded spots of emerald green lawn illuminated by the lights set along the dark pathways. The color of those tiny flecks in Lilli's eyes. "I can't."

"I'm sorry, brother," Teja said quietly.

"I don't know why I called. Perhaps to say it out loud to someone."

"What will you do?"

"I will enjoy the time I have left with her. And then I'll find a way to accept that she must leave. What else can I do? I understand perfectly well this woman will never want to be in a real relationship with a man who does what I do for a living."

"Then give it up, if she's that important."

"You make it sound so simple, Teja. But you know I need the money if I'm ever to open my own business. I've wanted to open the spa for years; it's everything I've worked for. But it's going to take a lot of money to do it properly. I won't do it if I can't afford more than some shoddy operation. This is my only chance to make it happen."

"I've told you a dozen times that I would help finance you—"

"And I've told you a dozen times I must do this on my own." He realized he'd spoken harshly and softened his tone. "But I do appreciate the offer. I also know that even if I were to give up my job here, it's unlikely she would want anything from me other than our days together in this place. I have nothing else to offer her. My fascination for her, my feelings for this woman, are nothing more than . . . a misguided fantasy."

They were both quiet as he walked the length of his living room, turned, and went back to the window. The sky outside was the deep dark velvet of the desert at night, studded with the faint twinkle of stars, the early moonglow hidden by a passing cloud. Beautiful, as always. But it looked cold to him now, too. Empty.

"Teja, I will figure this out."

"I have every confidence in you, little brother."

"That would sound infinitely more sincere if you stopped calling me that."

She chuckled, a low, soft sound. "I know. Ring me and let me know how you decide to handle this."

"I will."

If only he had some idea of where to start.

Caroline had left an hour ago, but Lilli needed some time alone to think. Not that she'd come to any useful conclusions. Finally, she had sent for Rajan. She couldn't stand to be away from him any longer.

And what does that mean?

God, she didn't know. No, a part of her she wasn't ready to explore too closely knew exactly what that was about. But right now, she couldn't even focus on that. All she could think about was the expectant flutter of her pulse, waiting for him to come to her.

She heard his soft footsteps on the tile, and he lifted the curtain aside, stepping into the room. So beautiful, this man. He smiled, and she went warm and loose all over.

He moved toward her, and her entire body lit up with need, almost as though her very flesh reached out for him. He came to stand in front of her, mere inches

away, and she breathed in his exotic scent. God, she had
to touch him. And once more, she felt a bit like crying.

"I missed you." The words were out before she could
do anything about it.

He smiled. Absolutely dazzling. "Did you? I'm glad.
I'm glad you didn't make me stay at the lodge all night
without you. How was your visit with Caroline?"

"It was good. But I just wanted to have you back . . ."

Why did she feel this sense of desperation? Nothing
made sense anymore. Her body, her mind, seemed to be
operating of their own accord. All control over her
thoughts, her emotions, even her actions, was gone.
Swallowed up by the overwhelming sensation of Rajan
being near.

He was watching her, his dark eyes glossy, bottom-
less, nearly black. His gaze on her was making her shiver
all over, just a small trembling beneath her skin. She
needed him so damn much!

Then he moved in and took her hand in his, turned it
over and kissed her palm. Heat spread out to the tips of
her fingertips, her breasts. Into that softly beating place
in the very center of her chest.

Impossible, impossible.

But he was here with her, and she didn't want to
think anymore.

He led her outside, and they stood together on the
terrace, her back clasped to his chest. His arms coiled
around her waist, and they watched the sky in silence.
The clouds had passed, and the moonlight shone down
on them in a wash of faded silver. She leaned into him,
needing his warmth. He was so solid. So real. How
could he possibly be nothing more than a fantasy?

She was almost afraid to move, to destroy this

moment. At this moment, they were just two people, looking at the stars. It didn't matter who they were, who they would be by this time next week.

She could feel every muscle and plane in his body against her spine. Hadn't he said something in one of their late night conversations about one of the *chakras*, the seven energy centers in the body, being at the base of the spine? It was as though she could feel his pulse beating through her at that point of contact, a hot, driving beat that reverberated between her thighs.

She moved back into him and felt the firm pressure of his erection.

Lovely.

She pushed harder, until she heard his quiet moan. When she turned in his arms and tilted her face up to his, his mouth, lush and ripe, was only a breath away. Irresistible. She stood on her toes and crushed her lips to his. The feel of his mouth opening, the damp heat of his tongue, made her dizzy, made her feel a strange sense of power.

She pressed her body closer, her breasts crushed against his chest until she swore she could feel the erratic beating of his heart. Wrapping her arms around his neck, she deepened the kiss, her need for him a primal, driving force. Her body was on fire, her nipples two hard points, her sex damp and hot.

He was panting into her mouth, his hands cupping her bottom and pulling her into him, his cock growing harder, bigger. She could feel the pulse of it even through their clothes.

Too many damn clothes.

She pulled at his shirt, and understanding, he pulled back long enough to sweep it over his head while she untied the knot at her shoulder, the sari falling in a silken pool at her feet, leaving her naked. She moved back into him, her skin against his heated flesh.

Ah, so good...

She didn't wait for him, but took his mouth again in a frenzy, pushing her tongue between his lips. She kissed him harder, until it hurt, bruising her lips. She didn't care.

He pulled back and a broken moan escaped her.

"No, Rajan. Please..."

His hands were in her hair, rough, forceful, pulling her head back so he could look into her face. Through gritted teeth he said, "Lilli. If we don't stop now it will all be over. You're so hot beneath my hands. I want you too much. I...I am too out of control. Do you understand?"

"Yes," she breathed. But did she? She was too far gone to take in his words. All that mattered was his big body still pressed up against her, the rigid shaft of his cock pushing into the soft flesh of her stomach. Her sex clenched.

"Lilli, come with me now. I want to slow down. I must."

He took her hand and led her to one of the padded lounge chairs. Stepping out of his pants, he sat down on it with one leg on either side, straddling it. His cock jutted from between his strong thighs, washed in the silver moonlight.

"Come and sit, facing me, and drape your legs over mine."

She did as he asked, yielding to whatever he wanted of her, and he slipped his arms around her back, pulled her closer. His cock was so close, yet not touching. And in this position, she was wide open to him. If she tilted

her hips another inch forward he could slide right inside....

"We are going to do some Tantric breathing. Do you
know anything about this?"

She nodded. "I've heard of it. But you'll have to tell
me what to do." She didn't care what it was, as long as
she was close to him, touching him.

He let his arms fall away from her body, laid them on
top of her thighs, palms up. "Lay your hands over mine.
Don't clasp, just let them rest there, palm to palm."

His hands were hot against hers, making her pulse,
her stomach, flutter.

"I want you to close your eyes and listen to me. This
is all about measuring your breath, synchronizing with
mine. This is an ancient esoteric practice. It's meant to
be meditative. But it is also a means to becoming more
attuned to your body—and to mine, so that we are perfectly aligned. It's another way to experience sex as a
spiritual practice. And it's a way to control orgasm, and
to make it more intense."

She nearly groaned aloud at simply hearing him talk
about it. His palms were burning hot against hers, and
she could hear his breath hitch as he spoke.

"Now, take a deep breath, and breathe into your di-
aphragm, your stomach. Use the muscles to pull the air
in, then to push it out. Yes, that's it. I'm going to breathe
with you for a while."

All she could hear was her own breath and his. In for
a few long moments, then out again, slowly. Her body
was still hyperaware of every point of contact: his muscled thighs beneath hers, his strong, beautiful hands.
And with every breath his exotic scent filled her mind
like a caress.

She did her best to follow his lead, her body relaxing, yet becoming more sensually aware of him at the same time. She didn't know how long it went on. Finally, he spoke again. His voice was low, calm.

"Now we begin the *Kundalini* breath. It is pure sexual energy, which we will channel into our bodies as we channel out everything else. As you breathe I want you to visualize the air as light, which travels through your body to each of the seven *chakras*, those energy centers, from the base of your spine to the top of your head. Hold the breath for as long as you can, and keep your stomach tight. As you exhale, visualize the light going back up your spine, and push the light out with your breath. Focus on me, follow my breathing. Open your eyes now, and look into mine. Focus, Lilli."

She nodded once, took in a deep lungful of air, trying to see it as light filling her body. She kept her gaze on his midnight eyes, and that intense gaze seemed to touch her all over.

She shivered. How was that possible?

She breathed in, held it, pushed the air out. And again. Her body fell into the pattern of it, as she fell into step with Rajan. Her muscles went loose. And his dark eyes stared into hers, became part of the breathing, part of the air filling her lungs.

"Rajan..."

"Shh. Allow it to happen," he whispered.

She was still aware of him, his scent, his skin. Hyperaware. Her own skin was warm, as though she were slowly being stroked all over, more and more intense as the air went into her body, out, and into his.

They breathed together, as one entity. Her mind was letting go, and all she could see was him. *Rajan.* He was all she could feel; his warm breath, his warmer skin, his pulsing cock at the opening of her body.

Her nipples were swelling, her skin tingling. With every inhalation the sensation built, as though he were touching her everywhere. But she was able to melt into it, to simply accept the pleasure coursing through her.

He leaned in closer, those glowing eyes swallowing her up, black and open as the night sky. Her body surged with heat, with desire, with pleasure. With each indrawn breath, she drew in his excitement, and with each exhalation, her skin became more alive, more needy, until looking at him was almost too much.

Their breath came faster now, a long pant, then another. Her nipples hardened until it was almost painful, yet lovely still at the same time. Her sex grew wet and hungry, wanting him inside her. Yet she could do just this forever, this exchange of sensual energy.

His breath shifted once more and so did his hands. His gaze hard on hers, he touched her open cleft and she cried out. Her desire pooled there, hot and damp. His fingers dove inside her and her entire body clenched. She was dazed, trembling. His lips only inches from hers, he drew her breath into his mouth, nearly kissing her, his eyes a dark blur.

He moved his fingers inside her and she bore down, into the sensation rocketing through her body. His thumb brushed over her hard, tight clit and she almost came. But he pulled his hands away, leaving her empty, bereft.

"Breathe, Lilli. Deeply. Yes, hold it now, then let it out slowly. Good, now do it again."

She followed his instructions, her body calming a little. She inhaled slowly, let it out, and he started once more. His fingers pushed inside her, his thumb brushing her clitoris in slow circles. In moments she was back on that precipice, closer this time, shivering with the need to come.

Again, he pulled his hands from her body and told her to breathe. And again she followed his lead, calmed that aching edge. Then once more he pushed his fingers inside her, pressed against her clit, until her orgasm threatened.

She almost couldn't believe it when he took his hands away this time.

"Rajan!"

"Shh. Breathe, Lilli."

She pulled in a deep breath, breathing him in, let it out, did it again, and again. And sighed against his mouth when he touched her.

Oh yes.

His fingers pushed deeper into her core, and her sex clasped hard around him. This time, when he pressed onto her clit, he rubbed hard, faster and faster, his dark eyes swallowing her up. Her whole body seized with pleasure. Unbelievable, how hard she came, like a million fireworks going off low in her body, behind her eyes, blinding in its intensity.

She swore she felt the climax in her breasts, her throbbing clit, her arms and legs, her skin. Pleasure burned, pulsed everywhere at once. The waves crested, pouring through her body in a sharp, scorching tide, easing off before beginning again. She cried out, over and over, her body jerking, shivering; his gaze boring into hers making it all the more intense, as though she were coming into *him*.

She was left shaking, weak, spent. His fingers were still buried deep inside her. His panting breath was all she heard. It was a few moments before she realized he was trembling as much as she was.

"God, Rajan." Her voice was nothing more than a whisper.

"Lilli . . ." His was strangled with desire. She'd never heard anything more purely erotic in her life.

She needed to feel him inside her body. Needed . . . *him*.

He inched forward, touched his lips to her hair and a shudder of desire surged through her veins. He was shaking harder now, and the idea of it, that he was that turned on, made her want him even more.

She moved onto his lap. Oh yes, she was that eager. Had to have him. *Now*.

She tilted her hips over him, used one hand to guide the swollen tip of his cock into her aching slit. She paused there, wet and wanting. Unendurable, the degree of wanting, but she had to spend a moment savoring it, seeing that same hard need in his eyes. Then she slid her body down, impaling herself on his thick flesh with a cry.

"Oh!"

Rajan groaned, pleasure shafting through him like shards of glass; that keen, that painful, yet glorious at the same time. He had to draw in a breath, hold it, command his body so that he didn't come in an instant. Even with his years of training, he could barely hang on. He shook with the effort. And if he dropped his gaze from her incandescent eyes to her lovely, lush mouth . . .

He groaned again, and she raised herself, her tight sheath moving up his shaft inch by excruciating inch. Pleasure reverberated through his system: in his chest, his belly, his balls. He whispered a silent prayer to the gods.

Even her creamy thighs against his sides were almost too much for him. And her breasts, hanging full and ripe before him . . .

"Lilli, hold still," he commanded her, desperate.

She did as he asked.

He closed his eyes and spent several moments concentrating on his breathing, the tightening of his stomach muscles, until he thought he had himself under control once more. He prayed to Shiva for the strength and the will to hold out. Pushing the lust singing in his veins down to the base of his spine, to his *Kundalini chakra*, he let it linger there only long enough to honor it, then breathed it out.

When he looked up at her, her cheeks and her breasts were flushed a lovely pink. Her eyes were glossy, her mouth swollen and bruised-looking. Her face held such a raw expression of naked desire, it went through him like a bolt of electricity. He had never in his life seen any sight more beautiful.

He wrapped his hands around her waist, feeling her strength and her delicacy at the same time. His need for her pulsed in his swollen cock. But now, the need belonged to him, to do with as he wanted.

"Now, Lilli," he told her, his voice unwavering, "turn over, onto your hands and knees."

She lifted her body from his, shifted. Using his hands, he positioned her, until her arms were spread out before her, her head resting on the cushion beneath them, her knees spread wide, and she was doubled over until her stomach, her breasts pressed against the tops of her thighs. Then he went down behind her on one knee, the other leg bent at her side. His hands wrapped around her tiny waist, he pulled her tightly against him. The head of his cock slid right in, and with a small thrust of his hips, he buried himself deeply in her body.

He heard her quiet exhalation. She was soft all over, yielding to him completely.

"This is called *Ekabandha,* the One Knot."

"Yes," she murmured.

She shivered in his hands, and he shivered in response, as though every sensation ran through one of them and into the other in a continuous arc.

The intensity was still there, but banked, even as it burned. He began to move, and with every thrust he felt that velvet clutch tighten around him. She was so hot inside, so luxuriously hot and damp. Heaven on earth.

He moved faster, driving into her, using his hands to hold her delicate frame firm against his body.

She began to shake, her stomach going rigid under his hands. Her insides shivered, squeezed, pulling at his swollen flesh. Her breath came in ragged gasps. Pleasure shafted into him like a hammer blow. Again, and again. And still he held his will, simply letting his body absorb it.

Lilli lifted her head and moaned, a long, keening cry that grew louder as her body clenched around him. The heat coming off her skin was incredible. She was shaking, caught up in the ecstasy of her orgasm, as he pumped harder into her. And his own body took in her climax, absorbed it as he did his own pleasure. Pleasure flooded his mind, his body, in a liquid surge, like the waves of the ocean—that powerful, nearly drowning him in sensation. Yet still he held on. But just barely.

She was like a doll in his hands as he rose to his feet and lifted her; that passive, that malleable. Guiding her into position once more, he bent her over the lounge chair, so that she braced her hands on the seat. Her lovely, rounded bottom was high in the air, her legs spread so that he could see the faint hint of damp pink between them.

His cock gave a sharp jerk. He moved in behind her, slipped his hand between her legs, feeling that slick heat on his fingertips. Lord, she was so hot and tight. He felt it surge into his cock, a tight pulse of pleasure that nearly sent him over the edge. This woman was going to be his undoing. He bent over her and replaced his fingers with his cock, ramming into her.

"Rajan..." Her voice was a gasping pant. "What... what is this position?"

He groaned as he sank into her, deep, deeper, pulled out, plunged in again so hard he would have knocked her over if his arm hadn't been so tight around her waist.

"This is me fucking you, Lilli...."

A long groan from her that hummed into his body. Too good, too good. Too perfect to comprehend, this woman. And the way she took it, gave herself over to him...

Her groan turned into another climax, her insides gripping him, milking his cock. He gritted his teeth as the edge of orgasm pulled at him, as his cock hammered with pleasure. Blow after blow as she came beneath him, *for* him. He drove into her lovely body, tried to hold on. When she surged back into him, taking him even deeper with a harsh cry, he came apart. He shattered, his come flooding into her body in long, hot spurts. He yelled her name, shaken to the core that this woman had done this to him. Made him lose control. It had never, ever happened to him before.

And it came to him all at once.

He was falling for her. Falling hard. And it was going to be a crash landing.

7.

LILLI LAY IN RAJAN'S ARMS, side by side on the lounge chair. Her skin was damp and sticky; she was damp and sticky between her thighs. And she loved it. All around them was the faint whirring of crickets chirping, the splashing of the pool fountain. And the sound of her heart beating in her ears.

What had just happened to her?

"Lilli?"

"Yes?"

"How are you? Are you alright?"

"Yes, of course. Why wouldn't I be?" She didn't need to tell him how her head was spinning.

"I have never . . . I'm not normally so rough with a woman."

"I liked it," she said, realizing how true it was. Then, more quietly, "I loved it."

He was silent for a while. "So did I. I loved the way you gave yourself to me. It was ... amazing."

"Yes." It *was* amazing. She still couldn't quite believe that had been her, so completely wanton, allowing him to do anything he wanted without even questioning it. Without giving any thought to what she must look like. It had been one of the most erotic experiences of her life. She'd felt beautiful. And so in the moment she hadn't thought of anything else.

She'd been missing so much all these years. Missing out because she hadn't been able to let go of her insecurities. Because she hadn't been with Rajan.

When he silently stroked her hair, her heart tumbled in her chest.

Oh no, no, no! Her mind whirred with the warning, but it was too late. She felt that gentle touch in the very center of her body. That warm rush was quickly followed by panic. It wasn't supposed to be like this! This was supposed to be about sex, about finding herself as a woman, rediscovering her sensual side. How could she be falling for this man?

But how could she not? He was amazing. Tender and commanding all at the same time. Sexy. God, he was sexy. And he was intelligent, spiritual, a man who actually bothered to look inward. What more could a woman want?

She could want a man who didn't make his living sexually servicing other women.

She couldn't expect a man like that to ever be happy with just one woman. But why was she even thinking these things? As though this was going to lead to a relationship in the usual way? And after what she'd been through with her marriage, her divorce, she was totally unprepared to even consider a relationship with anyone.

She looked up at him, at the heavy lids of his closed eyes. He seemed content to lay there with her in silence, a lazy fingertip stroking her cheek.

Her chest tightened, but she pushed the feeling away. She was here to enjoy the *now,* not to think about the future, or the past. And there were only a few days of the *now* left. And being with him, right now, was absolutely amazing. She didn't want to waste a moment of it on questioning anything, on self-recrimination, on those lingering feelings of poor self-worth left over from her disaster of a marriage. So she was falling for him. So what? She couldn't help it. She would deal with the fallout later.

She realized with sudden, aching clarity how her habit of worrying about everything prevented her from enjoying each moment, enjoying *life*. Evan's constant demands, his perfectionism, his ridiculous expectations of her, had only fed this negative tendency. Wasn't it time she stopped giving him so much power over her? That she took some responsibility for herself and stopped blaming him for her troubles? No more. She had a right to enjoy her life, and everything—and everyone—in it.

For now, Rajan's arms around her, his scent, his touch, all felt too good. In this moment, it was enough.

She laid her head on his chest and let the muffled beat of his heart lull her. And with his body as her pillow, she let herself drift to sleep, to dream about Rajan making love to her under a golden moon, with the sounds of night birds in her ears, and the scent of him all over her skin.

She came awake with a cramp in her back from spending the night on the padded lounge chair. It was early yet. The rising sun shone in her eyes, and cast a golden glow across Rajan's naked skin. The even rise and fall of his chest told her he still slept.

In her dream, she and Rajan had come together, a beautiful, symbiotic joining. But now with the dawn came the self-doubt she had talked herself down from last night. Thinking back, she still didn't quite understand what had happened. A small pang went through her, but she ignored it. Too early to be so dramatic. Why did everything feel more real, more harsh, in the light of day?

His voice was soft in her ear suddenly. "What are you thinking, Lilli? I can almost feel your mind working."

"I'm just . . . I'm thinking about last night."

"So am I."

"No, you don't understand. Last night was so intense. So different from anything I've experienced before. And I have to stop and wonder what that was about. The intensity. Is it because of some dynamic between us? Did we make that happen, you and I? Or is it simply a by-product of your . . . profession."

She felt him go tense beside her. "Rajan, I don't mean to insult you. I need to get a grip on what's happening to me. I just need to understand this."

He breathed in, let the air out on a quiet sigh. His muscles loosened a little. "Then understand these days with you have been the first time in far too long that I've been able to truly be myself, to not have to pretend.

That being here with you has made me question myself and my own motives, in a way I believe I have needed to for some time. That being with you means something to me."

She sat up, her heart pounding, tears stinging her eyes. "Why would you say such a thing to me?"

"Because it's the truth." His dark eyes were blazing suddenly as he bolted upright.

She didn't know what to believe.

She shook her head. "How can it be? I'm nothing but a . . . a customer. Just another customer."

"No. You were never just another for me, Lilli."

The tears pooled behind her lids, spilled over before she could do anything about it. "Don't lie to me, Rajan. Please don't. I can't take it."

He reached for her, but she pulled away. And was shocked at the hurt on his face. A sob welled in her chest but she clenched her teeth and held it back.

"Lilli, you must believe what I tell you. I have no reason to lie. This is not the sort of thing I've ever said to anyone else."

She wiped at her eyes with her fingers. "You mean to your other clients?" She hadn't meant to sound so bitter.

"No. I mean to anyone. Ever."

She looked at him, and the sincerity on his face made her chest knot up. Warmth, confusion, all tied up and weighing down on her.

He reached for her again, and this time she didn't pull away as he took her face in his hands. He used his thumbs to wipe the tears from her cheeks.

"You must believe me," he said again.

She shook her head. Her heart was hammering in her chest. "It's not that I don't trust you. I know it seems that way. I just . . . it's hard for me to trust after what I've been through with my ex. I know it's not fair to put that on you. And . . . God, I shouldn't even say this . . ."

"You can say anything to me, Lilli."

She shook her head mutely, still fighting the tears down. How did this all get so complicated? "Rajan, I'm not condemning you but, you work here. I mean, you spend your life as a professional . . ."

"Gigolo?" he whispered, his eyes shuttering, but not before she saw the flash of pain there. Real pain!

"I don't mean to label you that way. But surely you must realize . . . it is, after all, what you do for a living. Making women like me feel good. And isn't it part of your job to do whatever you can to boost our self-esteem? So you must be able to understand why I have to question if what you're telling me is true, or if you're simply doing your job."

He was silent for a moment, then he let her face go and used one hand to sweep his hair away from his eyes, his fingers tightening in the curls.

When he spoke, his voice was so quiet she wouldn't have heard him had they not been only inches from each other. "Yes, this is my job. And yes, I understand why you might think part of it is being insincerely flattering. But that is something I never do. I can find something lovely in every woman. I don't lie. I don't have to. That's not who I am. But with you, it's more than that. More than searching for something true to say. It's right there. I don't have to search with you." His hand fisted at his chest, his eyes blazing once more. "How do I convince you that what I feel for you is real? I am not your ex-husband, Lilli."

"No, of course you're not. I know that."

"Do you?"

It was her turn to be silent. Did she know how different Rajan was from Evan, deep down in her soul, where it really counted? Was she being fair to him?

"Rajan, I'm sorry." She reached out and took his hand, curled her fingers around it. "This is hard for me. I don't know what to think, what to feel. Can you understand why I'm confused?"

His features softened and he pulled her hand in, holding their clasped fingers to his cheek. "I do understand. Sex has always been a spiritual matter to me. And I am suddenly seeing how that very thing, which I thought was noble somehow, has prevented me from finding real intimacy with any woman. As though I had some higher purpose. I've been very vain."

"No, not vain, Rajan."

"Or perhaps I was waiting for you."

Her heart swelled at his words. And she realized this was exactly what she wanted him to tell her. Yet she still didn't know what to do now, what to do about all of these emotions between them. Or about the vast differences in their lives, in what they each wanted. The situation seemed impossible.

"I have no idea where we go from here." His words echoed her thoughts exactly.

"Maybe we just enjoy each other until my time here is up? Then we can figure out the rest later." What other solution was there?

He nodded, his fingers tightening around hers. There was urgency in his voice. "I don't want to waste a single moment with you."

The tears threatened again. But she didn't know how much was joy and how much was pain. But at least, with Rajan, she had found the joy.

The next four days melded together, a seamless continuum of pleasure. Rajan taught her more about Tantra, about the Kama, the "Aphorisms for Love," as he explained the Sanskrit translated to. He took her through the Preludes, the delights of kissing, nibbling, sucking, and all the myriad names for every small brush of the lips, every teasing sweep and plunge of the tongue. He showed her the ten thrusts of the penis, and she found she loved the *Manthana,* called the Churning; the *Avamardana,* where he used pillows to raise her hips high in the air; the *Nirghata,* which was a sharp, steady thrusting that made her come in moments, her body shattering with unexpected pleasure. And there was a name even for this: *Samputa,* the Jewel Case, that involuntary shuddering of orgasm which both shocked and delighted her.

He showed her how to meditate, which they did early in the morning on the terrace overlooking the pool. She loved those peaceful times with him. They were often quiet during meals, and there seemed to be something almost sacred about being able to simply exist together.

She sat now on the terrace, draped in an embroidered silk sari in the same shade of pink as the sun setting behind the distant mountains. Rajan was inside, bathing before their dinner was brought to them. She'd wanted a few moments of quiet time. Needed it, on their last night together.

Sex with him was amazing. The physical aspects were far beyond anything she had ever experienced before. Her body had never been so well-used, so adored. She felt cherished, for the first time in her life. And he'd made her see that giving herself over to her own desires, to him, was not a sign of weakness.

He had taught her that she was beautiful.

And all of this had made her a stronger person. Or maybe he had simply shown her the strength she already had inside, but had failed to recognize on her own.

But she was still leaving tomorrow.

She wasn't sure how this was going to play out. She wanted to be with Rajan. But was a relationship really possible? That wasn't what she'd come here for. She had expected to leave here feeling more like a woman, and she had that. She felt more whole. More serene. Except when her heart was aching at the idea of leaving him behind.

He hadn't pushed her. On the contrary, they hadn't spoken again of what they would be after she left Exotica. Maybe that was part of the problem: not only what they would be, but what he would be.

She could not have a relationship with a man who was, by his own admission, a gigolo of sorts. Even if he'd gone into this with a more spiritual attitude, that's what it amounted to. She could not attempt a relationship with someone who slept with other women for a living.

God. She was really going to leave him.

Her chest knotted up, and she suddenly went weak all over, her limbs like water.

She heard the soft scuff of feet on the tiles and then Rajan's hands came to rest on her shoulders. He was quiet, but she felt reassured simply by his touch. How was she ever going to do without it?

No, don't think about it now.

"Are you hungry, Lilli? Dinner should be here in a moment."

"A little, maybe."

He moved around in front of her and knelt down, his hands on her knees. He watched her face, the muted flame of the dying sun setting the tips of his black curls on fire. "You don't have to be sad, Lilli."

"I know. I shouldn't waste any time being sad. I wanted to enjoy our last night. But it's hard."

"That's true, but it wasn't what I meant." He stared at her as though willing her to understand.

She shook her head. "What are you talking about?"

"You don't have to leave like this. I can go to the wedding with you. To offer my support, my strength."

He wanted to go with her?

"Rajan...I appreciate your offer, but I have to do this on my own. I don't think your going with me would solve anything." She paused, stroked a hand over his cheek. "I've learned so much since I've been here with you. In some ways, having to face my...my feelings for you, and having to face leaving here, has helped me to see my own strength. But now I have to do it, to follow through to the end. As much as I'd love to have you with me, I have to go alone. Do you understand?"

"Of course."

But he was quiet for several long moments, making her wonder if he truly did.

A maid arrived with their dinner tray, that same delicate woman with her long braid over one shoulder, her brilliant saffron-colored sari, her flashing black eyes.

She silently laid the tray on the table on the terrace, as Rajan directed her to. She paused to turn the pool lights on before giving a small bow, hands in prayer position, then left them alone once more.

Lilli stared at the pool for a moment, at the way the light shone through the ripples caused by the fountain in the center of it, at the flower petals spilling from the fountain to float on the tiny waves. So serene here. So lovely. She would miss this place.

Rajan had sat down in the chair next to hers and was busy taking the plates of food from the tray and arranging them on the table between them. She watched him, as she often did, his hands and body in motion.

She had truly never seen such a purely beautiful man, she thought for the millionth time. Not that his features were perfect. But the way his face, his body was put together, his natural grace, the aura of calm about him. No, she'd never met any man like him. And never would again.

So, why was she leaving him behind, with their future nothing more than a vague uncertainty?

She had to stop this. She was only torturing herself. It would ruin their evening if she was unable to get it under control. She would figure it out later, once she was away from here. There was no way she could figure it out now, with her emotions running so damn close to the surface tonight she had to fight nearly every moment not to cry.

He looked up from his task and smiled at her, that flash of white teeth making her melt a little, as it always did. She smiled back.

"Dinner looks wonderful, Lilli. Let me prepare your plate."

"I'm not very hungry. Really."

"Ah, but you must eat something. You'll need your strength tonight."

There was a wicked gleam in his smile now, and she couldn't help but laugh, some of the horrible tension draining out of her.

"Alright, then."

He moved his chair closer to hers, and spent the meal feeding her from his plate. There was something so utterly nurturing about this gesture. So *him*. So Rajan. He fed her, told her stories about the elephant god Ganesha, about his childhood spent in Mumbai, and she relaxed without even realizing she was doing it.

After dinner they sat on the terrace, watching the velvet dark of the desert sky, drinking a little wine, holding hands in the way that lovers do. She was consciously aware of every single moment of his body, his presence next to her, the exotic scent of him.

"We should go inside, Lilli. It's growing chilly."

"Yes, let's."

He took her hand and led her through the silk curtains. The maid had prepared the suite as she did most nights: flower petals were scattered on the bed and on the floor around it. Candles and incense had been lit, the golden glow and the scents of sandalwood and amber in the air making the setting all the more exotic. Sitar music played, but faintly, so that it seemed almost like a gentle afterthought.

Rajan led her to the foot of the bed and pulled her to him. He looked at her, his eyes simply roving her face. He murmured, "My beautiful Lilli. My princess."

Her legs went weak. She could barely stand that he

said such things to her! Yet she drank it in. And when he stroked a hand over her hair she wanted to cry again. How could she be so utterly happy at the same time?

He took his time unwrapping her from her sari, kissing her shoulders and her arms as he worked. In the soft glow of the candlelight she watched the ripple of muscle in his arms, his bare shoulders, the fall of jet-black hair. And his lips on her skin were lovely. Electric.

Her flesh was already on fire by the time the silk fell from her body into a soft pool at her feet. She watched Rajan as he untied the string at his waist and his linen pants fell to join her sari on the floor. God, his body never ceased to amaze her. Even his cock was beautiful, thick and every bit as strong as the rest of him.

He pulled her in close, pushing her curls from her face, his thumbs stroking her cheeks. She moved in closer, her breasts crushed against the solid wall of his chest. Leaning in, she buried her face in his neck, drew in his scent on a deep breath, held it in her lungs, wanting to hold it inside her forever. When she kissed the tender flesh there he moaned softly. Her tongue darted out, tasting the salty sweetness of his skin.

So good, yes, she had to have more. She pressed her open lips to his skin and swirled her tongue, as he'd shown her, then began to suck. He groaned, a low sound. He held her head there, his hands fisting in her hair. She loved it, loved the pull of it, the almost-pain.

Rajan let his head fall back, let her feast on his strong throat. She couldn't get enough of him. But there was so much more she wanted.

Snaking one hand down, she took the weight of his cock, wrapping her fingers around him. Loved the immediate tension in his body. Pleasure shot through her as though she could feel his response. Yes, it was hers, every sensation shared.

His hands dropped to her waist, his arms winding around her back, his hands moving lower to cup her bottom, pulling her hips closer. Angling her body, she spread her legs apart until she straddled his strong thigh.

Even the touch of his thigh on her throbbing cleft was almost too much for her. Desire streaked through her like fire, hot and intense. She shivered with the heat, pressed her mound harder onto his leg. And Rajan lifted his head, pulled her face from his neck, and bent in to take her mouth.

Such lush lips. She'd never felt anything like it, the way this man kissed her. Then his tongue was in her mouth, exploring, pushing into her, all wet heat and driving need.

When he moved his thigh and one hand slipped between her legs, she pulsed all over with pure pleasure. Just a gentle brush of his fingers over her wet slit, then again. Her hips tilted into his touch, and he slipped a finger inside her.

Oh God, yes. More...

As though hearing her silent plea, he added another finger, pushed in harder, deeper. She was impaled by the pleasure shafting through her. Her nipples were rock hard against his body, the hair on his chest scraping her skin as she writhed against him. The taste of him was salt on her tongue, the scent of him filled her nostrils, his cock was a velvet weight in her hand.

She squeezed a little, stroked her fingers up the shaft, tightened for a moment before stroking down, and loved it when he moaned into her mouth.

She wanted to hear his every moan, his every sigh of pleasure, but kissing him was far too good to stop. The wet tangle of their mouths was every bit as erotic as his hand between her thighs. But, oh, that was good, too. . . .

The first edge of climax came, bearing down on her, and her body tensed in exquisite anticipation. Rajan pulled his mouth away. She tried to recapture his lips, but his free hand came to her face, held her chin.

His voice was a raw gasp. "You are going to come, Lilli."

"Yes!"

"I want you to look at me. Look at me while you come into my hand."

She caught his fevered gaze, his black eyes burning hot. With desire. With emotion. She had to look away, her heart fluttering in her chest, aching every bit as much as her hot, throbbing sex.

"No, Lilli. I need to see you. Need to . . ."

His hand on her chin tightened, forcing her to face him, to see those dark eyes on hers, flooding her with emotion and the purest need she'd ever felt for another human being. She needed to come. She wanted to cry.

He worked her mercilessly, his fingers pumping into her, his thumb circling her clitoris. She was shivering, desire pumping through her veins. And his gaze locked on hers only seemed to feed it more.

"Look at me, Lilli. And come."

One more deep thrust and she came apart in his hands. Pleasure stabbed through her: her aching sex, her full breasts. Her blood was on fire, seized by the over-whelming heat. And her heart was as scorched by the fire as her body, melting in her chest.

She was shaking, wide open, tears in her eyes. And Rajan's gaze never wavered, his eyes filled with emotion.

She cried out, over and over, and still that hot wave of pleasure and desperation crushing her, until she fell into his arms.

He laid her on the bed, covered her body with his. She was still coming in tiny waves, aftershocks coursing through her. His weight on top of her was exactly what she needed; to feel that close to him. But it wasn't enough.

"Rajan..."

"Shh, yes I know," he murmured. "I need you, too. Need to be inside you."

He parted her legs, pushed until her knees were level with her shoulders, both her feet flat against his chest as he lowered himself over her and slipped right inside.

"Oh..."

"This is *Indrani*," he whispered, pushing deeper. "This is when you become the goddess. Where together we share an encounter with the Divine Essence. A token of love."

He drew his hips back, slid into her again as pleasure hummed through her in rippling waves.

He was watching her still, his beautiful face torn with raw pleasure, with raw emotion.

She ran her hands down his sides, felt him tremble beneath her touch, felt the power of it. She didn't need even the spirituality of the Kama Sutra to tell her what she already knew. Wrapping her hands around his strong buttocks, she pulled him deeper, needing to feel all of him.

The pleasure was nearly incalculable: his cock pushing into her, his smooth skin under her hands, his gasping breath. And his eyes, dark and glittering.

She reached up and pulled his head down to hers,

kissed his mouth. Just kissed his lips, over and over as he plunged into her, quickly bringing her to the peak once more.

His gasps turned into a series of groans. She felt the sound reverberate in his chest, felt his body tense, and knew he rode the same edge she did.

She pulled back to take his beautiful face in her hands, wanting to see him this time.

"Rajan..."

"Yes. *Now.*"

And together they came, shuddering with the force of the climax that seemed to flow through one and into the other, building and building, until it was almost too much to take. She could see herself reflected in his eyes, like two dark mirrors. What she saw there was pain and love and indescribable pleasure, both his and her own.

And she didn't know how she would ever live without it.

8.

SHE WOKE IN THE DARK, hot and sweating beneath the silk sheets, despair tugging at her until she found Rajan beside her. Her hands moved over the contours of his face, assuring her that he was still there.

He woke and kissed her searching fingertips drowsily, pulled her into his arms, soothing her. Yet her heart wouldn't stop racing, pounding in her chest. She stared into the near dark, her eyes having adjusted to the gloom. She could make out the archway leading onto the terrace, and the faint moonglow behind the silk curtains. And it struck her that she really did not want to leave this place.

These rooms felt like some sort of haven to her. Safe, warm, comforting. But also the place where she knew Rajan. Would he even be real after she left?

Once more, she had to touch him to be certain. Her

hands went again to his face, her fingers tracing his cheekbone, his jaw, his lips. And again those sweet kisses on her fingertips.

He pulled her closer, and his erection pressed against her hip. She rolled to face him, curled her arms around his neck, lifted her face to kiss him. Greedily, desperately. She would never get enough to take away with her.

Her chest was a solid knot, heavy over her heart. She kissed him harder, wanting to lose herself in the sweet play of his tongue against hers.

Her body came alive, needy, wanting. She slung one leg over his hip and moved closer, using her hand to fit the head of his cock inside her. With a groan, he thrust his hips forward and slid home.

"Rajan..." she whispered.

"The fifth position of the Perfumed Garden," he told her, his voice low, smoky. "But it no longer matters, Lilli, what it's called. It's you and me here. Together."

They were silent as they made love, clinging to each other, kissing, caressing. And all the time the tears burned behind her eyes.

When she came it was in a lovely, warm rush, and the intensity was all about what was happening in her head, in her heart, and in the emotion mirrored in his every touch. The languid beat of her climax ran through her veins, until she felt it all over, felt *him* all over. And still, neither of them said a word.

After, she drifted to sleep in his arms, and slept the deep, unworried sleep of the innocent.

A faint breeze drifted through the curtains, along with the watery glow of dawn. Rajan opened his eyes, his heart pounding until he saw that Lilli still rested in his arms. He had no idea how he would get through this day.

But he would. For her. After she left he would allow himself to feel the pain of her leaving. To spend some time figuring it all out. But not yet.

She was still here, warm in his embrace, her lashes resting against her pale, smooth cheeks. Her hair was a wild cascade of strawberry curls that glinted golden in the early sunlight filtering into the room.

Would he ever see the sun in her hair again?

It wasn't right, that she could leave like this, leave him behind. He understood well enough her need to go to the wedding alone. But then . . . what happened then?

It came to him once more, although more clearly than it had before, that *he* held the answer. That the only chance they had was if he left Exotica, found some other way to earn a living. What he really needed to do was to open his business. He'd had his business plan completed and in place for the last six months, but he still needed many thousands. And without it, what did he have to offer her?

This was the first time in his life he had ever felt entirely helpless.

He *was* helpless, where Lilli was concerned. Helpless against the way he felt about her. The question was, what could he do about it? And was it pride once more that made him feel he needed to have more to offer her? Or was he simply being realistic?

Lilli let out a soft moan, turned a little in his arms. Her lashes fluttered, her eyes opened. He felt that glossy golden-green gaze like an arrow of heat in his chest. She smiled, but very quickly her features shifted, her brows drawing together.

"Shh, Lilli. Don't say it."

She shook her head mutely, bit down on her lip. And reached for him, pressing her mouth to his. He kissed her, hard, his hands going into her hair.

He pulled away long enough to ask, "How much time?"

"Not long."

"Then we will have to be quick."

She smiled brilliantly. "I was hoping you'd say that."

He turned her onto her back, covered her body with his. Ah, just the feel of her satin skin against his...

He lowered his head and kissed her face: her smooth cheeks, her eyelids, the tip of her nose. Then he moved lower, kissing the fleshy curve of her breasts, drinking in her sweetness for a few moments before taking her nipple into his mouth, which was hard and swollen against his tongue. He moved to the other, licked, sucked, until she moaned and her hands dug into his shoulders.

"Rajan, I can't wait. Please..."

"Yes."

He moved up, settled between her thighs, and immediately his cock found the heat of her body. With a groan, he slid right into that wet, welcoming warmth. Her body surrounded him, squeezed him tight.

Sex had never been simple for him before. Now all he needed was to be inside her body, to have these last moments with her. He didn't care about the Kama anymore. He raised himself up on his elbows, wanting to see her face. Lord, she was beautiful. So beautiful.

Moving inside her, thrust after thrust, pleasure

moving through his body in exquisite ripples. She tensed beneath him, and he heard her ragged gasps. And when she came, her tight sheath clasping around him, he felt her climax rip through him. He shattered, spilled into her body while they cried out together. There was no one to hear in the clear morning air. But at this moment, nothing—and no one—else mattered.

It was only an hour later that they'd showered, dressed, and Lilli's small bag was packed and waiting. They'd only eaten a few bites of fruit. She wasn't hungry; she only ate because Rajan insisted. But he hadn't eaten any more than she had herself. Food had become a sensual ritual for them. Neither one of them could take it now.

She sat in a chair, listening to the low murmur of Rajan's voice coming from the alcove as he called for the cart to pick her up and take her to the main building. Her pulse was racing, her heart twisting into a tight ball of pain in her chest.

He came out from behind the curtain, dressed only in his loose linen pants. Had she ever appreciated enough the breadth of his shoulders, the texture of his brown skin? She ached to touch him. But she was afraid if she got her hands on him, she'd never let go.

He knelt on the floor before her, and she remembered with a deep shiver the last time he had knelt at her feet in front of this chair. Remembered the tender, sensual touch of Rajan painting her hands.

"Are you certain you won't let me come with you?" he asked.

She shook her head, doubt flooding her mind. But she knew she'd made the right decision. "I have to do this on my own. Show my strength. *Feel* my strength. I have to know I'm healed, Rajan."

"I had to ask one last time." He paused, took her hand in his. "And when you come back?"

"I . . . I don't know. It depends on so many things."

She didn't want to say it out loud, that she could never be with him if he continued to work here. She didn't want to lay down an ultimatum. How could she force him to make a choice? It wouldn't be fair; she had no right. No, she wouldn't ask that of him. And he hadn't volunteered.

Pain lashed through her once more. How was this possible? That she had come to this place, fallen so hard for this man? And how was she going to deal with it?

Footsteps on the tiles and a young man in uniform appeared. "I'm ready to take you now, Ms. DeForrest. Shall I get your bag?"

She nodded, her throat too tight to speak. She looked again at Rajan. His eyes were flashing darkly, full of banked emotion. And yet, he still wasn't promising her anything.

He stood and helped her from the chair. "Do you want me to go to the gate with you?"

"No. I can't."

"I understand."

He took one step back, letting her hand go. She looked at him, the torn expression on his beautiful face, and a wild desperation surged through her. She lunged for him, took his face in her hands, and crushed her mouth to his. He opened to her, deepened the kiss, and the taste of him filled her, made her heart leap in her chest.

His hands fisted in her hair, tightening until it hurt.

She didn't care. How could she feel so joyous and so utterly sad at the same time?

They broke apart, and he whispered, "We will figure this out, Lilli."

"Yes."

His gaze locked on hers once more, then he blinked a few times. Nodded his head, smiled at her.

She stepped back. And before she could change her mind, she turned and walked away.

Lilli hardly noticed the emerald green expanse of lawn around her, or the peacocks strutting beneath the tall palm trees as the little golf cart followed the path toward the main building. The driver remained respectfully silent while she clenched her jaw against the tears.

The cart stopped and the driver helped her out. Caroline waited for her at the door at the back of the main building.

"Lilli, come and talk with me for a few minutes before the limousine arrives."

She followed Caroline inside, into her office, and Caroline shut the door. "Sit down, and tell me why you're so pale. Are you alright?"

Lilli sat next to her friend on the beige leather sofa, remembered sitting in this same spot, trembling with nerves, on her first day. How had so much happened in only seven days?

"I'm okay."

"You're not okay."

Lilli sighed. No, she supposed she wasn't.

"Caroline..." But what to say? The words choked

her. She shook her head, her eyes filling, burning with tears.

"Lilli?" Caroline put a hand on her arm. "Talk to me."

"God, Caroline...I just...God. I think I'm in love with him."

The truth of the words hit her as they spilled from her mouth. "I'm in love with him," she said again.

"Ah." Caroline sat back, paused for a moment. "And does he love you?"

"I think he does."

"Well, then this is good, isn't it?" When Lilli didn't answer, she repeated, "Isn't it?"

Lilli covered her face with her hands. "I don't know!" She dropped her hands into her lap and looked at Caroline. "Yes, it's good. It feels good. It feels wonderful. But it's all so impossible. How did this happen in a week?"

"A very intense week where you hardly left each other's sides. Most people don't get that much time together in a month of dating."

"That's true, I suppose. But, Caroline...this was not that sort of scenario. This was going to be a sexual adventure, to open me up, to help me rediscover that side of myself. This wasn't meant to happen. This isn't some fairy tale romance."

Caroline said very quietly, "Maybe it is."

Lilli shook her head. "I just don't know. How can I? We've been cloistered in this rarified environment. This is all fantasy. I won't know what's real until I leave here, get back into the world. Deal with some of my baggage."

"The wedding."

"Yes, the wedding." She sat a minute, bit her lip. "He offered to go with me, you know."

"Rajan?"

"Yes."

"But you're leaving here without him."

"Yes. This is the way it has to be."

"I'm sure you know what's best, Lilli...."

"Do you think I'm crazy? Leaving him behind?" Lilli pushed her hair from her face. "Would you do this?"

"I can't say. It's been far too long since I felt that way about anyone. What do you think will happen? Later, I mean. Down the road."

"I have no idea. I have to get away, to think."

Caroline nodded at her. "Then do that."

"Caroline, I want you to know that coming here has taught me so much. It's been good for me. And I think ... well, forgive me for saying this, but I think this is something you could use, to experience yourself. Not that you'll end up as foolishly confused as I am." She wiped a tear from the corner of her eye. "Not that you'd want to. But when we talked before, well ... it seemed to me then that this might be exactly what you need. And I'm even more convinced now."

"I understand what you're saying, Lilli. But I can't. These people are my employees. I can't do it once those roles have been established."

"What about the new section opening up? The Arabian Nights?"

Caroline's brows rose. "What about it?"

"Maybe someone new, someone who hasn't actually begun to work for you yet?"

"I hadn't really thought about it."

"Maybe you should. Really, Caroline, this experience has opened me up in ways I never expected. Physically, emotionally, spiritually. It's helped me to put my past with Evan behind me. To unlearn those self-deprecating thought patterns he instilled in me. Maybe you can do the same. Put what happened with Jeff and Sarah behind you. Work through your response to it. I know what you've been through is so much worse than my pathetic story. But I think it could help you." She reached out and squeezed Caroline's hand. "Just think about it."

"Maybe. No, I will think about it. I promise." Caroline smiled. "And now I think it's time to get you to the airport."

"Yes." Another quick flash of pain in her chest, but she pushed it away as she rose to her feet and gave her friend a tight hug. "Thank you for this."

"You're welcome. Send me an e-mail. Or better yet, call me. Let's not lose touch, Lilli."

"We won't."

Outside, the driver held the door for her and she slid into the cool interior of the limousine, the leather seat slick against the back of her thighs. Such a sense of déjà vu, sitting there. But this drive would be so different from the day of her arrival. Instead of that lovely nervous anticipation, her heart lay heavy in her chest. Her entire body felt heavy, weighed down.

She could hardly stand to think about leaving Rajan. And she didn't really want to think about the wedding. But she'd have hours of travel in which to prepare herself.

If only there were something she could do—anything—to help her figure out where her life was headed next.

And whether or not the man she loved would be a part of it.

The rising sun lit the sky with streaks of pink and amber, shooting across the dark purple that was quickly fading to blue. Rajan, standing thigh-deep in the pool, bowed to the east, praising the gods one by one, and asking them for peace, for clarity. He hadn't practiced the ancient ritual in many years, but he needed it now.

He'd asked Caroline if he could stay one more night in the Kama Sutra suite. It wasn't normally done, but she had allowed it. The next client wouldn't arrive until tomorrow, anyway, a client one of the other Kama Sutra companions would cater to, adore, pleasure.

He would not do it again.

He couldn't bear to leave this place yet, where Lilli's scent still clung to the pillows, her essence everywhere. But he had many things to take care of today. Things which would change his life. If only Lilli would be a part of what he was about to do. But he had to have it to offer her first. And even then, there was no guarantee she would choose to be with him.

All around him the earth was coming alive. The air was crisp and fresh, and still cool with the dawn. It would heat up quickly. But before it did, he would be gone from these rooms. Never to return.

Bowing once more, he left the pool, naked in the pale light. He dried himself with a towel, put on his loose linen pants and went inside, and paused for a moment, looking at the room. His gaze roved over the inlaid mosaics on the walls, the high carved bed, the mussed sheets. He moved to the bed, touched his fingertips to her pillow, put them to his lips. He felt absolutely crushed, in a way he'd never felt before in his life. But all the more determined.

He ran a hand through his hair, his fingers tangling in the thick curls, blew out a long breath. He knew what he had to do. Turning, he strode toward the entrance of the building, down the twisting garden path. He hadn't bothered to call a cart. Instead, he walked across the wide green lawns, using the motion to rid himself of the tension that strung every muscle in his body in tight cords. When he reached the lodge he passed through the empty common rooms, took the elevator up to his apartment, and went immediately to the phone.

His sister picked up on the second ring.

"Teja, it's me."

"Raj!"

"I need to talk to you. Are you busy?"

"With that tone in your voice, brother, I'd make the time, no matter what. But yes, I'm free. Talk to me."

Suddenly, the words choked him. How to begin?

"I have been the worst kind of fool. I've let my ego run my life. I've been self-indulgent, all in the name of offering a spiritual service to the planet. Hah!"

He paced, the phone at his ear. "Now I need to let that pride go before I lose ... everything."

"Rajan, slow down and tell me what's going on."

"It's Lilli. I can't let her go. But the only chance I have at holding on to her is to face my pride, to rid myself of this sin. To change my life, Teja."

"Okay, Raj, just calm down a moment and we'll figure things out."

"I've already figured it out. I know what I need to do." His heart was racing. He walked faster across the hardwood floor, one hand in his hair, his fingers tightening. "This is not only about Lilli. This is about me. About not fooling myself any longer into thinking I have some higher purpose. I finally do, Teja. Don't you see?"

"I'm not sure I do see, Raj. Tell me."

"I am in love with her."

He stopped. A powerful wave of emotion rolled over him, the words, their meaning, reverberating like a drumbeat in his chest.

"Ah." His sister's voice was soft, and he knew she was absorbing what he'd just said. Lord, so was he. "What do you need from me, Rajan?"

"You have offered several times to go into business with me, to help me open the spa. And I have refused you. I thought I needed to pursue my dreams on my own in order for them to be worth anything. Pride again. I see now how foolish that is. That doing it on my own accomplishes nothing, proves nothing."

"I tried to tell you that, little brother."

"Yes. But I wasn't ready to listen. I'm ready now, if the offer is still available."

"You know I believe in you, Raj. And I've loved this idea from the first moment you presented it to me. I truly believe it would be a sound investment. Luxury spas are making money everywhere. I think we could do very, very well with it, especially if you still intend to find a location in one of the L.A. beach areas. Do you have your business plan ready?"

"I've been working on it for three years. I've learned much at Exotica, have spent my time here improving on it. I have every detail worked out. I've simply been waiting to earn enough money. You know that's why I'm here."

"Then you can't look at it as wasted time. And you met her there..."

"Yes!" His heart pounded, just picturing Lilli's face, as he'd first seen her, only a week ago. Those golden-red curls, her eyes glossy with nerves, her lips such a lovely, tempting pink.

Teja's voice was certain. "Let's do this."

His mind was going a thousand miles an hour. "Yes, I need to go to L.A., look for locations, buy equipment. I will write up whatever contract terms you like."

"I'll have my lawyer draft something. But don't worry about that now. Are you going to her?"

"Not yet. I must have something to present to her first. I can't go empty-handed."

"Pride again, brother?" Teja questioned him quietly.

"No. For the first time, no." He gazed out the window, his eyes taking in the wide lawn, the sprinklers dusting the brilliant green with tiny diamond-like droplets of water sparkling in the early morning sun. "Not pride this time. Simply an understanding of what she needs from me. I'll have to prove myself to her. She has doubts, and I can't blame her."

"Do what you have to do, Rajan. I'll wait to hear from you."

"Teja, thank you. For believing in me. For trusting in me."

"I always have. I'm glad you finally believe in yourself."

9.

BOSTON WAS COLDER than Lilli remembered it. Or maybe it was just that she'd spent a week in the glorious sunshine of Palm Springs. The heat of it had seeped into her bones, but it didn't keep her warm now. As much as she looked forward to seeing her niece—Evan's niece, she corrected herself—she just wanted to get this over with.

She was dreading seeing Evan with his wife, the woman who had once been his mistress, and who was now pregnant with his child. It didn't upset her the way it once had. She knew she had Rajan to thank for that, in part, anyway. His gentle touch, his encouragement, his devotion had healed a place in her heart. Still, she knew the meeting here would be unpleasant, knew Evan's vindictive little wife would do whatever she could to rub Lilli's face in the situation.

The cab pulled up to the church and she paid the driver and got out. The building was beautiful, an old Catholic church with Gothic arches and lovely stained glass. Evan's family church for several generations. A few people lingered on the steps. It was almost time for the ceremony; she'd come late on purpose.

Just see Nikki, wish her and her groom well, get through the reception, and go.

She smoothed her ice blue silk suit down over her hips and walked up the stairs and into the interior of the church, slipping into a seat in the back row. Classical music played faintly, and she breathed in the scent of furniture polish and flowers, trying not to remember her own wedding in this church. It seemed like a century ago. She felt like an entirely different person. She was. She'd been so insecure then, so frightened of everything. Did she even know that girl anymore?

The first notes of the wedding processional began and her heart lifted a little. Weddings were always special, that day, those moments. Most people didn't know on their wedding day if they were marrying the wrong person. Not until later, she thought with a hint of the old bitterness she'd been fighting to rid herself of. Or maybe she was the only one who'd been so foolish. But no, Nikki would be happy. She would try to focus on that today.

She watched her niece walk down the aisle, beautiful and graceful in her white gown, and cried a little as Nikki and her groom spoke their vows. Such lovely sentiments.

There was only one man she wanted to say such things to. And he wasn't there with her. Her choice, she knew, but she couldn't help that moment of regret.

She watched the new couple make their way back down the aisle, waited until most of the guests had filed out of the church before joining the crowd on the front steps to see the bride and groom into their waiting limousine for their ride to the reception. Lilli smiled at familiar friends and relatives, most of them people who hadn't spoken to her since the divorce. That was fine. They were *his* family, *his* friends. She had a different life now.

Suddenly, a fierce sense of relief washed through her.

Although Nikki had been a favorite, most of Evan's family were strict, conservative people who tended to be fairly narrow-minded. Like Evan himself. And all of them with that sense of superiority that she supposed often came with being an old Boston blue blood, people of wealth and power. They had intimidated her, as Evan had. Not anymore.

"Well, you came."

She'd know that voice anywhere. Direct, utterly confident, perhaps a bit smug. She turned and found her ex-husband standing two steps below her, his wife held close to his side.

He was the same Evan, all tall, blond, Ivy League good looks and exuding a confidence bordering on arrogance. She knew instantly he was pleased to run into her under these circumstances: her alone at his family wedding, him with his pregnant young wife. What he didn't know was that it didn't bother Lilli in the least.

It truly didn't.

The idea struck her like a small shock, yet a thoroughly pleasant one. She smiled at Evan, at his wife, who wore her smug grin for all to see as she ran a hand over her round belly.

"Evan, Patricia, how nice to see you. You look well. I hope the pregnancy is agreeing with you?"

"Yes, it's going perfectly," Evan answered.

Oh yes, speak for the little wife. He hadn't changed one bit. And of course, everything was perfect, as always.

"You look like you've had some sun, Lilli." Some negative insinuation lay beneath the words. No compliment from him. But had there ever been?

"I've been spending some time in Palm Springs."

He suddenly reached out and pulled one of her hands into his, a frown on his sculpted features. She had to suppress a shudder of revulsion. "What else have you been up to, Lilli?"

She glanced down at her hennaed palms and smiled again. She looked back at Evan. "All sorts of wonderful things, Evan. Things you could never even dream of. Things you never let me dream of."

He snorted and dropped her hand. "What a ridiculous thing to say."

She shrugged. She realized she didn't care what he thought about what she said, what she did. And with that dawning understanding came a profound sense of freedom. For the first time, she truly felt like her own person.

So why that underlying yearning to have Rajan there, by her side?

She didn't need him there; she simply wanted him. But there would be time to figure all that out later. For now, it was enough that she'd found her own sense of power again, through him.

She nodded to Evan and Patricia. "I'll see you both at the reception." And without waiting for an answer, she stepped down and moved past them, leaving them behind.

Lilli moved through the house she'd bought shortly before her trip to Exotica. It was an airy, open space, with an amazing wall of windows overlooking the beach in Malibu. She loved the crash of the waves against the shore, the call of seabirds. The sunsets from her living room were not to be rivaled. She'd paid a small fortune for the place. But then, she'd made a small fortune in her divorce, something she no longer felt any guilt about. She'd more than served her time with Evan; she'd earned this.

Evan. She reflected back to the wedding, seeing him and his wife. She was still a bit surprised by her new indifference. Why was it so hard for her to accept how she'd grown?

Her confidence had been ground into dust beneath the critical foot of her ex-husband. He'd done plenty of damage. And the worst part was that she'd let him. But that was over.

Part of it, she was certain, was that her feelings for Rajan gave her something else to focus on. A lot of it was about Rajan, really: who he was, how he made her feel about herself. He'd shown her how to see herself through his eyes. He'd helped her to open up, which in turn had led to her finding her own strength. Strength that had been there all along, if buried inside her. But it was out in the open now, a part of how she operated on a daily basis. She would be forever grateful to Rajan for showing her this side of herself.

If only they could figure things out, a way to be

happy together. But she'd been back from the wedding for nearly a week and she hadn't heard one word from him.

Her heart twisted in her chest. She was going to have to find a way to accept that he would go on living his life. And she would go on living hers—without him.

The drive up the Pacific Coast Highway from Marina del Rey to Malibu wasn't a long one, but it had already been far too long since Rajan had seen Lilli, spoken with her. His pulse was racing as he passed, unseeing, the stunning coastal scenery tourists came from all over the world to look at.

He'd just locked in the perfect property down in Marina del Rey for his new business. It was all about to happen, thanks to his sister's generosity. But he understood his life would be incomplete without Lilli. If only she would accept what he had to offer. It was only because of her that he *had* anything. He must communicate that to her somehow.

She had changed him, and there would be no going back. But those changes were all good, changes he'd needed to make without even knowing it. He thought he'd been doing just fine, but only after he'd met Lilli did he begin to see his life for what it really was: empty.

He gunned the engine and rounded a curve, spotting the street that led to her house. He made a right turn, then a left, and followed the narrow street up onto the hill that looked over the beach, a wide crescent of golden sand against the thundering green and blue of the Pacific Ocean.

Caroline had given him Lilli's address. He hadn't

been certain she would, especially after he'd quit his job without notice, but she'd seemed to understand his need. He'd had Lilli's cell phone number, but he didn't want to talk to her until he truly had something to say. And now, he knew he had to do it in person.

He found the house, one of those long, low, thoroughly modern structures that dotted the Southern California coastline. The place was surrounded by lush vegetation, reminding him for a moment of the gardens around the Kama Sutra suite. The gravel in the driveway crunched beneath his tires as he pulled through the open gate and parked next to a small Mercedes coupe.

This was it. His chance to show her how much she meant to him. To tell her about all she'd taught him.

His heart was hammering, with nerves, with pure need for her. This had to work.

The chiming of the doorbell took Lilli by surprise. Today was Sunday; she wasn't expecting the pool man or her housekeeper. She was a mess today, her hair uncombed, dressed in an old pair of sweatpants and a cotton tank top. Who could be at her door? She took a moment to run a self-conscious hand through her unruly curls and went to answer.

She swung the door open and it took a moment for her to understand that it was Rajan standing there. Her heart stuttered in her chest, and she was overwhelmed by an odd mixture of joy and pain.

"Lilli."

God, had she forgotten how purely beautiful he was?

"Rajan. What are you . . . what are you doing here?"

"I had to see you, talk to you. May I come in?"

"What? Yes. Sure."

She stepped back and unconsciously inhaled as he moved past her into the foyer. She went dizzy for a moment, from his scent, from the shocking realization that he was actually there.

He walked right into the living room, went to stand before the windows, silhouetted in the glare of sunlight reflecting off the ocean.

She had never seen him fully dressed before, she realized. He wore a pair of black slacks, a crisp white dress shirt. His shoulders looked even broader than they had naked.

She went warm all over, her body throbbing with yearning. It hurt, to see him standing in her house. To want him so badly.

"Rajan, what are you . . . I mean . . . I've been back for a week."

"Yes. I know."

"Then why . . ." She stopped, not wanting to sound desperate. Even if she was.

He took one step toward her and she took a defensive step back.

A look of hurt crossed his features, and she felt momentarily crushed that she had caused him pain. But she had to know why he'd waited so long to contact her. And why had he shown up now, unannounced?

"Lilli, I wasn't even sure if I should come here like this. Except that I knew I had to. Lord, I'm not making sense, am I?" He ran both hands through his dark curls, pulling his hair back from his face. And that was when she saw how dark his eyes were, how full of emotion.

She wanted to cry just looking at him. But she also felt the need to hold herself back from him. Because even though she knew she loved him, she was every bit as aware that he could hurt her, too. Every nerve in her body was on fire, pulling her toward him, wanting, needing to touch him. But she was too afraid she wasn't going to hear what she needed to so desperately. Why did that make her angry?

"Lord, Lilli, I didn't mean for it to be like this." He looked absolutely helpless standing there.

"Like what, Rajan? Difficult? How else could it be between us?"

"You can't really believe that."

"This whole thing was crazy from the start!"

"Alright, I admit that. But it doesn't mean we can't make it possible."

"How are we supposed to do that?" She hated that her lip was trembling, that tears burned her eyes. "Rajan, you are who you are. And I learned so...so much from being with you. And I'm grateful for that. But I have no right to ask you to change. I understand that."

"What if I want to? What if I've come to realize that I must?"

Her throat was closing up on her and she could only shake her head in silence. What was he trying to tell her? Hope welled up, along with the tears, but she choked them both back.

He went on. "Lilli, you made me come to a few realizations about myself. That I have been full of pride, that I've been operating from that place. I was too proud to do what needed to be done in order to really begin my life. But I know now how wrong I was. I thought I could do everything on my own. Thought I had to. But I was wrong. And you were wrong, too."

"What do you mean?"

"You thought you had to go to that wedding with your newfound strength all alone. But don't you see, Lilli? We aren't any weaker if we allow ourselves to lean on someone. The strength is still there. And neither of us has to prove that to anyone. Being strong is enough." He moved toward her, took hold of her hands before she could protest. "I can say this about you because it's true for me, too. I can see it. Just as I can see that you love me, as I love you."

The tears spilled then, flowing over her cheeks. She shook her head, speechless once more as emotions warred in her mind, her heart. He loved her! But what did it mean for them? It was almost too much to take in all at once.

He bent down and pulled her hands to his lips, laid gentle kisses over her fingers while her body went soft and warm all over. He looked at her through a fringe of midnight lashes. "I love you, Lilli. I have since the first moment I saw you. And I can't allow my pride, or yours, to stand in the way of us being together."

She was crying in earnest now, sobs welling in her throat, making it hard to breathe. Finally she managed to take in a gulp of air. "But . . . it can't be that simple."

"Why not?"

"There are still so many things . . . too many reasons . . ."

"You mean my career, such as it is?"

She nodded. "It's impossible to ignore. How can I?"

"You don't have to. It's over. I quit."

She shook her head. "I didn't want to force a choice on you. You have to live your life, Rajan."

"My life is with you." His dark eyes bored into her, until it felt almost as though he were touching her, deep down. "Lilli, I didn't change my life because of you. You simply made me see the necessity."

She still couldn't figure it all out. "What will you do now?"

"I'm opening a business, with my sister. A luxury spa in Marina del Rey. This is what I've been working toward these last years. Why I became a companion at Exotica to begin with. I was there to learn about that sort of business structure, and to make as much money as I possibly could. And I was waiting. I thought I was waiting for the time to be right. But now I believe I was waiting to meet you."

"Rajan..." She shook her head. He was opening a business, moving to L.A.?

"Lilli, if I don't kiss you I swear I will lose my mind."

There was nothing more in the world she wanted. He moved in, pressing his lips to hers, softly at first, then hungrily. His kiss reverberated through her, a thrumming of heat and pain and love.

He pulled back. "Tell me you love me."

"I love you. God, it feels good to say it to you."

He kissed her again, pulling her close, until she felt the steady beat of his heart against hers. She never wanted him to stop kissing her, holding her, the scent of him surrounding her.

When they pulled apart it was only so they could look at each other, to touch fingers to cheeks.

He was right. Giving in to love only made them both stronger. How had she not known it before? But there was so much Rajan had taught her. There would be more, she was certain.

She was flooded with relief at the thought that they had a chance now. And with remorse at her lack of faith. In herself, in him. But all that mattered now was that they could be together. They loved each other. And together, they could do anything.

PART TWO

Nine Days of Arabian Nights

11.

LUXURY. Exotic silk. Hot, sultry nights. This was the first impression Caroline had as she followed Exotica's decorator into the new Arabian Nights suite.

The marble-lined room was enormous, with alcoves here and there along the walls. Some were nothing more than niches which held stone urns of flowers, perfuming the air. Some held tall wooden mirrors, carved and inlaid with mother-of-pearl, and in some stood enormous bronze statues of horses, tigers, and enchanting female figures.

In the center of the room, beneath the sixteen-foot-high mosaic ceiling, was the bed. It was round, enormous, covered in a heavy gold damask spread, and four tall brass spires rose elegantly toward the high ceiling. And above it a gossamer drape of silk in a pale shade of cream with gold threads shot through it hung from the vaulted ceiling, suspended by a golden framework. The sheer fabric was drawn around the head of the bed and draped down each side, but she could still clearly see the mounds of silk-covered pillows in cream and gold, with a few in rich jewel-toned purples, reds, and deep blues.

More pillows were piled here and there on the floor next to low tables of delicately carved and inlaid wood; larger ones meant to sit on, smaller pillows heavy with gold embroidery, and bolsters in every size. The marble floors were scattered with Persian rugs in gorgeous colors and patterns. The entire place spoke of sybaritic luxury. Decadence. An environment made for sex, which is exactly what it was.

"Denise, you've done an incredible job."

"I'm so glad you're pleased." The petite blonde decorator smiled, her eyes lighting up at the compliment.

"Really, just incredible, this place." Caroline moved to the bed, ran a hand over the fine fabric. "I can't believe you finished ahead of schedule. Thank you for all your hard work."

"You're welcome. This was my favorite project here so far. I'm only sad you don't have plans to build another theme area."

"Oh, you know we always come up with something new for our clients. I'm kicking around a few ideas already. I'm sure you'll be hearing from me before the end of the year."

"I hope so." Denise glanced at her watch. "I'm sorry, Caroline, but I've got to go. I have an appointment with a client in Rancho Mirage."

"Of course. Go ahead and take the golf cart. I want

to stay for a while and look around. I can call another cart when I'm ready to leave."

"I'll check in with you in a couple of weeks, after your first clients have seen the place and given you some feedback. Meanwhile, let me know if I've missed anything."

"You never do. I'll talk to you soon."

Denise walked toward the high, arching doorway, her heels clicking on the marble floor, leaving Caroline alone to take in the beauty of the place. And to sit a moment and peruse the file of the newest Exotica employee, one of the recently hired companions for the Arabian Nights area.

She sat on the edge of the bed and opened the file she'd only been able to glance at before Denise had arrived at her office earlier. But that brief glance had been enough. She'd kept it gripped in her hand this whole time.

Amazing-looking man. One look at his photograph had her heart pounding as though she'd run a mile through the desert heat.

Lilli's words ran through her mind. *Just think about it.* Yes, she would think about it. Hell, she could barely think of anything else already, which irritated her and intrigued her all at the same time.

She ran her fingers over the edge of the manila folder in her lap, staring at the eight-by-ten image of her new employee. Jet-black hair barely brushing his shoulders. It swept back from angular features set off by an impossibly lush mouth, and hazel eyes that burned even through the photograph. How much more magnificent would he be in person?

In person in this room, in this place designed to titillate the senses? She could imagine the possibilities just sitting here, on this big bed where he might...where she might...

Her cell phone rang and she was momentarily startled by the sound. She flipped her phone open.

"Yes?"

"Caroline, it's Lilli."

"Oh, hi. How are you? How's Rajan?"

"We're fine. Perfect. Ridiculously happy." Lilli laughed. "I'll stop now before I really start to gush. How are you?"

"Me? Oh, I'm...fine."

"You sound a little breathless. Did I catch you at a bad time?"

"What? No. I'm just...I'm down in the Arabian Nights suite. It turned out beautifully. You should see it."

"And?"

"And...I have this file in front of me. The new companion. And he's...God, he's incredible. I'm telling you, Lilli," Caroline said into the phone, "this man has got to be the one, if I'm ever going to...try to work past my issues. Already I feel things I haven't felt for such a long time, just looking at his photograph. I feel strange telling you this, even though we've talked before about... my problem. But I've never seen a man who looks like this."

Such strong features; pure male beauty at its finest. All so strong except for that gorgeous full mouth. She could read utter confidence in the way he held his shoulders, in his smile. Nothing sexier than confidence in a man. And those eyes, framed by dark, thick lashes...

"Caroline? Are you still there?" Lilli's voice sounded as though she were a million miles away, rather than at her house in Malibu, a mere two hours from Palm Springs.

"What? Oh, sorry. I was ... I wasn't paying attention."

Lilli laughed. "No kidding. So, what do you know about him?"

"His name is Kian Razin. He's thirty-six years old. He's of Jordanian descent, but was apparently raised all over Europe and the U.S. And since Collette sent him I'm sure he's educated, refined. He speaks six languages."

Her attention wandered again as she focused on the man in the picture. Broad shoulders in his finely cut suit. A custom made suit, if she wasn't mistaken. But if he could afford such a suit, what was he doing coming to work as a companion at Exotica? Perhaps one of Collette's ... indulgences? Not that Caroline begrudged her anything. Collette Fournier, the owner of Exotica, was a more than generous employer. Caroline made a rather insane salary working for her. But she didn't like the idea of being with one of Collette's cast-off playthings, and from what his file said, he was coming from Paris, where Collette lived. Perhaps there was a way she could discover the nature of their relationship?

"He sounds perfect, Caroline. I'm so glad you're seriously considering doing this. You know I believe this is exactly what you need. And you sound enthusiastic about it, finally."

"Maybe." But her cheeks were flushed and hot just staring at his picture. She couldn't stop staring.

"When does he arrive?" Lilli asked her.

"Sometime today." Her stomach gave a small squeeze. Was she really going through with this mad plan?

"Good. It's time you did something just for you."

"I'm still not quite sure about it, Lilli. About what to tell him. God, I can't just come out and say that I'm... frigid. Damaged." She gave a wry laugh, her throat a tight knot. "That sounds so pathetic."

"You don't have to tell him. Tell him you just need to open up, that it's a journey of self-discovery. That's the truth, isn't it?"

"Yes." Caroline smoothed back her already perfectly smooth hair. She'd pinned it into a tight bun this morning, a defensive gesture that made her feel less vulnerable. But even considering being with this man was making her feel raw, open. "It's just that he's so... so incredibly good-looking. The prospect is overwhelming. And you know that, working here, I've seen some of the most beautiful men on the planet. I don't understand why this man is affecting me this way."

Lilli said quietly, "Maybe because you've already given yourself permission to let him touch you. To really try to let him inside. That must be a very powerful thing."

Caroline's skin tingled. Powerful indeed. It had been so long since she'd let anyone touch her. Longer since anyone had touched her and really gotten through. Not since Jeff. Five years was more than long enough to have shut herself off from intimacy, from feeling anything, even the most basic physical response. And looking back, she wasn't certain how far she'd ever let Jeff in, even before he'd betrayed her so horribly. Yes, too much of her mother's cool blood in her veins. Her mother who had never needed anything from her, even as she lay dying of cancer, and who had given nothing emotionally, to Caroline or to anyone.

She could almost hear her mother's voice in her head now, judging, and finding her lacking, as always. Her mother, who had blamed her for what happened to Sarah. She'd never said so out loud. Never anything more than those small, biting remarks about Caroline being impetuous, not thinking things through. How ironic that Caroline was the most controlled person she knew. That it was her very inability to let go of that control which had made her shut down physically, emotionally.

Stop.

This was not about her mother. This wasn't about Jeff, or even Sarah. Lilli was right. This was for *her.*

She ran her fingers over the slick surface of the photograph once more. What would it be like to feel that mouth on hers? She shivered with a small rush of heat. Perhaps she wasn't entirely frigid after all?

"I really have to pull myself together, Lilli. I feel like some schoolgirl with a crush! It's absurd. Just looking at his picture is making me—"

She looked up at the sound of footsteps. Her breath hitched in her chest.

Kian Razin. What was he doing here? But he was even better in person. Her face went hot, absolutely burning. God, had he heard any of her conversation?

"Lilli, I'll have to call you back." She snapped the phone shut without waiting for her friend's answer. And closed the file just as quickly, but not before she saw his eyes darting there.

"Can I . . . can I help you?" Was that really her breathless, stuttering voice?

He walked toward her with his hand outstretched, all cool elegance in his crisp white shirt. "Kian Razin, at your service, Miss Winter. Your secretary told me I'd find you here."

She stood and offered her hand, an automatic gesture.

But when his fingers closed around hers, an electric current hummed through her skin, into her veins, heating her blood.

Oh yes, much better in person. That face, that smooth European voice.

He held her hand a few moments too long, long enough for his intense hazel gaze to bore into hers. His lashes were even thicker, duskier, close up. She felt her cheeks go warm and released his hand.

He smiled, a devastating flash of perfectly white teeth. Lord, he was almost too beautiful to be real. And he exuded a certain undeniable aura of power. She had to remind herself that he was her employee.

Don't think too much about that or you'll never be able to go through with this.

Better just to look at him, talk with him.

"Please, let's sit down." She gestured to a pair of heavily carved chairs flanking a small table inlaid with mother-of-pearl.

He moved to hold her chair for her, a charming gesture that flustered her. Then he took the other chair, settling into it in an entirely relaxed manner. Graceful, self-assured. Almost, but not quite, cocky. But then, why wouldn't a man who looked like he did be utterly confident?

Pull yourself together.

She cleared her throat. "Collette sent me your file, and I've looked through it. It seems you're a perfect candidate to become one of Exotica's companions. Our Arabian Nights section opens in nine days, so you'll have some time to settle into your apartment in the lodge and to familiarize yourself with the setup, with the two other companions and the staff in your theme area. I'm sure Collette explained to you how everything works here?"

"Yes, I'm familiar with the procedures."

His voice was deep and smoky, and held an accent she couldn't quite place. Definitely a bit of the Middle East, but also that European edge she'd first noticed.

"I'm curious...how did Collette discover you?"

"I've known her all my life." He leaned forward and plucked a flower from the small vase on the table. Caroline watched as he stroked the petals with his fingers before her focus shifted to his hands. Fine, strong hands, with a sprinkling of black hair. He set the flower down on the table and looked at her. "And I've known about this place since she opened it."

"Your whole life? She's a friend of your family, then?"

He sat back in his chair. "You could say that."

"Would you like to go to your apartment now and rest from your trip? You must be tired after your flight from Paris."

"Not at all. I spent a few nights at the Beverly Wilshire, then drove down this morning."

The Beverly Wilshire? Either Kian Razin had his own money—a lot of it—and was here for the thrill, or he was one of Collette's boy toys. But he'd said Collette was a friend of the family...which told her exactly nothing. Was she imagining that his answer had been vague?

God, she was making herself crazy with this stuff!

She shook the thought away. "Then perhaps we can talk a bit now?"

"We can do anything you wish, Miss Winter."

Why did that make her shiver? "Please, call me Caroline. Everyone does."

"Caroline, then. A lovely name, if a bit reserved."

He watched her, his eyes glittering gold and brown and a bit of silver. She had a sense that he was gauging her response to his words, his flirtatious tone. Oh, he was smooth. And why would he have said that, about her being reserved? Her cheeks went warm again. She cleared her throat.

"May I offer you something to drink?"

"No. Thank you, Caroline."

Intimate somehow, him saying her name like that. She shifted in her chair, crossing her bare legs beneath her short linen skirt.

"Well then." She smoothed a hand over her hair. "Tell me, Kian, why do you want to work as a companion at Exotica?"

"Ah, we're in interview mode now, are we? Alright. I did speak with Collette about all of this, but I'm sure you know that."

"Yes, of course. But I like to get to know my staff myself."

The heat flooding her cheeks now was anger. Or annoyance, at the very least. She hated being reminded that she was to be his boss. It made her ideas about him seem wicked, somehow. But it wasn't as though they were in banking or software development. This was a sex fantasy resort. And after all these years of keeping her sexuality so tightly wrapped, it was time to indulge her own fantasy. Or at least, to try. But she was distracted again, while he sat there watching her with that glowing hazel gaze.

"I came to work here because I love women, everything about them. Because I think I'll be good at it. And

I don't mean to appear narcissistic. I simply think it's the truth. Because, quite frankly, the idea of doing this appeals to me on a very deep level. It intrigues me. I believe what you do here, what *we* do here, is a celebration of female sexuality. Don't you agree?"

"What? Yes, I do agree." Her palms were sweating. She rubbed them together beneath the table. She wasn't sure she liked that he seemed to be more in command than she was.

"I'd love to see the rest, Caroline. I came right in without stopping to admire it all. Won't you give me a tour?"

"Yes, of course."

She stood, perhaps a bit too quickly. She felt awkward suddenly. And completely off balance.

He's just a man.

Yes, just a man, like the dozens of other men who worked here. All of them handsome, confident, intelligent, charming. But none had ever had this effect on her.

He rose as well, and it was then she noticed how tall he was. She was five foot seven herself, and was wearing heels, but he towered over her, making her feel small. Vulnerable. Feminine.

Lord, what was wrong with her?

She gestured to the high arched doorway. "Shall we go?"

They moved through the entryway. Here the floors and the walls were again done in a pattern of white, gray, and the precious pale pink marble that had been imported from the Middle East. The foyer was bare of anything other than an enormous mirror with a carved wooden frame that was inlaid with mother-of-pearl.

Caroline paused, waiting to make sure Kian followed her, then moved through another archway and out to the front terrace overlooking the garden.

Date palms towered on either side of a sandy path, green vines twining around their narrow trunks. Shorter palms, cypress, olive, and blossoming orange trees made up the landscape, along with the trailing, bright pink bougainvillea that grew everywhere at Exotica.

"It's lovely here," he said. "Let's take a walk."

This man was clearly someone who was used to being in charge, and she had to wonder again what he was doing there. But something in her was responding to him, to his air of command. "Alright."

He pulled a pair of sunglasses from a pocket and put them on. Armani, she noticed. Slipping her own dark glasses on, she had a moment to look at him unnoticed. His chiseled jaw, his cheekbones, really could have been cut from stone. Yet his mouth was full and frankly sensual. What would that mouth feel like? Taste like? She looked away, her cheeks warm.

"The landscaping is all new," she told him as they walked down the shallow flight of marble stairs and stepped onto the narrow path. "It should grow in a bit more, in time. And we ordered several statues that haven't arrived yet." She gestured toward the building behind them, and they both turned to face the tall stone façade of the miniature palace, the towering archways with their detailed scrollwork, the new green vines just beginning to twine their way around the supporting columns. "The structure is modeled largely after a palace in Damascus."

"Azem Palace."

"Yes. Exactly."

"I've been there. It's so ancient. So beautiful." He lifted his sunglasses, resting them on his dark hair. The sun glinted in his eyes, making them glow with a golden light. "Your architect did a very good job here. The stonework is very similar to the original structure; that pattern of light and dark, the mosaic tiles on the ground. And the detail on the stone archways. Remarkable, really." They walked on, approaching a low, square pool, the intricate blue tile work on the inner surface shining through the clear water. "This is exactly like the one in the courtyard of the palace. Exquisite."

"We do our best at Exotica. We want our clients to truly immerse themselves in the environment."

"Yes, I can see that."

He moved closer to the pool, touched his fingertips to a delicate fern in a tall stone urn next to it. "Beautiful," he murmured. Then he turned to her and took her hand. "Yes, beautiful."

His smile was dazzling, and his touch burned into her skin, making her entire body feel as though she'd suddenly become weightless.

Must get control of yourself.

She drew in a deep breath. "Shall we go back inside? It's getting warm out here."

She pulled away from him and walked up the shallow flight of marble stairs and into the suite. But inside, surrounded once more by the decadent luxury, she wasn't sure this had been the wisest move.

Kian came to stand beside her. "An incredible place, Caroline. You've done an excellent job here."

Why should his words please her so much? Why were her cheeks so hot?

"We use a decorator. I do often come up with the

initial design ideas, but she takes over after that. This is the first time I've seen the finished product myself."

She sensed him moving in closer next to her, caught the heady scent of expensive aftershave, something woody and spicy. Masculine. Something very *him*.

"So, tell me Caroline, when exactly do I begin?"

God, was she really going to make this proposition to this man? She wanted to. Needed to. Lilli was right about that. And the way she was responding to him physically told her there was no better man for the job. But just thinking about saying the words made her stomach tie up in a hard knot.

She took a step back, needing some distance from him. She ran her fingers over her hair, then, feeling self-conscious, dropped her hand to her side. It was now or never.

"Actually, I'd like for you to begin tonight."

Had she really said that? Her pulse was racing, her blood hot and thick in her veins.

"You have a client for me already? Not that I mind, of course."

Now, Caroline!

"No, not a client." *Just say it. Say it as though it's the most natural thing in the world.* "You're going to work with me."

2.

ONE OF KIAN'S DARK elegant eyebrows arched as he smiled. Why did it seem predatory? But he looked pleased. Inordinately so. "With you?"

"I . . . I always audition our companions." The lie slid off her tongue. She felt half relieved, half guilty.

"Do you?" He paused. She kept quiet, watching his reaction. Oh, he definitely looked pleased. And there was something else in his eyes, but she couldn't tell what it was. "I would be honored to begin my work here with you, Caroline."

"Well, alright then. We have nine days before this area opens to our clients, so it's free for . . . our use."

"Do we begin now?"

"Now?" Impossible. She needed some time to prepare herself. Time to . . . she wasn't sure what. Catch her breath, maybe? "Well, no, not right this moment. I have to finish out the workday. There are some things in my office I have to . . . no. We'll meet here tonight. And I'll arrange my schedule so that I can spend some of those days here, with you."

"Only some?"

She swallowed, hard. "That depends on . . . how it goes."

God, she could barely breathe. This was all too real, suddenly.

Pull it together!

He nodded, as though this weren't unusual in the least. "I'll drive you back to the main building, then, so you can finish work and I can get my bags. I didn't see another cart outside."

"Yes, thank you. That would be fine." Not that he'd phrased it as a question.

He nodded, motioned toward the door with a graceful hand. How had he taken over the situation so completely? But she walked across the marble floor and outside. He followed, then took her elbow in a familiar, Old-World gesture that she half-loved, even though part of her was appalled at the way she was responding to his commanding strength.

They were silent as they made the short walk through the garden, to where one of Exotica's golf carts was parked. He handed her into the passenger side and went around to settle into the driver's seat before she had a chance to think about the fact that helping her into the open cart had been completely unnecessary.

Who was this man? He started the cart and drove off, his posture relaxed, in control. Caroline lowered her sunglasses over her eyes once more and tried to ignore the palpable sensual energy of Kian Razin.

The sun shone down on the emerald lawn that made up the central park-like area around which the themed suites of Exotica were built. She tried to focus on the backdrop of rugged gray mountains in the distance, the crystal clear blue of the desert sky, but every nerve in her body was alive with the awareness of Kian next to her.

"Collette tells me you've worked here for several years," he said. That lovely voice again, exotic, like some expensive imported liqueur.

"Yes. For three years."

"And do you like it, working here?"

"I do like it. I love my job here, actually."

"An unusual occupation," he remarked.

"And so is yours about to be."

"Touché." He turned to smile at her, and she cursed silently as her limbs went warm and weak.

They pulled up to the door of the main building which housed her office. He immediately jumped out to help her from the cart, another unnecessary gesture. Why did it cause a small thrill to ripple over her skin, even as it annoyed her?

"Thank you."

Kian made a small bow. So gallant, despite his cockiness. Such an unusual man. Her head was spinning with contradictions.

"I'll retrieve my bags now, Caroline, then wait for you in the Arabian Nights suite. Come whenever you're ready. I will be sure to have everything prepared. I'm very much looking forward to our evening."

She nodded. She couldn't think of a single thing to say.

Her brain emptied completely when he took her hand and brushed a soft kiss across her knuckles before he backed away and walked around the side of the building. She just stood and watched him for several moments, her breath hitching in her chest.

She was on dangerous ground with this man. Danger she had volunteered for herself. But she'd had no idea what she was getting herself into until she'd met him. Of course, she'd asked for this, hadn't she? But Kian Razin was far too good to resist. Too good, and too bad. Which made him just about perfect.

Kian scattered rose petals on the enormous and luxurious bed in the Arabian Nights suite. The petals were soft, silky, as he knew Caroline's skin would be. He held a handful of the deep red blossoms to his nose, inhaled. Such sweet perfume. Almost too sweet for the enigmatic woman he'd met a few hours ago.

He hadn't been able to stop thinking of her since. Complicated. That was a perfect description of the manager of Exotica. And beautiful. Oh yes, undeniably so. With those high cheekbones, those wide, dusky blue eyes. And that full mouth that belonged on a porn star. He loved that she wore it bare of anything other than a bit of gloss, the natural pink shining through making him think of naked bodies, of sex. Or maybe it was just her, all of her.

She was not what he'd expected when he and Collette had talked about him coming to work here. But what had he expected? He hadn't given much thought to the manager. All he'd thought of was the experience, living as a companion here, exploring the business from the inside. And the thrill of doing this, working in this extreme environment.

He bent to arrange the cascading piles of silk pillows. What an opportunity for a man who loved women the way he did. There was an art to seducing a woman, and he'd always had an eye for art. Women themselves were pure art to him. And, short attention span that he had when it came to the female sex, this was the perfect job for him. A perfect way to celebrate the carefree existence he'd always lived, now that he would soon be faced with real responsibilities. He didn't mind. He understood very well that life had been extraordinarily kind to him. He'd led a charmed life, really. If he had only six more months in which to indulge his whims, so be it.

Finished decorating the bed, he moved to a curtained alcove and set the basket of blooms on a table, picked up a box of matches, and moved back into the room to light the candles that sat on every surface, as well as the filigreed brass lamps which hung suspended on delicate chains from the high ceiling.

What was Caroline's story, exactly? Who was this woman her staff called the Ice Queen behind her back? Oh, she was controlled enough. Or she tried to be. Except that nerves radiated off her like an electrical charge whenever he moved near her, flirted with her, smiled at her. He recognized sexual attraction when he felt it, and the chemistry between them was explosive. But she did her best to keep it reined in.

Yes, control was crucial to her. That much was obvious. But what was hidden beneath that smooth surface? He'd had a glimpse. And he firmly believed that sort of absolute restraint could only be fueled by a person of immense passion.

This experience with her would be a great challenge. He loved nothing better than a challenge. Especially one which involved a beautiful woman.

He had one brief sting of guilt that he hadn't told her exactly what he was doing at Exotica. But he couldn't do it. He understood that. And he was a man who honored his word.

He moved back over to the bed, stripped off his slacks and shirt; his shoes he'd already removed when he'd come inside. He picked up the heavy swath of midnight blue silk from the bed and pulled on the full-legged pants that were as much a part of the Arabian Nights fantasy as the luxuriously detailed setting. He was surprised at how comfortable, how natural he felt dressed this way. Perhaps part of this job was for the companions to sink into their roles as much as the clients did. He smiled at the idea.

He thought Caroline would like to see him dressed like this. Yes, as of now, it must all be about what she might enjoy. His job here was to please her in every way possible. He had never lived to serve anyone other than himself before. Surprisingly, he relished the idea, his blood heating at the thought. Even though he knew she was lying.

He knew quite well that she never auditioned the companions. So why had she chosen to do so with him? What could her motivation possibly be? He was intrigued by it; that she had lied in order to have him. Not that the lie was at all necessary. She was a beautiful woman. Incredibly attractive, really, with her long, long legs, that gorgeous, lightly tanned skin. And that lovely, elegant face. He could only imagine how exquisite her breasts would be beneath her tailored blouse. He was getting hard just imagining the feel of those soft mounds of flesh in his hands.

Yes, Caroline Winter was a most fascinating woman. He could hardly wait to unlock the mysteries buried deep in that beautiful body, in that complicated mind.

Of course, he hadn't been exactly forthright with her, either. But there would be plenty of time for that later. He tried to tell himself it didn't matter, but another small surge of conscience nettled him.

Why was he suddenly questioning his motives, his actions?

A faint shuffling on the marble in the foyer, and he knew it was her. His entire system sprang to life.

Ah, and now it begins.

Caroline walked into the Arabian Nights suite, awed by the change the evening had brought. Everywhere candles and lanterns glowed, sending the sensual fragrance of sandalwood into the air. Rose petals were strewn in a path across the floor from the doorway to the bed, like some crazy romantic fantasy. Almost too much. But a part of her she could barely admit to loved it.

On the bed, reclined, relaxed, with a confident smile on his gorgeous face, was Kian.

He was wearing the loose silk pants made especially for the Arabian Nights companions and nothing else. His bare chest glowed golden in the soft light. The fact that he was barefoot made him seem all the more naked for some reason. Oh yes, the perfect Arabian Nights fantasy man.

The back of her neck grew warm and her mouth went dry. She stood, frozen, in the doorway.

"Caroline." That deep, accented voice turned her knees to water.

"Yes..." She didn't know what to say to him. This had all seemed like a good idea earlier, but now that she was here, all she wanted to do was run, to hide from her hammering pulse, from the heat building on her skin.

But no, that was a lie. All she wanted to do was touch him. Strangely. Urgently. She didn't want to admit that, either.

Too late.

He rose from the bed, strode across the room, every inch the regal Arabian knight. All he needed was a scimitar and a white horse. She shivered as he took her hand. And when he raised it to his lips and kissed it, just a gentle brush of his lips across the knuckles, a surge of warmth flooded her system.

Yes, she remembered this sensation. Lust. Desire.

"Come and sit with me," he said, leading her across the room. Her stomach tightened as she took in the big bed, piled with luxurious pillows. Could she lie in that bed with him? She didn't know how she was going to do it.

He stopped at the foot of the bed and turned to her, never letting go of her hand. His was warm, large, his fingers wrapped around hers in a way that was at once protective and possessive. And God, his shoulders were so broad, muscular. His skin that perfect golden shade that made her think of honey, of the sun. She swallowed, hard.

He dropped her hand and slipped around behind

her, his movements like some sort of dance. Having him where she couldn't see him made her pulse race even more. Was it fear? Excitement? What was this man doing to her, in only the few moments since she'd entered the room?

His hands landed on her shoulders and she flinched.

Damn it.

That flinch was too telling, she knew. And she hated that she'd done it.

"Just relax, Caroline. Take a breath. Do you trust me?"

"I...I don't know. I don't trust easily. You should know that."

"And yet, you asked me to be here with you."

"Yes."

He slid his hands down her bare arms, leaving a trail of hcated flesh behind. She bit her lip, trying to escape the sensation.

"I can see you're struggling, Caroline. Tell me why."

She didn't want to talk about this. Not now, not ever. She just wanted him to touch her, to do his job without her having to explain anything. It was too awful, too humiliating. She shook her head mutely.

He came around to face her once more, searched her eyes. His were like molten gold, shimmering in the flickering candlelight. He said softly, more gently than she would have expected from him, "What is it?"

She shook her head again, looking away as her throat closed up.

Keep it together, Caroline.

"I can see it's something." He reached out and stroked her cheek with one fingertip. She trembled at the tender touch, with emotion, with need. "Is it simply that this is an . . . audition, as you said?" He paused, then murmured, almost as if to himself, "But no, that wouldn't make sense."

He was going to figure her out for the fake she was!

"Let's not talk about it now, Caroline. Let's not think about it." His tone dropped even deeper. "For now, let us just be together. Let me touch you, open you up. I believe you need it. Leave everything to me."

When had she had that kind of offer from a man? And something about his tone made her believe him.

She nodded once more. He slid his hands down her arms, and again she had that sensation of heat trailing his fingers.

"Yes, that's it. Enjoy my touch."

Somehow, his simple, murmured words were helping her to give herself over to him. She had to swallow the part of her that wanted to get angry, defensive. That wanted to tell him to go to hell.

Just do it.

A hard lump formed in her throat as he untied the light sweater from around her shoulders and let it fall to the floor. Then he methodically unbuttoned her blouse, one small button at a time, as though he had all the time in the world. She stood stiff, trying to breathe, to will herself to relax, to at least fool him into believing she belonged here. But by the time he slipped her sleeveless silk blouse from her shoulders she was trembling all over.

He moved in and laid a soft kiss on her shoulder. Desire poured through her, fought against the tension in her body. The fear. Yes, fear. She hadn't realized she was actually afraid of getting close to a man until this moment.

Kian trailed his fingers over her neck, bringing up gooseflesh, and she let him, let him pleasure her skin. So hard not to struggle, not to fight off the desire. It felt dangerous, letting go even this much.

When he leaned into her and kissed her neck she shivered, then tried to pull away. He moved back and looked at her.

"Do you want me to stop, Caroline?"

"No. No, I don't."

"Are you certain? Because if that's what you want, I will stop. Now. Whenever you ask me to."

"No. It's not that. I need to . . ."

Her throat was closing up again.

"Do you mean for me to continue, even if you flinch away? Even when you aren't enjoying my touch? Is this some sort of test?"

"I can't explain." Her voice was shaking. "But yes, that's exactly what I want you to do."

"Then I shall."

He reached out and drew one finger over her jawline, across her lips, then made his way down her neck to the curve of her breast.

He said so quietly it was almost a whisper, "I see your breath, coming fast and hard. I see your excitement, but something else, as well. Perhaps that is my challenge here, then? To discover what it is that holds you back. To break through that boundary. Am I right?"

It was a moment before she could answer. "Yes. Yes, that's it."

"Alright then. But I must ask that you trust me, as much as you can. You must try."

There was something comforting in that tone of authority, his confident insistence. As though he were entirely secure in the belief that he could give her whatever it was she needed.

Perhaps he could.

She had a feeling she was about to find out.

Kian swept his hands over Caroline's smooth shoulders. The woman was strung as tight as piano wire. Nerves, yes, but an exquisite sensual awareness, as well. There was definitely something going on with her. Something to do with the lie she'd told him about "auditioning" him. Something to do with pain. What had happened to her to make her like this? He would discover what it was, would find a way to loosen her up.

He was right: Caroline *would* be a challenge. One he was certainly up for. Even more so because it was her. This woman whose very presence, whose scent, made his stomach, his groin, knot up with lust.

He had to have her. And he would. But not yet.

He could feel that shallow trembling in her body beneath his hands. But her nipples were coming up hard beneath the pale pink satin of her bra. He had to remind himself to take it slow. Wasn't this exactly the sort of control he'd have to exert while working with the clients here at Exotica? And somehow this idea made his job here even more exciting. Yes, it would be all about control, commanding both himself and his partner.

He stroked the smooth skin of her arms, slowly down, then back up again, simply allowing her to get used to his touch. After a while her eyes fluttered closed.

"Yes, that's it," he whispered. "Only the two of us here, my hands on you. It's all new now. You must let it happen. The trust will come later."

And so will you, my Ice Queen.

Yes. He could hardly wait. To see her come apart under his hands. How much more delicious with a woman as cool and controlled as Caroline. Of course, she was losing that control already, and all he'd done was touch her arms.

He slid his fingertips over her collarbones, felt her flinch once more as he inched his way over the top curves of her breasts. But he didn't stop.

Lovely breasts. Not too large, just enough gorgeous flesh to fill his hands. She had one of those trim, athletic bodies that showed she took good care of herself. Probably exercised religiously, spent hours in the gym. That control again. Yes, Caroline was the kind of woman who would have to have perfect mastery over her body. Not that he minded the results.

Most men of his culture liked their women to be curvier, more heavily fleshed, but he loved her lithe figure. Loved the clean lines of her face.

He watched her as he slipped his palms around the undersides of her breasts. Another sharp intake of breath as he filled his hands with that warm flesh. But she let him do it, kept her eyes closed. And that small gasping breath made his cock go hard as stone.

He stepped in closer, tugged at the zipper to her skirt, let it fall around her ankles. Such perfect thighs, lean and taut with well-toned muscle. They'd be strong wrapped around his back while he sank into her....

But no, that wasn't going to happen now. Not yet. Whatever was going on with her, he knew he'd have to take this slowly, more slowly than he ever had with a woman in his life. Hell, he usually had them in bed before the first date was over. This would be a new experience for him, holding back his own need. He brushed her nipples with his thumbs, felt those tips come up hard against the satin. Yes, a new experience he would enjoy thoroughly.

By the end of their time together, Caroline Winter would be the Ice Queen no more. He would take those walls down, brick by brick.

His cock throbbed as he stroked her nipples through the fine fabric of her bra. It was killing him, to touch her, knowing he wouldn't fuck her. But yes, whatever he had to do, he'd do it. Even if it killed him.

It just might.

3.

CAROLINE PULLED in a deep breath. How long had it been since she'd felt so stimulated? Since she'd allowed herself to? Yes, just as Lilli had said, she'd given herself permission, making it a little easier for her to allow this, for her to feel . . . something. Anything. Just that chink in her armor . . .

She was feeling plenty right now, as he rubbed her swollen nipples through the satin of her bra.

Her sex was beginning to swell, just from his hands on her breasts. A part of her was embarrassed, humiliated, even as desire poured through her in a warm rush. She was trying hard not to think about it.

He was so quiet, just touching her. But she could hear his breathing as it became more ragged, could feel the warmth of it on her cheek. Something about the fact that he was obviously turned on made it easier to handle. Gave her a sense of control over the situation.

How could he want her, as she stood there, frozen, as still as a statue, so unresponsive?

No, don't think about it now. Don't ruin it.

It was obvious he did want her, and she took pleasure in the thought. If even for this moment, simply because he had his hands on her. She would accept that. It was enough for now.

Of course, Jeff had wanted her at one time, too. Until he'd changed his mind and wanted her best friend. And look how that had ended.

Don't, don't, don't!

Why did she always do this to herself? She had to stop. But the only way she thought she could was to be so swept up in the moment, she couldn't possibly think of anything else.

Which was why she had chosen Kian. He was the first man she thought might be able to do that for her. To her.

Focus!

His hands were exploring her now, sliding over her rib cage, her stomach, tracing the top band of her pink satin panties. And her body was responding, despite the thoughts roving through her mind. It seemed she could control everything in her life, except for those memories, and her reaction to what had happened.

"Caroline," came his soft voice. "Where are you? No, don't answer. But be here, with me, at this moment. Do you understand?"

"Yes." The word came out on a whisper.

He moved in closer, until she could feel the heat coming off his body, his skin only inches from hers. God, he smelled good.

"Block out everything but my voice, Caroline. My touch. Yes, keep your eyes closed. Don't think. Feel."

Total command in his voice. There was no point in trying to argue.

His fingers slipped beneath the lace band at her abdomen, just an inch, but it went through her like a shock. But rather than bolting, she let it happen. Her sex went warm, wet. A soft sigh escaped her.

"Ah, yes, that's it. Beautiful."

His hand slid down, until his fingertips caressed the curls between her thighs.

"Oh God . . ."

"Shh . . . it's okay."

How did he know how hesitant she was, how frightened? But it felt so good, his hand on her body. That was exactly what scared her so much.

He stayed there, just brushing softly over the curls, while her body heated up, even as she trembled. She could hardly believe she was responding to him this way. It had been so long. What was it about Kian that made her let go?

But only so much. When he dipped lower, his fingertips grazing the lips of her sex, she stiffened all over. She wanted to pull away. She wanted to cry. She wanted him to do it again.

He moved in even closer, so that he was pressed right up against her, his bare flesh against hers. His skin was absolutely burning. So was her sex, her breasts. But her mind was a whirling mass of confusion, a war of want and fear and denial of her own need.

"I . . . I'm sorry. I'm not sure I can do this."

She stepped away from him, her cheeks burning, wishing she could hide. He put a hand on her arm, drew her back to him, pulled her right up against the solid planes of his chest. Taking her chin in his hand, he tilted her face. His eyes burned into hers, those elemental eyes that reminded her of tiger's eye, of molten gold touched with silver.

He said in a low voice, "I will let you go if you want to. Of course I will. But I don't think you want me to. Do you?"

It was too hard to lie to him, with his gaze boring into hers. "No. I don't know . . ." Then, more firmly, "No."

He smiled, dazzling her, then guided her to the bed.

"I have an idea, Caroline. But you must trust me. You must turn yourself over to me. Can you do that?"

She took in a long breath, held it a moment. "I think so. It's not in my nature. It's not . . . I just don't know."

"Do we stop now, then?" His eyes burning into hers again.

Inside, she felt as though a storm were raging, pulling her in every direction. She couldn't seem to think straight.

"No. I don't want to stop. No."

He stared at her for a long moment, his gaze challenging her. She was shivering, but she stood her ground, lifted her chin a little higher.

Finally, he nodded. "Lie down on the bed." His hands on her shoulders, exerting a gentle pressure, but enough to force her onto the bed, to lean back on the pile of pillows. "Just do as I say. I will do everything."

Fear flowed through her. She didn't like it one bit. She wasn't used to it. It made her feel lost. Powerless. But she had to do this. This was her chance to truly heal.

A weaker man would never have worked, and she'd never met anyone as strong as Kian in her life. She did her best to swallow the fear, the embarrassment; not at her near nakedness, but at the fear itself.

He began to stroke her skin in long, fluid motions: her neck, her chest, her sides, down over her thighs. He caressed her calves, even her feet. Then back up again, until his fingers traced the curves of her cheeks, her lips, her chin. Her skin was warm and alive, her body buzzing with desire. She had no control over that, either, she realized, to her response to him.

"The lingerie, as pretty as it is, will have to come off."

She swallowed. How much more vulnerable would she feel naked? But the more he touched her, the more she wanted to be.

She nodded, but he was already unfastening the catch on the front of her bra. It took him mere moments to slip off the pink scrap of panties. Yes, vulnerable, so naked. She was more aware than ever of the scented air touching her skin as she lay back on the pillows once more.

"Beautiful, Caroline. You are so beautiful. I love the long line of your legs." He drew a finger down her thigh. "That tempting triangle of curls." He swept his fingers over her, so lightly she could barely feel it, yet it made her tremble with longing. "I want to discover what's hiding there, the secrets of your body. And I'm going to."

God, to have him talk to her like this! She was shivering all over.

He was still touching her, his hands wandering in a slow, sweeping caress. Her breasts ached for his touch, but he spent long minutes avoiding them, avoiding going too near her sex, which was aching harder than her breasts were. She could not believe her body was

responding this way! It felt almost like a betrayal if she
let herself think about it too much. She closed her eyes.

"Yes, that's good. Sink into it. I'll do everything."

His touch seemed to amplify somehow, the moment
she shut her eyes. It was as though she was more able to
focus on what was happening to her without distraction.

When he cupped her breasts her body arched off
the bed.

"Oh!"

"Shh." He squeezed gently, and her nipples came up
hard against his palms.

It took her a few moments to unwind again, to allow
her muscles to loosen. And as though he sensed her body
relaxing, he brushed his fingers over her hardened nipples.

She moaned.

He took those swollen tips between fingers and thumbs
and began to roll them. The sensation was exquisite,
buzzing through her body in shimmering waves. She
could almost feel her blood undulate with desire. And
her sex was wet and wanting.

When one of his hands slipped between her thighs
she jumped.

His hand immediately went to her stomach, pressed
there. "It's alright." He was quiet for a moment while she
drew in a deep breath. Then, "I think you need this...
yes. I will return in a moment. Keep your eyes closed.
Keep breathing."

She did as he asked, a small part of her mind wondering what he might do next, but mostly she was mor-
tified. How was she going to get through this? She was

barely able to hold still from one moment to the next. And as much as her body was on fire from his touch, she was fighting it so hard inside. He would have to sedate her, for God's sake, to *make* her...

"I am going to tie your wrists, Caroline."

Her eyes flew open. He stood at the foot of the bed, a rainbow of silk scarves in his hands. Purple, blue, red, gold. Her hands went to cross over her bare breasts.

"You can't mean that."

"Oh yes, I can. I do. I think it will help you."

"No. I don't see how..."

He came and sat next to her on the bed, one hand sliding over her arm, her shoulder.

"It will help to relieve you of responsibility. To free you to simply enjoy."

She was suffused with anger suddenly. "What makes you think I need help?"

He looked at her, his burning gaze on hers. "Caroline. We both know there is some issue here. And we both know that is why you are 'auditioning' me. I don't have to know why. But we must be honest with each other on some level in order for this to work."

Her cheeks burned with shame. "I just...I need to..." God, how utterly humiliating.

"You're afraid." It wasn't a question.

"Yes," she whispered.

"Fear is nothing to be ashamed of. But it should be dealt with. I believe that is why we are here together. Am I correct?"

She nodded. "Yes."

She hadn't expected this sort of insight; not from this kind of man. A man who looked the way he did, with his absolute confidence, didn't need to be so sensitive, so intuitive. Yet he was.

"Close your eyes again. Let it happen."

He touched her hair, his fingertips lovely, soothing. And the other hand slipping over her stomach made her body burn with need once more. His hand moved up her arm, to her wrist, and then he circled it in silk and tied a loop. He tied the other end to a bedpost.

Pure panic filled her for a moment, then he bent and kissed her wrist, soothing her, before doing the same with her other wrist. He sat on the bed beside her again, running his hands once more over her heated skin.

"So lovely. Even more so like this, in the act of yielding. Do you understand how beautiful this is?"

Did she? She couldn't seem to make sense out of anything at the moment. And her mind just emptied out when he slipped one hand between her thighs. Just a momentary feathering of his fingers, but again she felt it as though it were a shock. Her sex blazed with heat, and she bit back her moan.

"I'm going to tie your ankles, as well, Caroline. Don't be afraid. It will make you feel more vulnerable at first. But it will also give you a sense of safety, once you realize you can do nothing but give in to it."

He pulled her leg out to one side, opening her sex. She did feel vulnerable as he looped the silk around her ankle and tied it to another bedpost. Even worse when he put his hand on her other leg and moved it aside.

She'd never felt so exposed in her life.

Her heart hammered, and she pulled against the silky restraints. Yet she was flooded with desire at the same time. Absolutely burning with it. Shocking. Even better when he smoothed his hands over her naked skin: up her legs, over her stomach, and back to caress her breasts.

Oh yes...

He pulled at her nipples, rolled them, tugged until it almost hurt. And they were harder, more inflamed, than they'd ever been in her life. Sensation was washing over her: her breasts, her belly, straight to her sex. Something about being so wide open to him was an incredible turn-on, even though the idea of it was terrifying.

Just don't think.

He was right, being bound was freeing, she realized.

Don't think. Don't analyze.

With a conscious effort, she turned her brain off, and let herself float on sensation.

As though he felt that moment when she was finally able to let go, he brushed his hands down the front of her body, between her thighs, and right into her wet heat.

"Oh! Kian..."

"Lord, you are so wet. So tight." His voice was rough. "I would do almost anything to be inside you. But I won't do that tonight. Tonight is all for you."

He pushed two fingers into her, used his thumb to press onto her clitoris, and she cried out. Searing pleasure moved through her, making her legs, her arms, weak, liquid. Yes, that was exactly what it felt like: liquid heat, liquid need. And she was dissolving beneath the force of it.

Higher and higher, he drove her on. He never stopped caressing her sex with one hand, his fingers moving inside her, while with the other hand he teased her nipples, rubbing, plucking, rolling them. She felt overwhelmed by sensation; it was almost too much to bear. And yet, exquisitely keen at the same time.

Higher still, until she began to pant. Unable to resist the tide of pleasure. Panic. Pleasure.

Don't fight it.

"Yes, my lovely Caroline. That's it. Let it go. Come now. Come for me. I want to feel you come. I want to watch your face, want to hear your cries of pleasure."

It was too good, to have him say these things to her. Her body hit a new peak, began to clench. She was trembling with the force of it as she poised on that edge.

"That's it." He pumped his fingers inside her, pressed onto her clit harder. "I can almost feel your climax in my hands. I can feel you shivering with it. Come, Caroline."

So close, so damn close. She squeezed her eyes shut, tensed the muscles in her thighs. His hands on her felt incredible. Indescribable pleasure washed over her, and yet she couldn't quite reach the crest that hovered just out of her reach.

"You can do it," he encouraged her.

But she knew it was impossible. It had been too long. She groaned her frustration and let her body go limp.

"Don't, Caroline. I can take you there. You must relax, have patience."

"It's no good." She hated that the words came out on a half-whispered sob.

He leaned in and kissed her then, pressing his soft lips to hers. So sweet. She wanted to cry. She wanted his tongue in her mouth.

He kept kissing her, until she couldn't think anymore. Better that way. He just kissed her lips, over and over, soft kisses. His mouth was impossibly lush against hers. He swept his tongue across her lower lip and she opened for him.

Warm and wet and so damn sweet, his tongue explored her mouth. The man could kiss like a demon. Perfect, every single moment. Her body lit up with need, her skin tingling, her breasts tightening, her nipples rock hard. Oh yes, this was exactly what she needed. Her muscles went loose all over. She wanted to wrap her arms around his neck, hold him to her. She didn't ever want him to stop kissing her.

When he did, her breath was coming in ragged pants. Her lips felt bruised.

She wanted more.

When she looked into his eyes they were glittering. She could see desire there, and felt a small surge of satisfaction.

His voice was quiet, a rough whisper. "Have you ever used a vibrator, Caroline?"

"What? Yes. Of course. But it never . . . it never worked."

"I think it might now."

He leaned over and pulled open the door of the night table, which she knew held a variety of sex toys. From it he drew a phallic-shaped vibrator in a soft shade of pink. It was textured all over with small bumps. Her sex clenched just looking at it. Yes, maybe it would be different if *he* used it on her. She wanted it. Wanted him to do it.

She licked her lips, trembled in anticipation. He watched her for a moment, then smiled.

"I can hardly wait to touch you with this."

She could hardly wait, either.

When he switched it on she tensed in anticipation. He kept his eyes on her face as he lowered the instrument between her thighs.

The first moment of contact went through her like a bare bolt of electricity, and he'd only touched it to her mound. Then he used his fingers to spread the lips of her sex apart, and ran the vibrator over the sensitive flesh.

God, she could barely breathe, it felt so good. Too good.

"Kian!"

"Shh. Let it happen. Allow yourself this pleasure, Caroline. And know it is my pleasure, as well. To see you responding this way, to see the expression of ecstasy on your face. I'm as hard as I've ever been in my life, I swear it."

He used his fingers to spread her lips wide and pushed just the tip of the vibrator inside her. She felt it reverberate throughout her body.

"Oh!"

"Yes, it's good, isn't it?" he murmured.

He pushed it in another inch, and her sex clamped around it. Then he began to move it, in and out, slowly, and with his other hand he circled her clit. She pulled hard on her silken bonds, felt the safety of them, as he had said. And something else she hadn't expected; that being bound made every sensation more intense, more concentrated.

She was overcome by pleasure, on the verge of climax. Her body wanted to give in, but her mind held her back.

Let go, let go, let go.

She'd never felt anything like this before. So good. He leaned down and took one nipple into his mouth, nearly sending her over the edge. His wet, sucking mouth, his fingers, the vibrator moving deeper inside her now. She was entirely helpless.

The edge was right there, just waiting for her to fall over. But she couldn't do it.

"Kian, I can't. Please. Just stop. I can't do this."

Tears rolled down her cheeks. But he didn't stop.

A wave shimmered through her sex, her very center, an almost-climax, before it faded away.

"I can't, I can't . . ."

"You can," he murmured against her breast. He moved to the other nipple, pulled it between his teeth. A little pain, a lot of pleasure, shooting to her sex, heating it up all over again. The lovely brush of his hair falling over her skin. And still his clever fingers working her clitoris, the vibrator moving inside her. And again, she came so very close before the sensation washed away on a wave of self-doubt.

"Kian," she panted. "Please, no more. It's not going to happen. Please . . ."

"I won't give up on you, Caroline. Even if you give up on yourself." He lifted his face, looked into her eyes. "Let go of the control, Caroline," he commanded.

"I can't! You don't understand."

"I don't have to. All I have to know is that you can do this. Do it, Caroline."

He shoved the vibrator deep into her sex, took her clit between his fingers and rolled it, tugged on it. Pleasure shot through her body like shards of glass, so intense it hurt.

"Oh! Oh, oh . . ."

Again, that peak rose before her. She didn't want to go there, couldn't lose control of herself. But he was licking and sucking on her skin, her nipples, the vibrator and his fingers working the needy flesh between her thighs. Until she had no choice.

It slammed into her like a fist, that powerful, that shocking. A storm of pleasure, drowning her in sensation that hummed through her in sharp, stinging currents. She cried out, and another wave flashed through her. Still, his mouth all over her, his hands, the vibrator, all sensations blending together, melding. Pleasure, lust, as sharp as a knife blade lancing through her sex, her breasts, her belly, her arms and legs.

Tears poured down her face, and still the tremors shook her. Intense, too intense. It hurt. It felt good. Unbearable.

Finally, the shock waves subsided. Her entire body was on fire, shaking. Kian was still there with her, kissing her breasts, her neck, untying her hands, then her ankles. She could not believe it had happened. That it had been *her* shivering and screaming on the bed.

She rolled onto her side, curled up into herself.

No, no, no!

She couldn't help the tears, the anger that came right behind them. He had made her do this. *Made* her let go, lose control.

The anger swelled, until it swallowed up the fear, and she was suffused with nothing but pure, clean fury. She sat up, dragging a pillow to cover her nakedness.

He was watching her, his expression wary.

"You . . ." But she was too choked to finish her sentence.

"Caroline. It's okay." He reached out to touch her but she flinched away.

"No, it's not! It's not okay. It never will be. I can't do this!"

"But you just did."

"Don't patronize me, Kian."

"I'm not. I swear it. Why the anger, Caroline? What is this about? Because I know perfectly well it's not about me."

He had her there. She had to pause, to drag in a deep lungful of air. She blew it out slowly. "No. It's about ... it's about me."

"Are you going to tell me?"

"No. I'm not."

There was a long pause. Then, "What now, then?"

"Now ... now we stop. I can see this was a mistake." She was still shaking inside, but at least half of it was rage. Rage and a deep need to be in command of herself again.

"You're going to tell me that orgasm was a mistake? Because I don't think I've seen a woman come so hard in my life."

"How dare you?" She wanted to slap him. She might have if he'd looked the slightest bit smug. But he didn't.

"Caroline, we both understand that this is some deep issue for you," he said quietly.

"Why should you care?"

"I simply do."

"Is this some sort of personal challenge for you? Is that how you see it? Make the frigid girl come?"

"Perhaps that's part of it, yes. Would you rather I lie to you about that?"

She could not believe he was saying these things to

her. "This was a mistake," she repeated. "One I won't make again."

She started to scoot off the bed, taking the big pillow with her, wildly glancing about for her clothes.

"Caroline. Wait."

"Why? So I can humiliate myself further?"

Her eyes were burning, tears gathering behind her lids.

Damn it.

"Perhaps so that I can redeem myself."

She stopped, looked at him. His soft voice, the expression of sincerity on his face, made the fury die down a little. He came and put a hand on hers, held on gently.

"I have a proposition for you."

She waited in silence for him to continue.

"Give me these nine days."

"What for?"

"To help you work through this...whatever it is. You don't have to tell me. But let me try."

"What exactly do you intend to do?"

"To make you come, every day and every night. Until it becomes natural for you. Until you stop fighting it."

"That's ridiculous!"

"Is it? I don't see your struggle as ridiculous. I see it as something which prevents you from fully enjoying life. Am I correct?"

She looked away, whispered, "Yes."

"Then do this with me."

"And if it doesn't work? What then?"

"Then...then you will have the opportunity to do to me whatever I have done to you. No argument. You will have total control."

She had to smile at that. "Are you serious?"

"Perfectly."

"You're very confident."

"Yes. Always." He smiled, that beautiful, devastating smile. "So? Are we in agreement?"

How could she resist? Either he would help her, or he would spend some time under her command. She was still angry enough to think that retribution could be a lovely thing.

She nodded. "Yes. We are in agreement."

She couldn't stop shivering. Was she really rational enough to make such a deal right now? The shivering got worse. She clamped her jaw tight.

Stop it!

But she couldn't stop. She was horrified when the tears spilled over, poured down her cheeks. Even more so when Kian pulled her into his arms.

No, no, no!

But it was too late for that, wasn't it? She was afraid she'd already lost the fight, with herself, with Kian. And she didn't have the strength left to fight anymore.

4.

LONG, SILENT SOBS shook her as Kian held her in his arms. He let her do it, let her cry it out. He was in a state of shock himself. He'd never seen a woman go through anything like this. He felt a deep sense of honor that she had chosen him to be the one to experience this with. At the same time, he had a hard time understanding his own reaction. He felt... opened up by her. As though her vulnerability had reached inside him and found some raw spot he hadn't known existed.

He felt elated and exhausted at the same time. And he was still rock hard. Still wanted nothing more than to push into her body, to pound into her, to feel the satin length of her legs wrapped around him. But that would have to wait.

What had happened to her to make her like this? It

must have been horrific. Had what he'd done with her tonight helped her? Would she forgive him for forcing her orgasm on her?

Why did he care so damn much, as long as she had agreed to continue?

He'd never truly cared when it came to women. Not on any personal level. His life had been far too easy; he'd never been taught to care. Why was he suddenly feeling that perhaps he'd missed out on something? Strange. Shocking, even, this idea. But it made him want to hold her tighter.

Finally she stopped shivering and relaxed a bit in his arms. He looked down into her tired face. She was pale, her eyes red, yet still as beautiful as ever. Beautiful and tragic.

"You need to sleep now," he told her.

She nodded, let him tuck her into the big bed as though she were a child.

"Do you need anything, Caroline? Something to eat? To drink?"

"No. I just want to sleep."

"Then sleep. I will join you in a few minutes."

Her eyes were already closed, her lashes dark and dusky against her pale cheeks. Her breathing was shallow, and he knew she slept already.

He got up and went out to the terrace. The dark silhouette of the mountain range rose against a deep blue velvet sky scattered with stars. The moon was a crescent hanging above him, casting a pale blue light. Drawing the night air into his lungs, he tried to cool off, to rid himself of the images of Caroline plaguing his mind. Her lovely face, twisted with pleasure, and her inner struggle against it. Her breasts with their dark, luscious nipples, hard and swollen and eager for his mouth. Her long legs, her silken skin beneath his hands. Ah, the slick folds of her pussy, the tight clench of her sex around his thrusting fingers . . .

He groaned, his hand pressing on the solid erection that wouldn't calm any more than his mind would. The clean, bracing air of the desert night wasn't enough. He looked through the open doorway to where Caroline lay curled on the bed. The sheet had fallen away, leaving her succulent breasts bare. Even in sleep, her nipples were hard, as erect as his cock.

He groaned again, then moved across the hard, cool floor, passing the bed on his way into the bath. He ignored the big marble tub there and reached into the shower, blasting the hot water. Stripping the loose silk pants off, he stepped into the cavernous marble stall, turned a few knobs until all four shower heads rained down on him. Standing under the steaming water, he willed it to take away the edginess in his body. But the sting of the hot water on his skin only seemed to make it worse. His cock throbbed, hard and ready and needing Caroline's body. But he couldn't have her. Not tonight.

He reached down and wrapped his fingers around the heavy shaft, and pleasure shot through him. The image of her naked body was clear in his mind's eye as he began to stroke.

Yes, those breasts, high and firm and perfect. The nipples so deliciously dark. He remembered the way they elongated as he tugged on them, going hard beneath his fingers. And in his mouth . . . her flesh was so damn sweet on his tongue. He stroked his cock harder, faster, pausing to run his fingers over the swollen head. Desire, sharp and fierce, rose in him, made his cock swell impossibly.

Pleasure burned hot in his veins with each stroke, making his legs shake.

How he wanted to touch the head of his cock to her slick folds, so pink, so hot. To be enveloped by the wetness there. He could imagine what it would feel like to press his cock into her opening, to slide inside. Ah yes...

He groaned aloud. He was going to come. Too fast, hardly even time to enjoy it, but he didn't care. He needed it too badly. Needed to fuck her. Needed to taste her. To push his tongue deep inside her. To push his cock deep inside her.

Yes...

Yes!

With one final, hard stroke, he came, his semen spurting out over his hand, as the heat of the water fell all around him, and his mind danced with images of the beautiful woman who slept in the next room.

Caroline woke as Kian slid into bed beside her. She had no idea what time it was; there were no clocks in the suites at Exotica. But she had a sense that it was very late.

The soft murmur of crickets was the only sound. And in the deep silence she was hyperaware of Kian's warm body, of the rhythm of his breathing. She held perfectly still, not wanting him to know she was awake. She didn't want to talk about anything right now. Couldn't deal with it. Didn't even want to think about what had happened.

She was surprised when she felt the gentle touch of his fingers in her hair, heard his sigh. What did it mean? She lay awake for a long time wondering about that, about what he could possibly be thinking, this incredibly confident, smooth man. He'd been so surprisingly...tender with her. That was the only way she could describe it to herself. Totally unexpected. How else might he surprise her?

Normally, the unknown factor would trouble her, make her anxious. But there was a certain luxurious excitement in not knowing exactly what would happen next. Maybe that was part of it for her, part of what would make this work. Part of what had made her agree to his Scheherazade deal. That she didn't have everything lined up, assigned to a neat little cubbyhole. She had to give up some of her control because the simple fact was she had very little control over this situation. All she really had any choice over here was when to stop, if she wanted to. For the first time in far too many years, that was enough.

Almost unconsciously, she inched back toward the heat of Kian's body; not quite cuddling up to him, but the warmth of him next to her in the big bed was soothing. She allowed it to be. She didn't want to think about why, didn't want to think at all right now. Instead, she closed her eyes and listened to the crickets. To his breathing. A long time later, she slept.

Caroline felt the morning sun against her closed eyelids. She didn't want to open them, wanted to stay in that floating cloud of sleep. She pulled the covers over her head, only to have them drawn back a moment later.

"Wake up, Caroline. Time to wake up." Kian's voice came, soft and low, along with the scent of incense in the air, the muted sounds of exotic music: sitar, cymbals.

"No, not yet," she mumbled, rubbing her eyes.

"Then I'll wake you slowly."

It began with a soft kiss pressed to her bare shoulder, then another, and another. It turned into a trail of hot kisses along her collarbone, up her neck to that sensitive spot just below her ear. Despite herself, she smiled. Her body was still lambent with sleep, but lighting up with desire just from his gentle kisses.

He dragged the damask bedcover away, leaving only the thin silk rose-colored sheet covering her body. He pulled the sheet tightly across her, tucking it in under her sides.

"Kian? What are you doing?"

His voice was low, quiet. "You will see. Before you wake up, while your mind is still in that twilight place. Relax." A gentle command, yet he was clearly in charge. But it helped her to do as he asked.

He moved down her body, pulling and tucking until she was mummified within the fragile silk from her shoulders to her toes. And then he began to touch her.

A long, slow sweep of his fingers against the silk sent a chill over her skin. Somehow, the sensation was entirely different with the layer of silk between her body and his fingertips. She watched him as he ran his fingers over her belly, his face intense, entirely focused on his task, his jaw firm, his hazel eyes glittering.

Again that lambent stroking over her skin: her belly, her ribs, between her breasts. She shivered.

"Caroline, close your eyes."

"What? Why?"

"Because it will allow you to focus on what is happening to your body, to shut out the rest of the world, distractions. And because I asked you to."

Anger wanted to rise up in her at his cocky assumptions. But instead she melted a little inside. If she'd thought about it, she could work up a decent amount of ire over his attitude, at the way he sometimes spoke to her. But she found she went most willingly to him when he issued orders, when he spoke to her with that utter authority. But he was still touching her all over, and it was too hard to dissect it all now, to work into a good fight. Desire was pumping through her body, hot and needy. It was too hard to think about anything else. Her eyes closed.

His hands moved up her body, stroked the undersides of her breasts for endless moments, teasing her. Her nipples went rock hard beneath the sheet. Yet still he didn't touch them. Instead he circled the curves of her flesh, pulling the silk against her skin, abrading her nipples, making them harder and harder. She wanted to squirm. She wanted to cry out. Somehow she remained still, her jaw clenched against the sensations shivering over her skin, arrowing deep into her body.

When he moved his hands down to stroke her thighs she jumped. She didn't know why. It felt good, too good.

"Shh, Caroline. Let me touch you. All you have to do is feel, receive."

Her sex went wet, ached with wanting. His voice was rough with desire; she loved hearing it. And his fingers dragging over the tight silk were lovely, excruciating. She wanted to part her thighs for him, to let him slip his hand between them, but the silk held her so tightly she could barely move. Why was that reassuring? Why did it make her feel more truly that he was in control?

He was silent as he touched her, while her body tingled and swam with a hot current of slowly building need.

Down the sides of her thighs, over her calves to her feet, where he stroked her arches. Her toes curled, pleasure wafting through her. She'd never felt this odd sense of relaxation and sexual stimulation before. It was as though she could almost fall back into sleep, yet she was as turned on as she'd ever been in her life, her sex, her breasts, pulsing and warm.

Kian worked his way back up her legs, this time stopping to run his thumbs over her hips in small circles, moving closer and closer to that aching vee between her thighs.

She sighed.

"Ah yes, Caroline. I know what you need. And I will give it to you. I'm going to shift you a little. Move with me."

He loosened the sheets from around her legs, slid them, used his hands to guide her thighs until they were spread apart. He wrapped the sheet around her legs tightly, then tucked them in once more. She felt vulnerable, as she had the night before, even though the sheet still covered her. And as the silk ties had the night before, the binding sheet made her feel safe somehow. As though she had no choice in the matter, and therefore, no responsibility.

"Lie quietly, Caroline. Hold still."

She trembled at the sound of his voice, at his command.

Don't think about why. Just let it happen.

She was shaking before he even touched her again. But when his hands came down on her belly she moaned, squirmed a little.

"Hold still." A little sharper this time, but she loved it.

Then his hand slid over her mound and pleasure shot through her body like a rocket.

"Oh!"

"Yes, you like that."

"Yes," she gasped, barely able to breathe suddenly.

He used one hand to hold the silk tight against her mound, then with his other hand he stroked her through the sheet.

Yes...

He kept stroking, a slow, even rhythm that seemed to flow with the music in the background. Her sex was soaking wet, needing his touch. Needing him to make her come again. She was so engorged it hurt. But she didn't care, as long as he kept touching her.

A shock of pure pleasure went through her when he pinched one of her nipples. Almost hard enough to hurt, yet she immediately wanted more.

"You like that," he said again.

Again she whispered, "Yes."

He pinched once more, harder this time. Excruciating pleasure, hot and fierce, made her tremble, made her squirm. It was almost too much, his hand stroking between her thighs, his wicked fingers on her nipples. And without any prompting, she murmured, "Yes..."

"Ah, you're too beautiful, Caroline." He leaned in, until she could feel his breath warm on her cheek, and whispered, "Do you have any idea how badly I need to touch you? To fuck you? My cock is so hard it hurts with wanting you." He paused, pinched her nipple again, sending an electric jolt of desire racing through her body. "I'm going to fuck you, Caroline, today, tonight. Or maybe not until tomorrow. You're going to beg me for it. And you're going to love it."

Oh yes.

"But first, I'm going to make you come. With my

hands. With my mouth, perhaps. Oh yes, with my mouth. You'll like that."

Yes!

Before she had a chance to think anything more, he lowered his head and planted his hot, wet mouth over the sheet stretched across her mound. She could feel the heat of him immediately through the thin silk. Pleasure, hot and fierce, made her legs shake, made her stomach tighten up. Her entire being seemed to be concentrated at that point between her thighs where his mouth rested, where his tongue began to lick.

Oh God . . .

And then he began to pull on the sheet, so that the wet fabric rubbed back and forth across her aching cleft, along her slit, even as he licked at the hard nub of her clitoris. The sensation was amazing, muted yet multiplied by the silk.

Her hips began to pump; she couldn't control it, didn't want to. Her body was absolutely on fire: desire, pure and animal, raging in her system. What little control she'd been hanging on to slipped away with the motion of the silk sheet, with the heat of his wet mouth. She bucked into him, the pressure building. He worked her harder in response, his hot, sucking mouth on her clit, pulling on it through the silk. The sheet rubbing her wet and swollen flesh. The only other thing she knew was the exotic music, which had somehow become part of it, melding into the physical sensations, making it all the more dreamlike.

Pleasure built in her body, gaining speed. Her pulse hammered in her veins, carrying that animal desire into every pore: into her full, aching breasts, the hot, rock-hard tips of her nipples, even her limbs. And low in her belly, her climax began to tremble, shivering deep inside her.

No, no, no!

Some part of her mind rebelled, refused to let it happen.

"Kian..."

"Don't fight it," he murmured, before returning to his task.

He kept at it, sucking, licking, rubbing her mound with the sheet.

Let go, let go...

She tilted her hips, moving harder into his face, his wet mouth. He worked her harder, faster, his mouth rough on her, hurting her a little. But she knew she needed it. Needed him to *make* it happen.

Again the pressure built, taking her to the edge. She wanted to fight it. But she wanted to fall over that edge even more. And she did.

She fell, hard, spinning out of control.

"Kian!"

Lights flashed behind her eyes, her mind emptied out, taken over by pure ecstasy, thundering through her. Spasm after spasm of hot, clean pleasure, stabbing into her body, shaking her to the core. She shivered with it, her muscles clenching all over, loosening, only to clench once more as the next wave hit. Until finally, she lay there, exhausted.

Even then, tiny tremors flittered through her sex, deep inside her body. She couldn't open her eyes.

She felt Kian's hands through the silk, running over her thighs, her stomach. He kissed her body, the muted warmth of his mouth through the sheet soothing, lovely.

She was so sleepy, so utterly sated she couldn't have moved if she tried.

Then his face was next to hers, so close she could feel his breath warm on her skin, could smell her own ocean scent on his lips.

"Sleep now, Caroline. Rest."

His fingertips brushed over her cheek, her lips, her closed eyelids. She'd never felt more relaxed in her life. Her limbs were heavy. She was so tired. Once more, she slept.

This time, when she opened her eyes, the brilliant desert sunshine was muted by the silk curtains drawn over the enormous windows. She immediately looked for Kian, but he was nowhere in sight.

She stretched, feeling languid still, lazy. Her body was heavy with too much sleep, but she felt good. Wonderful, in fact.

She wanted Kian to fuck her.

Where had that come from? And in such...crude terms? But it felt sexier, somehow, to think of it as fucking. And it was true. Even now, just thinking about it, her sex was growing warm and damp. Yes, suddenly, that was all she could think about. That and the fact that he had made her come. Twice.

She didn't want to question it too closely yet. She was afraid to break whatever spell had settled over her, the spell that allowed her body to open to him.

Maybe Kian was the key to the spell?

She sat up in the bed, yawned, then got up and padded on bare feet to the bathroom. There, she spent a few moments washing up, then found a short silk robe on the back of the door in a pretty shade of sapphire blue, like the loose silk pants Kian had worn last night.

Kian, in those pants and no shirt, his bare chest and shoulders, broad and muscular. His abs as tight as any she'd ever seen.

I'm going to fuck you, Caroline...

A sharp, hot clenching of her sex at the thought.

God, what had gotten into her? But there was no doubt her body was ready for more of him. For all of him. Almost torturous that she hadn't had him yet. She squeezed her thighs together briefly before she slipped the robe on and tied it at the waist, and went back into the suite to find him.

It was still as empty as it had been before, just the mussed bed sheets, the incense in the air, the muted music. She wandered to the high arched doorway leading to the terrace, and saw him sitting at the mosaic-tiled table there. She watched him for a moment, as he lounged in the padded wrought iron chair. Even though his pose was casual, relaxed, he looked regal, as though he knew the entire world was there for the taking. Perhaps, for him, it was. She wouldn't be surprised.

He was dressed in those loose blue silk pants again, the folds of fabric draped around his strong thighs. His head was leaning against the high back of the chair, his eyes closed against the late morning sun. So beautiful, his chiseled profile. His face was all stark male beauty, and made more so by the incongruous lushness of his mouth. A small tremor ran through her just looking at him.

She stepped onto the terrace, the patterned marble

beneath her feet pleasantly warmed by the sun. He looked up and smiled, that dazzling smile, making her melt a little inside.

"Good morning."

She loved his deep voice, the husky timbre of it.

"Good morning."

"Did you sleep well, Caroline?"

"Yes. I haven't slept that well in a long time."

He rose from his chair, held another for her. "Come and sit. I've just ordered breakfast. Then we can decide what we'll do today."

Why did that sound like a command? But she found she didn't really mind. It was even a bit of a relief to let someone else handle things, for once.

She sat in the chair, relaxing into the plush cushions and looked out at the view. The mountains from here were jagged points against a clear vault of blue sky. She loved the serenity of the desert, the dry emptiness of it. The simplicity.

Kian took his seat again across the intricate wrought iron table from her, and moments later a waiter dressed in flowing Arabian Nights white arrived with a heavily laden tray. He silently set it down on the table, nodded to them both, and left.

Yes, they paid attention to every detail here, she knew, from being the one who oversaw the entire operation. And yet now that she was the one immersing herself in this environment, even she was a bit carried away with it all. With the silk and the incense and the servants, the grand and exotic architecture, the tranquil music.

"I took the liberty of calling your assistant to ask what you normally eat," Kian said to her. "But coffee and

fruit isn't enough to fuel your body for our time together, so I ordered pastries and yogurt, as well. Here,
you must try these; they're made with honey, you'll enjoy them."

He was piling food onto a plate, which he set in front
of her.

"The coffee is very strong, like an espresso. But richer.
And the yogurt will be heavier than what you're used to,
but with a more mild flavor. It reminds me of my home
country. I was glad to find they'd brought in some special food items for this suite."

He took a pastry and bit into it, his strong white
teeth coming down on it. Licking the crumbs from his
lips, he groaned his pleasure. So beautiful, his mouth.

It was several moments before Caroline could tear
her gaze from the sensual act of Kian eating. The food
was as wonderful as he'd suggested, she discovered. The
coffee was dark, rich on her tongue.

"Oh, this is really good."

"Better than any American coffee. Not to be a snob.
But it's better than what we get in France, as well."

"So, you've spent quite a lot of time in France, then?"

He nodded, taking a bite of sliced melon. "I grew up
between France and Jordan, my father's country. Our
family owns hotels in Europe, in the Middle East. We
also spent some time in the U.S. A little of everything,
everywhere."

"We? Do you mean your parents? Or do you have
sisters and brothers?"

"I have one brother, one sister. And you?"

"I have a brother, but he's much older than I am. We
were never close. And I have two younger half-sisters,

but we . . . well, after my father left my mother, I didn't see much of him, so I don't really know my sisters."

"I find that sad. And your mother? Are you close with her?"

"My mother died several years ago. We were never close, either, at least, not in any healthy way."

Kian put his coffee cup down, leaned toward her. "Ah, we are finally getting personal. Tell me about your mother, Caroline."

She didn't want to do it. Didn't want to talk about her mother with him. With anyone.

She kept her gaze on the distant mountains. "I don't know what to tell you, really. She was . . . she was a hard woman. Cold. Critical. She had a brilliant mind, and always expected everyone else to be able to keep up with her. And she had little patience for those who didn't."

"You strike me as being a very capable woman. I'm sure she could find no fault with you."

"Oh, she always found plenty."

"What did she think of you coming to work here?"

"She never knew. I came to Exotica shortly after she died."

He was quiet for a moment, sipping his coffee. "So, this is a sort of rebellion, perhaps?"

Caroline shrugged, her throat tightening. "Perhaps. Does it matter?"

"Maybe not."

She pulled a pastry in two, then dropped it back onto the plate, dusted crumbs from her fingers. "She would hate me working here," she said quietly. "I've always known that. But I'm here, anyway. Because I want to be. I love my job." She paused, rolling her linen napkin between her fingers. "But yes, a little bit of rebellion, if I'm going to be perfectly honest about it."

"There is nothing wrong with a little rebellion."

She looked at him, and his hazel eyes were twinkling, a small smile on his face.

"And what about you?" she asked him. "Have you never rebelled?"

He shrugged, a ripple passing through the muscles of his bare shoulders.

Nice.

"My parents gave me little to rebel against. Truthfully, they have always been rather indulgent with me. I'm terribly spoiled."

It was her turn to smile. "I can see that about you. But I don't mind it, for some reason."

He leaned forward again. She could see the sunlight glinting golden in his eyes. "Since we're getting more personal, Caroline, do you want to tell me what happened to you?"

"What do you mean?" But she knew perfectly well what he meant. Her insides froze up, as though a sheet of ice had passed through her body. Images of Jeff, of Sarah, of that night flashed behind her eyes, everything moving in slow motion. Her fingers tingled with the reverberation of that one hard slap. Perspiration broke out on her forehead.

Stop it!

"Ah, I can see this is not the right time." He stood and came to her, lifted her hand and pressed it to his lips. "Forgive me. We never have to talk about it, if you prefer not to."

She nodded, looking away at the mountains again, pulled in a deep, calming lungful of the clean desert air.

Yes, those mountains were so solid and simple, just enormous rocks on the surface of the world, reaching deep into the earth. Permanent, unchanging. There was comfort in that. She had a feeling her life was about to change.

Perhaps it already had.

5.

KIAN PACED the marble terrace outside the Arabian Nights suite, cell phone to his ear, waiting for his mother to pick up the line. Finally, he heard her French accented voice.

" 'allo?"

"*Maman,* it's Kian."

"Ah." She switched to English, her French accent heavy. "And 'ow are you, my darling?"

"I'm fine, *Maman.* And you?"

"A little tired lately. Perhaps looking forward to my retirement."

"Really? You? Are you sure you're alright?"

She laughed. "Even I grow weary of working. But tell me, why are you calling?"

"There is something I have to ask you." He paused. His mother didn't like having her decisions—her decrees—questioned. "I'd like to tell Caroline Winter why I'm here."

"Absolutely not. There is a reason why I've asked you to keep that information from her for now. Why would you ask such a thing, Kian? You know my feelings on the matter. You must see the business from the inside, without anyone deferring to you, being on their best behavior."

"I don't think it would hurt, *Maman,* if we told only her."

"It is out of the question. Let us not speak of it any further. Tell me, 'ave you spoken with your sister? Your nephews are doing well in school. Although why they must live so far from me, I will never understand."

There was no point in pursuing the matter further. Once his mother had made up her mind, she was immovable. He hated lying to Caroline. But he would never openly go against his mother. This was, after all, her business. And she had given him everything, a good life, the best life. No, as much as he wanted to tell Caroline the truth, he couldn't do it.

But he'd had to try. Because for the first time, a woman had gotten under his skin. Enough to make him question his own motives. And that woman was Caroline.

Caroline sat in her office, her fingernails tapping on the slick surface of her glass desk. She'd come there meaning to work, but found herself completely unable to concentrate. She could not get Kian out of her mind, or her response to him. While he was touching her, talking to her, she was fine, she could go with whatever was happening. But now, here, with some distance between them, she was beginning to question everything.

How could she have given her power over to a man the way she had with Kian? Frightening to think about it, that she'd done it. That she might do it again.

A part of her wanted to blame him, but she knew she had some culpability in it herself. Still, she was angry again. With him. With her own weakness.

What would happen to her if she let him . . . do whatever he wished? If she truly lost control?

She shivered, pushing the old images from her mind. *He is not Jeff. And there is no Sarah. Not anymore.*

Shit. That line of thought wasn't helping.

Her mind's eye began to wander, past images of Jeff's condo, of her turning her key in the lock, the sound of moaning from the living room. Voices yelling, that one hard slap across Sarah's cheek. *Her best friend!*

More arguing. Jeff's cell phone ringing, her anger when he paused to answer it. Then the two of them standing on the street, the blue and red lights flashing, the gurney being loaded into the ambulance, the face covered with a sheet.

Yet she knew that face. Knew what it looked like, what it felt like under her hand.

Her fault, her fault . . .

Her phone buzzed, and it slipped a little in her damp palm as she picked it up.

"Yes?" Her heart was hammering in her chest.

"Caroline, the new rugs for the Medieval Castle are here."

"You take care of it, Samantha."

"What? Um, sure. Of course. Is everything okay?"

"Yes. Fine."

"Okay. I'll check in with you later."

"Yes, do that."

She hung up, poured herself a glass of cold water from the pitcher she always kept on her desk, took a long drink, damping down the panic. But the anger wouldn't go away.

She shuffled some files on her desk, trying to pretend to herself that she was being productive. The anger burned brighter. She knew some of it was unfounded. But she wasn't able to stop it.

She punched a button on her phone and her assistant picked up.

"Yes, Caroline?"

"I'm leaving, Samantha. Probably for the day."

"I'm glad you're taking some time for yourself. We'll handle everything."

"You know how to reach me if you need anything."

"Of course."

She hung up with a small pang of guilt. She hadn't meant to be so abrupt. But she was absolutely boiling inside. She had to get out of there.

She went through the back doors and found a golf cart, drove quickly across the lawns and through the gates of the Arabian Nights area, followed the twisting, sandy path. All around her the flowers bloomed in tropical profusion, birds sang, but she hardly noticed. She parked the cart where the path narrowed and stalked the rest of the way to the miniature Persian palace, up the marble stairs and through the foyer.

She found him just coming in from the pool, naked and dripping, with a white towel slung over one shoulder. He smiled when he saw her.

"You're back early." He reached out toward her and she stopped in her tracks.

"Don't."

"Caroline? What's wrong?" Water hung in tiny droplets from the dark tips of his hair, fell onto his shoulders. She watched them slide over that sleek golden skin, over the muscle that lay like steel beneath it.

Beautiful.

But, no. She refused to allow the way he looked to confuse her.

"Nothing is wrong. I've just come to understand how manipulative you've been with me."

"Manipulative?"

She nodded, her throat dry. She hated that she wanted to cry.

"Caroline, I've done nothing but what you've asked me to do, what you've agreed to."

"Don't talk to me as though you're really in this to help me!"

His eyes smoldered, turned a fiery gold. His voice was flat, cold. "You accuse me of lying?"

"What man hasn't lied to get what he wants from a woman?"

He was silent a moment, that hard golden gaze on hers. "*I* have not. Ever. I don't need to."

"You always know how to do it, don't you? You always know exactly what to say."

He took a step toward her, menace in his gaze. Her stomach knotted. And her sex went wet.

What the hell was wrong with her?

"You wanted this, Caroline. You wanted me."

She shook her head.

His voice was a low growl. "It's the truth."

"No. I didn't . . . I had no idea what I was getting into."

He advanced another step. She stepped back.

"You knew exactly what you were getting into. And I've seen how your body responds to my touch. I've watched your eyes go glassy, your panting breath. I've watched you come, Caroline."

"Stop it!" She took another step back, felt the soft edge of the bed against the back of her thighs.

He kept moving, closing in on her until he was only inches away. His hands gripped her shoulders hard. Her heart was pounding, her head hot.

He slid his hands down, his voice a harsh whisper as he took her breasts in his palms. "You want me, Caroline, even at this moment. I can smell it on you."

Her nipples came up, two hard points. Her legs were shaking.

Bastard.

But she didn't say it.

"You want me to stop now, Caroline?"

She opened her mouth to speak, but nothing came out.

"I thought not."

He tore her clothes off so quickly her head was spinning. Or maybe it was the chaos of her fury and her desire mixing together until she could hardly tell the difference. She was soaking wet. Her blood burned with anger still. But the anger was slowly being swallowed up by her need for him.

When he had her naked, he pushed her down roughly on the bed, then lowered himself on top of her, forcing her thighs apart. His cock was hard and strong, pressing into her cleft. She was so damn wet, shivering with heat and a desperate, overpowering need.

"Spread, Caroline. Wider."

One hand curved around the back of her neck, pulling her head up. His hand tightened painfully in her hair. Her breasts, her sex, ached with the pulsing drumbeat of pure lust.

"Damn it, Caroline," he murmured, his brows drawn together. Then he pushed into her, one hard thrust. She cried out, clenched around him.

"Are you going to tell me now you don't want me?" he ground out.

"No. No . . ."

"Good. Because I plan to fuck you. And while I've never forced myself on a woman in my life, you tempt me . . . God damn it, Caroline."

He drew out, plunged again, slamming into her.

"Kian!" Pleasure coursed through her, cut into her like a knife blade, burrowing deep. Her arms went around his neck, her fingers twisting in his hair.

"I'm going to fuck you so hard, Caroline. And you will never be able to deny me anything. Do you understand?"

Another sharp thrust, pain and pleasure sending hot chills racing over her skin.

She gasped. "Yes!"

He really began to pump into her then, one long, hard thrust after another, a volley of blows, hammering into her body. Too hard, too fast to think. Pleasure pushed into her, deeper and deeper, gathering in her belly. She was pinned to the bed, crushed beneath him. She buried her face in his neck. He smelled like sex to her.

"Oh . . . Kian, God."

He paused, held himself up on his elbows, looked into her eyes. His were dark, glittering. His mouth was red and lush. She wanted to kiss him. She wanted him to fuck her even more.

"Come here," he muttered, pulling himself up onto his knees, turning her over as though she were no larger than a doll. "Spread for me, Caroline. Do it."

She moved her thighs apart, went down until her head was cradled in her arms. He spread her pussy lips with his hands and pushed in.

He was big; it was hard to take all of him this way. But she would. Oh yes . . . He pulled back, then plunged in again hard, and pleasure shivered through her system. She knew she wasn't thinking. She didn't care.

He bent over her, one hand going into her hair and pulling it tight. The other arm went around her waist, holding her against his body, his cock buried inside her. He started to pump into her again, harder, faster, driving his cock deep. And with every thrust was a wave of pleasure so intense she could barely take it. Pleasure and pain and *him*.

Kian.

She hovered on that edge, her body shimmering with the first waves of orgasm. Her sex clenched around him.

"You're going to come, Caroline."

"Yes!"

"Not yet."

"What?"

He didn't answer. Instead, he slipped out of her, leaned to the side, and reached into the nightstand, pulled something out.

"Don't move."

He used his hands to pull her buttocks apart, and she

felt something cold and damp on her anus. She knew what he was going to do. Her entire body shivered in fear, in anticipation. She didn't want to stop him.

Then his finger was at that tiny opening, working the lube in. Pleasure shafted through her in long, pulsing waves. Then it was the head of his cock, pushing in slowly, stretching her. Oh yes, even better. Her body was still pulsing with her near-climax. She spread her legs a little wider, opening herself to him, hardly believing she was doing it. His hand went into her hair again, gripping tightly, making her scalp tingle: a little pain, a little pleasure.

He pushed in a bit more and paused, and pure desire danced through her limbs, into her belly, her sex. She was so close to coming, helpless against it. His cock felt so big, hurting her just a little, yet she was amazed at how good it felt. If only he would drive in deeper.

He did, pulling back a bit first, then sliding in, one slow inch at a time. Tiny strokes, in, then out, then deeper. She stretched even farther, until her body was wet, open, shaking with need. She pushed back against him to take more of him in, her skin stretched taut around his thick shaft. She felt impaled, helpless. Lost.

"Kian, please."

He pushed in another inch and she moaned, twisting the sheet up in her hands. "More..."

He pulled back, poised for one endless moment, then very quickly he was buried deep inside her.

"Oh!"

She'd never felt so filled in her life. So taken over. And she had to recognize that part of her which gloried in being so physically dominated by him, even in the burning pain that was pleasure at the same time. That part of her which needed a man as strong as Kian in order for her to give herself over to what he was doing to her, what was happening to her body.

"Can you take it, Caroline?" His voice was a deep rasp.

"Yes. Yes..." Pleasure was a deep, dark pulse, carrying the heat of it through her body. Nothing else mattered.

He snaked a hand around and teased her clit, pulling and pinching it. Sensation layered on sensation, until she couldn't take it anymore. As he drove into her again and again, she exploded, just came apart under his hands, his body. He moved faster, pumping into her ass. She cried out. So did he. And as her body shook and shuddered with the power of her orgasm, he came into her, long hot spurts inside her body.

They collapsed together on the bed, and he rolled, taking her with him. They lay side by side, curled together, a tangle of limbs. She turned her face and bit into his shoulder, leaving marks on his golden skin. But he only smiled at her and pulled her closer.

He had dozed, he realized, coming awake. Caroline still lay in his arms. But he could tell from her breathing that she was awake.

"Caroline."

"Yes?"

He shifted so that he could see her face. "How are you? Are you alright?"

"What? Yes, of course." She searched his face, her eyes a deep and dusky blue. "Oh. You mean because of... you didn't hurt me, if that's what you mean."

He nodded.

"You do realize, though, that if you lose this bargain we've made..." She stopped, grinning at him. He'd never seen her so gleeful. It was a moment before he understood what she meant.

"Oh no. You will never have the opportunity to do that to me." Although, somewhere deep in his mind a small voice told him it might not be all bad. He was sexually adventurous by nature, sexually sophisticated, after all. And it was something many people enjoyed. But he wasn't going to tell her that. "I won't give you the chance. Because I will fulfill my end of the bargain, as I have been doing. As I intend to do again shortly."

He paused, watching her lovely face. Desire there, yes, and a new openness he hadn't seen before. "We have become intimate enough now that I see no reason to suppress any urges."

"Kian..."

"I want to do everything with you, Caroline." He paused, the thoughts forming only seconds before coming out of his mouth. "I want to know you. Everything about you. And I will admit to you, this is the first time I've ever truly been interested in knowing a woman. You must think I'm very shallow. Perhaps I am. But I am telling you my truth."

She nodded silently, as though expecting him to say more.

"I want to know your truth, Caroline. Tell me," he said quietly.

He didn't think she'd actually do it. Whatever she'd been through had left her too raw. But he'd *had* to ask. He didn't know why he felt so compelled to keep pushing.

"Tell me," he said again.

His voice was so quiet Caroline could barely hear him, yet it still held a clear air of command. What a relief to give in to that command. How strange that she should feel this way.

Don't think about it now.

No, now she wanted to simply do as he asked. To tell him the things she never spoke about with anyone, other than her recent talks with Lilli. She felt so completely loosened up now, after what they'd done together. She didn't want to analyze it for once. She didn't want to ask herself how she could possibly equate a sexual act with trust. She just wanted to tell him.

"I was engaged once." Her throat went tight and she had to stop, to take in a deep breath of the incense-laden air.

Kian nodded encouragingly.

"We met through mutual friends. Jeff was all the things a woman is supposed to look for in a husband. He was good-looking, he came from a good family, whatever that still means these days. He was an attorney, motivated, very dedicated to his job. As foolish as it sounds now, I thought... I thought that finally, I was doing something right."

"You agreed to marry him, then, not because you loved him, but in order to gain approval? From who? Your mother? From him?"

"Yes, both of them." Too perceptive, this man. But there was no point in not telling him all of it now, was there? "My mother's approval was always important to me. Far too important, I now realize, but then... I lived for it. Foolish of me. Nothing I did would ever be good enough for her. And I was certainly old enough to know better, to have grown out of it. But I didn't really come to understand that until after she died, a few years ago."

"And him, what was he like? Did he treat you well? Did he show his approval of you, in the end? Did he fill that need at all? Because it doesn't sound as though he did."

"I think in some ways he did, although not on purpose. He was so much the complete package, too perfect. But the problem was, because he was so complete, there was nothing I could offer him. He made that clear over time. Still, it made me feel good that a man like him was interested in me."

Kian gave a rough laugh. "I can't imagine any man *not* being interested in you."

She shook her head, her cheeks growing warm. "I never felt good enough, at that time in my life. Part of that came from my mother, and unfortunately, my relationship with Jeff only reinforced those feelings. It made me put him up on a pedestal. And he . . . he took advantage of that in small ways. I didn't see it then, of course."

"Everything in life is so much clearer in retrospect."

"Yes, that's it exactly."

Kian stroked his hand over her bare shoulder, reminding her that they lay naked together on the bed. The sheer canopy hung over them, so delicate it fluttered a little each time they moved. But it made her feel shrouded, somehow. Safe. Or maybe it was him?

"Go on," he told her.

"I had a best friend. Sarah. We were neighbors for several years, did everything together in the way best friends do."

She remained quiet for a few minutes, trying to figure out how to say what she felt she needed to say. She hadn't told anyone this story in any detail since it had happened, five years earlier.

"So. Jeff and I had been engaged a few months. I'd started to plan the wedding. Sarah would be my maid of honor, of course. I had this whole idea of what our life together would be like. I realize now that the image in my head held no personal aspirations for me, other than being Jeff's wife. Almost sickening to think about it now. I have my own degree in business management, but I didn't even care about that."

"We all do things we regret. Think and do things which we later realize don't make sense."

"Yes. But this could have been a tragic mistake. Well, as it turned out, it was tragic."

Could she really tell him this? It was getting harder and harder.

"What did he do to you, this Jeff?"

Kian stroked her hair from her face, and when she looked into his eyes, they were glittering. Fierce. Something deep and dark about the way he was looking at her. His tone was commanding again, a little rough this time. "Tell me, Caroline."

Her throat hurt, but she said it anyway. "I caught Jeff and Sarah in bed together."

"Bastard!"

"Yes."

The thought usually hit her in the chest like a fist. It had never stopped feeling so awful. Until now. Now it was a soft blow, one she was able to deflect. But the really bad part was still to come.

"And this experience, this man, made you shut down, yes?"

She couldn't do it. Couldn't tell him the hard part.

"I didn't . . . I wasn't with a man for a long time after that. I cut myself off from my other friends. I didn't feel I could trust anyone. I'm just beginning to renew an old friendship now, with my friend Lilli. I've known her since college. It was her idea to . . ."

"To what?"

"I . . ." How had that slipped out? But she may as well tell him, even though her cheeks were burning. "It was her idea for me to spend time with you. To sleep with you. To reopen myself sexually."

"Ah." He paused, then said quietly, "And so you lied to me when you told me you audition all of the companions at Exotica?"

Damn. Her brain was too fuzzy with emotions, with the afterbuzz of sex, to think of a way out of this. "Kian, I'm sorry. I didn't mean any harm. I just . . . I needed to . . ."

She couldn't speak. Her throat simply closed up. And tears sprang to her eyes. "God, this is why I'm no good at these kinds of discussions. Why I can't tell you the rest of . . . of what happened."

"But there's more?"

"Yes. There's more." Her stomach gave a hard squeeze, and she felt dizzy. "I can't. I can't do this. Please. I can't even think anymore . . ." A tear rolled down her cheek. "Shit."

He propped himself up on one elbow, looking down at her. She couldn't breathe, couldn't move, couldn't even turn her face away. The old pain was there, freezing her, making her whole body cramp up.

"Lord, Caroline, what happened to you? No, I don't mean for you to tell me now." He wiped her tears with his thumb, smoothed her hair, and pulled her in close.

She wanted to fight him at first, would have if she'd had any strength left. But talking about this, even without finishing the story, had taken everything out of her. She felt limp, exhausted. After only a few moments she couldn't even cry anymore.

"You're very beautiful when you cry," he said softly, almost reverently. "Tragic and beautiful."

She sniffed. "I understand more than anyone else that it is your job to say such things to me, Kian."

"I told you earlier, I'm very self-indulgent. I wouldn't bother to say anything I didn't mean. Especially to a woman who's crying. Especially to you. But I think you're done now, yes?"

She nodded, a little embarrassed. About crying. About what he was saying to her. "Yes."

At the same time, she felt a small sense of relief at having told him about Jeff, at least. About having confessed to lying to him. He hadn't even questioned her about it, had simply accepted it as she'd admitted the lie to him.

She curled into him, taking comfort from his warm body. And already, she wondered how she was going to do without him once this was over. To watch him work at Exotica with other clients. She couldn't stand the idea.

But neither one of them was here for anything more than this. It would have to be enough.

6.

WHEN HE WOKE HER it was dark. Moonlight shone faintly through the arched doorway to the terrace.

"Why are we up, Kian?"

"Because there is something mysterious and even a little magical about being up in the middle of the night. And because I need you."

"For what?" Her mind was still too fuzzy with sleep to understand what he was saying.

He growled and pulled her hand to him, wrapped her fingers over his stiff cock. Immediately her sex went wet, a warm rush of heat suffusing her body.

"Ah. And what would you do if I refused to wake up?"

"I would do what I did the first night here." His voice was low, smoky. "I would go into the hot shower and stroke myself, my cock swelling in my hand as I thought of you, lying asleep in the bed. Your lush breasts, that slick heat between your lovely thighs. Wanting you. Wanting to touch you, to kiss you. To fuck you as hard as I did tonight."

Her body was lighting up with need, making her breathless. "Do it now, Kian."

"Oh, I intend to. But first, you must get out of bed and come with me."

"What?"

"Don't ask any questions. Simply do as I say, Caroline."

God, that tone again. She shivered, small tremors of desire running through her. But she got out of bed silently.

He dressed her then, in a pair of dark, billowing silk pants, very much the same as he wore. Then he helped her into an intricately decorated sort of half top, jeweled and embroidered with golden threads that left her stomach bare and pushed her breasts together. He draped layers of long chains of gold and pearls around her neck, slid golden bracelets onto her wrists.

"A costume," she murmured.

"You cannot have the full Arabian Nights experience without it."

She'd known about the costumes, of course. She'd simply never considered wearing one herself. But he was right, it was part of the experience. And this was the perfect time. The magic of midnight, as he'd said. How had he known this is how it would work best for her? But then, he seemed to know everything about her, about what she needed.

"Come with me now, Caroline."

"Where are we going?"

"Out to the gardens."

Under normal circumstances, she would have questioned him further. But now, he took her hand and she followed him silently, their bare footsteps making small scuffing sounds as they walked across the marble floors, down the front steps, and onto the sand path.

Outside, there was music in the air, the delicate strains of flute and sitar and cymbals. They followed the path, and soon came upon a small clearing where costumed musicians played, seated on beautifully patterned rugs on the ground. And once more, even though she herself had arranged for all of these things to happen in this area of Exotica, she was surprised. Surprised that he had bothered to set up this scenario for her.

He looked down at her and she smiled. There was no need to say anything more.

He pulled her farther into the garden, and she could smell the lush greenery all around them, the perfume of night-blooming jasmine heavy in the night air. And she began to really sink into the experience, into the mood of the exotic setting.

They came to the low square pool that was a replica of the one in the courtyard of the palace in Damascus, and he guided her to sit on the flat edge, then sat beside her.

"Do you feel the magic of this place, Caroline?"

"Yes. It's impossible not to. With the costumes and the music and the gardens and...all of this."

"Don't think of it like that. Let yourself imagine that we are there, in the Middle East, in some exotic place where all of these things exist. There is nothing more now than the two of us, under the moon and the stars."

He leaned in and kissed her neck, sending a shiver of

delight through her, her nipples coming up hard and needy.

"The musicians are only a few yards away." She couldn't put that awareness of them out of her mind.

"Yes. And that will make this even better. To know that one of them could come upon us at any moment. Open the front of your top, Caroline. Bare your breasts for me."

She started to shake her head.

An imperious nod of his chin. "Do it."

With shaking fingers, she unfastened the hooks on the front of her silk top, the embroidered fabric a little rough under her fingertips.

"Ah, beautiful." Kian reached over and took her breasts in his hands, kneading them gently. A small sigh escaped her. "You have the most beautiful breasts, Caroline. So soft and full. And your nipples..." He paused to stroke them with his fingers, pleasure lancing into her body. "So perfect. So dark and ripe. I want to pinch them." He did, hard, and she gasped with pain, with pleasure. "I want to taste them, to pull them into my mouth and suck that pink flesh."

He gathered her breasts together in his hands, leaned in and ran his tongue over one hard tip, then the other. Her sex went wet, absolutely soaking in seconds. Her breasts ached exquisitely. Even better when he drew one nipple and sucked on it, hard, using his teeth to graze the sensitive flesh, before moving to the other side, and licking, sucking, and biting again. She loved it all, the small, sharp pain of his teeth on her, his hot sucking mouth. She was shivering with need, her sex swollen and hungry.

Then he was pushing her down, onto her back on the

hard stone edge of the fountain, and forcing her legs apart. And she didn't care. Didn't care that the stone beneath her hurt a little, that the musicians still played only a few yards down the garden path. All she cared about was that he was touching her.

His hands went into the loose folds of her silk pants, found the seam between her thighs and ripped the delicate fabric. She didn't say a word, just let him do it, her body getting hotter and hotter.

"Have to fuck you right here," he muttered.

He drew his cock out from the folds of his own billowing pants. She caught sight of it for a moment, rigid in the blue wash of moonlight. Her sex clenched.

"Yes, now, Kian!"

He held her down, his hand on her shoulder, pressing her hard into the stone beneath her. And with one smooth motion, he pushed into her aching heat.

"Oh!"

Pleasure knifed into her body, shimmering, spreading. He began to pump his hips, driving his cock into her in hard, fast strokes. So fast, so fierce, all she could do was wrap her legs around him and hold on.

And then he stopped.

"Kian, no!" She was panting, barely able to breathe.

He pulled back, stripped her pants from her, and dropped them to the ground. "On your knees, Caroline. Kneel on the fabric and rest the front of your body on the edge of the pool."

She did as he asked, too turned on to question anything. She loved that she never knew what he might ask of her next.

She felt the heat of him as he knelt behind her, was

surprised when he drew one of the long strands of pearls from her neck, over her head. He reached around the front of her body, pulled the pearls between her thighs, drew them up tight, until she could feel the small beads against her wet cleft. Then he began to move them, pulling them back and forth, so that the pearls massaged her slick cleft, the hard nub of her clitoris.

She groaned.

"Yes, I knew you'd love this." He pressed up against her, used one hand on the back of her neck, forcing her to bend over more. "I'm going to fuck you again. Spread for me."

She moved her thighs apart, sighed when she felt the tip of his cock against her waiting hole, gasped when he slipped inside, ramming her hard over and over. At the same time, he kept sliding the pearls over her clit. Her body shook with sensation, her pulse racing and hot, her skin on fire.

She was vaguely aware of the ground hard beneath her knees, hurting a little. Of the hard edge of the pool against her ribs. Didn't matter. All she knew was his cock deep inside her body, the luscious sensation of the silky, hard pearls moving over her wet cleft, her swollen clitoris. Pleasure washed through her in waves, centering deep in her core, until she was shivering all over with the need to come.

She was so close, at that keen and lovely edge. But she held herself back. Not to hang on to the control this time. But simply to hover on that edge of pleasure, so sharp and fine she didn't want to give in to it quite yet, wanted it to last.

"Kian . . ."

"I'm going to come."

"Yes. Come." She gasped as he pulled the pearls tighter, grazing her clitoris in hard strokes. And his cock really pummeling her from behind, driving deep. It was too much; her climax thundered through her body as Kian tensed, cried out. Pleasure, sharp and hot, pierced her body, from her sex to her breasts, spreading, trembling along her skin. A wet gush between her thighs as she came and came.

She was left shaking. Weak. Barely able to breathe. The sharpest edge of her climax faded, but small tremors kept shivering through her. Kian's softening cock was still inside her, his panting breath hot in her hair. His hand was gripping her hip, hard and hurting. She didn't want to move.

All around them crickets sang a rhythmic chant against the music still playing. She drew in a lungful of the soft desert air, and let her hands fall into the water of the pool. It felt like silk against her skin; that sleek, that cool.

Kian pulled her hair aside and kissed the back of her neck. So tender, especially after the roughness of the sex. She smiled.

He pulled out of her, turned her body in his big hands, and set her on the edge of the pool. He sat next to her, scooped up a small handful of water and drizzled it over her hot cheeks, let a few drops fall between her still bare breasts. He lifted her chin in his hand, his gaze meeting hers. The metallic gleam of his eyes seemed to draw her into him as his hand slipped around the back of her neck, holding her firmly.

His other hand, still damp from the water, moved

down between her legs, stroking her slick folds. She parted her thighs, and his fingers slipped inside her.

"Oh..."

He worked his fingers in deeper, added another, filling her. And with the heel of his hand, he ground into her clitoris, moving in circles. Pleasure upon pleasure as he pumped into her, pressed onto her sensitive flesh, and soon she was back on that lovely edge once more.

His gaze bore into hers, intense, powerful. And his panting breath matched her own as she went tumbling over the edge. She fell into that place that was all about fiery need and a pleasure so fierce she could barely breathe. And he went with her, somehow.

She felt it. Felt that odd moment, suspended in time, when his gaze reached beyond her eyes and right into her.

When it was over he was still right there, locked in with her. He held perfectly still, the sound of their synchronized, panting breath keeping time with the chirping of the crickets, the music. She was hot all over, shivering. He pulled her into his arms, and held on to her. She could smell his skin: like incense, like man, like sex.

His arms around her were strong, hard with muscle. She felt protected. Perfectly and utterly cared for. And she had to admit it was the first time in her life she'd ever felt this way.

Her mind tried to argue with her about the improbability of it, of what Kian made her feel. But she didn't care about logic anymore. She was too sated. Too worn out. Too lazy.

She almost had to laugh at that. She had never in her

life been lazy. Maybe it was about time she was. Maybe it was time for a lot of things. Her body had certainly opened up. And her mind, to some extent. It seemed her heart might want to follow, but could she really allow that to happen?

Far too much to figure out now. No, now was the time to enjoy Kian's body beside her, the night sounds all around them, the lovely scent of him. And the days still to come.

They had seven days left together. Anything could happen in a week. But what was it she really wanted to happen? She honestly didn't know.

In the morning she'd found him standing on the terrace, staring at the distant mountains, hazy in the early sun, as she often did herself. He was quiet, pensive. So was she.

Everything was usually clearer in the light of day, but she still wasn't certain that one stunning moment last night had even truly happened. She needed some time alone to sort her head out. And so she'd told him she had to go to her office to work for a couple of hours.

She sat now at her big glass desk, playing with the long golden chains she'd left around her neck from the night before. She was tired, and yet her body was humming with nervous energy. It was too hard to sit still in her chair, to concentrate on work. After two fruitless hours, she'd asked her assistant to hold all her calls and had given herself permission to spend some time brooding. But it hadn't helped. She'd tried to reason it all out. That was how she normally figured out anything, but she couldn't seem to fit it all together in a way that made sense.

Emotion was not her strong suit, she had to admit. No wonder her staff called her the Ice Queen. A flash of regret at the thought, but it was true. She was all hard, cold logic. But what she was going through had nothing to do with logic, and she felt utterly lost.

She needed help.

She picked up the phone and dialed Lilli's number, waited while it rang, prayed her friend was home. She tapped her nails harder against the cool glass, shifted her feet. Finally, Lilli picked up.

"Hello?"

"Lilli. Thank God."

"Caroline? What is it?"

"I'm such a mess, Lilli. I can't figure this thing out . . . I don't know what to do."

"Slow down, sweetie. What are we talking about exactly?"

"It's him, Kian."

"Has he turned out to be awful? I'd so hoped he'd be just what you needed. I'm sorry."

"No, no, it's not that. He's . . . he's perfect, if you want to know the truth. Absolutely perfect."

"Okay." She could hear the questions in Lilli's voice. But she was letting her tell it at her own pace.

"He's . . . it's as though he knows exactly what I need. On so many levels. He's made me lose all control, Lilli. And I mean *all* of it. You have no idea of the things I've let him do to me already. I hate it. And I love it, need it. I feel . . . adrift. Like I don't have a handle on anything anymore. And it's only been three days! How much worse will it get by the time this is over?"

Lilli was quiet a moment, then said softly, "Caroline, what is it you're so afraid of?"

Caroline got up, paced in front of the window overlooking the emerald lawns behind her office. Her gaze followed the twisting path that led back to the Arabian Nights suite. Back to Kian.

"I needed a break, Lilli. It's too much. And I don't know what to do with it all."

"With all of what?"

"With . . . with this loss of control. He brings that out in me. And it terrifies me. That I can be so vulnerable with another human being. I know that sounds stupid."

"No, it doesn't. Not after what you've been through. But I think it's time now to put it behind you. Don't you, Caroline? I mean, isn't that what this little adventure is all about?"

"I suppose it is. But this is no longer some little adventure." She paused, buried her fingers in her hair. Funny, she just now realized she'd been wearing her hair loose since her first night with Kian, when she normally wore it pulled back, bound into a tight ponytail or wrapped into a bun. "Lilli, this is already turning into something much bigger. For me, anyway. No, for him, too. I think. But I don't know this man well enough to know what's true, do I?"

"Sometimes you have to go with your instincts."

"My instincts are obviously way off!"

"Why? Because you misjudged Jeff?"

"And Sarah. My best friend. And . . . myself, most of all."

"That wasn't your fault, Caroline. You can't judge yourself for it."

"I know. I know it in my head, anyway. But the whole thing still tortures me, you know? I can still see that night so clearly in my head. I don't know that it will ever go away."

"Caroline, you have to make the choice to move on. To really move on. And it sounds to me as though Kian is helping you to do that, at least on some level. I think that sex can touch us in the most primal, basic way. The reason it can be so healing is because it goes so deep, down to where we're simply feeling, rather than thinking. And it's working. Am I right?"

"Yes." Hard to even get that word out. Because Lilli *was* right. And that meant Caroline had to face her past, to do the hard things she'd been avoiding for so long. "I told him. Not everything. But I told him about finding them together, Jeff and Sarah. I told him why I asked him to be here with me like this. I just don't know if I can do this. It's so intense already, the energy between us. You wouldn't believe it."

Lilli laughed. "Oh yes, I would. If anyone would."

Caroline smiled. She knew how quickly Lilli and Rajan had fallen for each other, how changed they both were by their connection. But it seemed unlikely, ludicrous even, that the same thing could be happening with her and Kian. Caroline's life just did not work that way. Despite the odd connection she felt with him. Despite the breakthroughs she'd had with him already.

"Lilli, I'm not you. I'm not open the way you are."

"Not yet. But it sounds as though perhaps you're on your way."

"I don't know. I don't know if I even should be, under these circumstances. My head is spinning."

"I can hear that in your voice. In fact, you sound an awful lot like I did not too long ago."

Caroline groaned. "I can't do this."

"Sometimes we don't know what we're capable of until we try."

Caroline was quiet, absorbing that. It was true. If she were being perfectly honest with herself, she really didn't want to stop what she was doing with Kian. She just wanted the emotions and the confusion that went with it to go away. But she wanted the full nine days, before the Arabian Nights suite opened to the public and Kian would have to serve his first real client.

Her stomach tightened, twisted.

Caroline began a slow pace again. "Maybe that's part of it. I don't know what I'm capable of in this situation, so I have no idea of what to expect. From myself. From him. And he's so different from my first impression of him. I keep trying to figure it out, to put everything in its logical place, but I can no longer find any logic in it."

"This stuff usually has nothing to do with logic, Caroline. Look, you're out of your comfort zone, but that certainly doesn't have to mean it's impossible for you to handle. It's time you took some risks, tried new things. This is a step in the right direction, regardless of where it leads. Try not to think that far ahead right now."

"You're right. I have to face this stuff. Face my fears. And Kian is the perfect man to do this with."

He was the perfect man in so many ways. Except, of course, that he'd come here to work. To Exotica. Not that she thought there was anything wrong with what they did here. But a man who volunteered for this sort of job . . . What sort of man could he be?

She didn't mean to judge him. But it was simply a

fact. One she couldn't escape, no matter how badly she wanted to.

Kian Razin was going to get paid to sexually service other women. And there wasn't a damn thing she could do about it. Even if she could admit she wanted to.

7.

Caroline's whole body was strung tight with nerves going back to the Arabian Nights suite. Her stomach fluttered, she was hot all over. She was nervous, yes, but also ridiculously excited to see him.

Strange that Kian's unpredictability was part of what excited her so much. He was so spontaneous, acting on his most basic impulses. So unlike her.

The exotic scent of the setting was all around her, something spicy in the air. Incense and flowers and something else . . . the scent of sex in that midnight garden. Her body was loosening with desire even as she walked up the garden path, then the marble steps, across the floor of the foyer, her earlier doubts draining out of her. She found Kian standing next to the bed, arranging the small mound of embroidered pillows. Getting ready for her, she imagined. Such a luxurious thought.

"You're back." He smiled, dazzling her.

"Yes." She didn't know what else to say to him. She felt like a girl at a high school dance; that off balance, yearning for him in that same way, as though she couldn't be sure if he'd want her. Yet she knew he did.

"Come, let's get you undressed."

"Undressed?"

"I do prefer you that way, yes, but it's warm today. And you've been working. I thought a bath would refresh you. Or a shower."

"Ulterior motives, Kian?"

"If you're lucky." He grinned. Then he moved toward her, powerful, graceful.

A small shiver raced over her skin, knowing he was about to touch her.

Silently, he undressed her. And silently, she let him do it, until she stood naked before him, other than those golden chains he'd put around her neck the night before. There was something sensual about the gleam of them, the weight of them on her skin. Some part of her, a part she had to recognize now, sank right into that place where he was in charge and she was . . . what? Yielding. More feminine, somehow. He smiled, his gaze drifting from her eyes to her mouth, pausing there before lowering to her breasts, her stomach. There was something overtly sexual about the way he looked at her naked body. Something she loved.

Impossible now to think about those concerns which had seemed so important only a little while ago.

"Bath or shower, Caroline?"

"Mmm...either." She didn't care. All she cared about was the idea of being naked with him, wet all over. And she'd been needing more and more to see him naked, to touch him, to give him the pleasure he so readily gave to her. Torture, really, that she had to stand there and wait one more moment.

He took her hand and led her into the big bathroom, let go only long enough to reach into the enormous marble shower to turn the water on. Steam floated on the air, making everything a little hazy, dreamlike, before a fan overhead drew it upward. That low white drone, mixed with the sound of falling water, made for a faint, sensual music, so that every sound, every movement was muffled, cushioned.

She watched his reflection in the mirror as he drew off his loose pants and stood next to her, both of them completely bare. His golden brown skin was a few shades darker than her own. He was so much more muscular, so utterly masculine. Her mouth nearly watered simply looking at his reflection in the mirror. She glanced up and caught his gaze in the glass.

He moved in right next to her, and said quietly, "There is something sensual in seeing oneself in a mirror. Something a little mysterious. Surreal. Even more so now, seeing you here, next to me." He slipped an arm around her waist, his hand coming to rest on her rib cage, then snaking up to cup her breast.

She gasped, his touch burning into her immediately, a lance of pure desire.

"Look, Caroline. See the flush on your cheeks, how it reaches even your lovely breasts. How your nipples grow darker. Especially if I do this."

He reached up and rolled her nipple in his fingers. She moaned, arcing into his touch.

"Ah yes. I love to see you like this. Surrendering to pleasure, to the needs of your body. Do you see how I love it, Caroline?"

He moved against her side, and she felt the thick ridge of his arousal press into her hip. She lowered her gaze to watch him in the mirror. His cock was hard, so long and swollen. So damn beautiful. Her sex squeezed, wanting him. Wanting him inside her body, in her hands, in her mouth.

"Have you ever watched yourself come in the mirror, Caroline?"

She licked her lips. "No."

"You are about to."

He turned, slipped his other hand between her thighs and right into her soaking wet cleft. She parted her legs for him. And for herself. He was right, there was a strange fascination in seeing herself in the mirror, his hand between her thighs, his fingers moving into her. Pleasure shafted through her; the physical sensation of his fingers rubbing over her slit, sliding in and out, but also watching him do these things.

"Yes," he whispered to her. "Open wider, Caroline. Let us both watch. You are so wet, so beautiful."

His cock was pressing into her hip, moving gently against her.

"I have to touch you, Kian," she murmured.

He sighed into her ear when she reached down and wrapped her fingers around his cock. It was like a silken length of steel in her hand; that hard, that solid, yet covered in the most gloriously soft golden skin. She watched in the mirror as she slid her hand gently up the shaft to the tip. And shivered when he moaned. And all the time, he was working her with his hands, his fingers buried deep in her wet sex, one thumb circling her clitoris, and the other hand kneading her breast, teasing her hard nipple.

She nearly hit sensation overload, desire blazing through her body. And the sight of them together, touching each other, was mesmerizing. Seeing and feeling his powerful cock in her hand. Knowing how much more powerful he would be inside her. The man fucked her so hard. Pure animal.

That thought brought her to the very edge.

"Kian..."

"Yes," he gasped, thrusting his hips, pushing his cock into her hand.

She squeezed him in her grasp, stroked him hard and fast. Her hips moved of their own accord. And still she couldn't tear her gaze away from the misty image of herself in the mirror, Kian's body next to hers, the glistening head of his cock in her hand and his strong hand working between her thighs.

Unbelievable, how this was affecting her. But she really didn't have time to think about it. Kian was pumping his cock in her tight grasp, and her own hips were moving in rhythm, her orgasm bearing down on her as his fingers plunged, his thumb hard on her aching clit, his other hand squeezing her nipple, causing shards of pleasure to stab through her, from breast to sex. Sensation met somewhere in the center of her body, pleasure upon pleasure, shafting into her.

"Oh! Oh, oh, oh..."

She stiffened all over as she came, a powerful tide,

hot and shimmering. And as her body clenched in pleasure, she watched the hot spurt of Kian's come flow over her hand, onto her hip, heard his groans, his wild, panting breath.

She was still trembling with the tiny waves of postorgasm when she turned in his arms and he pressed his mouth to hers. He kissed her hard, opening her lips with his tongue, plunging inside. His kiss was deep, desperate, his hands coming over her cheeks. He nipped her lower lip, pushed his tongue into her mouth again. So hot and sweet and wet, she could barely stand it. It was all too good, his hard body, his mouth on hers, the pure satisfaction of having made him come in her hand.

She had never experienced anything so erotic in her life.

She felt powerful. And a strange sense of freedom filled her, made her loose and warm all over.

Kian pulled his mouth away, smiled at her, moved her into the enormous marble shower and under the steaming water. Then he kissed her again, the heat of the water fusing with the heat of their bodies. He pulled her in tight, her breasts pushed up hard against his chest. So good, wet skin against wet skin. And he was still kissing her, pushing her wet hair from her face with his hands, sliding them down her shoulders, over her back, then cupping her buttocks and pulling her hips in close, as though he couldn't get enough of her. And she gloried in it all, in that feeling of being wanted this much.

Finally, he relaxed his hold on her, and took a cloth and a bar of soap, and washed her carefully. The soapy cloth felt lovely gliding over her skin; her nipples hardened, her sex tightened up once more.

The man was making her insatiable.

He used the handheld showerhead to rinse her off, and even the sting of the water felt good to her: on her belly, her breasts. With a wicked grin, Kian moved it down between her thighs, using one hand to push her legs apart.

"You'll like this, Caroline."

She had no doubt she would. She would do whatever he asked of her. Would enjoy it even if only because he wanted her to.

He knelt down on the marble floor of the shower, and parted her thighs with his hand, then spread her sex wide with his fingers. With the other, he held the showerhead, and sprayed the water right onto her clitoris. Sensation shot through her, stinging, intense. She gasped.

Kian murmured, "Yes..."

She spread her legs wider, and he moved the sprayer back and forth over her clit. His fingers holding her open felt good, just the idea of being so wide open to him, so vulnerable. Even better when he slipped a few fingers inside.

Her breath came out on a ragged pant. "I need you to fuck me, Kian."

He pushed his fingers deep inside her, began to pump. And still he moved the sprayer over her sex, her clit tingling, aching, the water and the heat and his hands all one sensation. Her climax washed over her, fast and furious, taking her by surprise. She shivered with it, thought she might collapse, but Kian stood and pulled her into his arms while he drove her climax on with his clever, wicked fingers.

"Oh God..."

He kissed her again, another long, deep kiss. And she

melted into him, let him hold her up. It was a long time before she could breathe normally. Kian still held her firmly in his arms. She tilted her head up and kissed his neck, wrapped her arms around his back and moved in to suck at the golden skin of his throat.

A soft moan from him, then a chuckle. "We may never get out of this shower again."

"I won't mind," she answered.

How lovely that would be, to stay in there with him forever. Warm and sensual, everything soft and slippery as a dream.

But this was no dream.

Still, it was far too soon to wake up. They had some time left. She would make the most of it.

They'd had a lovely, lazy day together, with a long nap after their shower. Kian had awakened at sunset with a raging hard-on, and had gone back into the big shower to relieve himself while Caroline slept. He was beginning to connect that shower entirely with sex.

Dinner had been on the terrace, with the dark silhouette of the San Jacinto mountains against the deepening blue of the sky. He loved that she watched the mountains in the same way he did, that she seemed as soothed by them. A small thing. Why was he even noticing such a thing about her? But he seemed to be catching every tiny detail.

A maid had taken the dinner tray away, and they sat now on the terrace, quietly watching the moon rise in the sky. He glanced over at her, took in the delicate bones of her profile. He reached out and touched her hand, just a whisper of his fingertips against hers. She turned and smiled at him. So beautiful.

He wanted to do so many things with her. He wanted to fuck her again. There was no question about that. Even now his body was hardening, simply thinking about the evening ahead. Imagining the ways in which he would touch her, make her come again and again. But there was more. He wanted to get out into the world with her, away from this place where she could only see him as an Exotica companion, a gigolo. He wanted her to see him as a man.

He didn't want to ask himself why.

They'd been sitting quietly together for some time when she said, "Kian? Do you think this is a sin? What we do here at Exotica?"

"I am here, aren't I?"

"Yes, of course. But for some, that aspect of sin makes it more appealing. I know that was part of it for me when I came to work here, for whatever twisted reasons I had at the time. Although now I'm used to the idea and it feels natural. But when I really stop to think about it..."

"Then you have a chance to see the sin in it, is that it?"

"Something like that." Her brows drew together, as though she were really trying to figure this out.

"I will admit we aren't saints, either of us. Nor any of those people willing to work here, to come here as clients. But I also somehow don't see that as important. I suppose I'm not accustomed to questioning what I do. What is it that seems sinful to you? Is it the sex?"

She bit her lip, into that soft pink flesh. A shiver raced over his skin watching her do it, making him hard for her once more. "Maybe. But I'm only now beginning to recognize that I feel this way at all."

"Part of that rebellion you spoke of before."

"Yes." She smiled. "I suppose it is. When do you think we'll be able to put all of that behind us, those archaic ideas about things planted in our heads early in life?"

"Planted by whom?"

"By my mother, in my case. What about you?"

"As I said before, my mother has always been very open with me, very permissive."

Be careful.

"And your father?"

He shook his head. This was not something he normally thought about. But did she have something there? "My father played a much less active role. With him, it was always about expectations. For my older brother, anyway. For the world at large. But he never seemed to have any of me. As I said, I was spoiled. Lucky to have been the youngest, I suppose."

"Lucky that your father never expected anything of you? It sounds almost as bad as my mother expecting too much."

He had to stop and think about that. And about the fact that she found ways to challenge him, his ideas about the world, about himself. He wasn't used to a woman doing that. But then, he'd never before given a woman that opportunity.

"I've always thought of myself as lucky. Perhaps I haven't appreciated it enough. But yes, fortunate to have been born into my family, into a life of ease."

"Ah." She leaned toward him, resting her chin in her hand on the arm of the chair. "I knew it."

"Knew what?"

"That you were someone who had been raised with money. I didn't really get it when you mentioned before that your family owns hotels. I didn't think about it. Not that it's a bad thing at all. But it makes me wonder all the more what you're doing here."

He twined his fingers around hers, stood, and tugged her to her feet, pulled her close. "I am here to make you happy, to fulfill your every desire."

He leaned in and took her mouth. Her soft lips yielded to him instantly, opened to him. Her mouth was hot and sweet inside.

Yes, just kiss her, get her into bed again.

He wanted her. His hardening cock was testament to that. But he had to get her off this course of conversation. It would be too hard to keep his secret if they talked anymore about his family.

He was begining to hate his secret. Hated even more that when it came out, as it eventually had to, she would think he was a bastard. Maybe he was. But for now, he just wanted her, whatever he could have of her. He would think about the consequences later.

Caroline felt as though they were floating as the limousine raced down the highway. Scenery passed in a blur of color through the tinted windows.

She'd always loved riding in a limo, had never outgrown that little thrill, that sense of luxury. Even better with Kian sitting beside her, opening a bottle of Dom Perignon, pouring the sparkling liquid into crystal glasses. That sense of utter luxury, yes, but also being there with him. Her pulse raced hot in her veins just looking at him: his aristocratic profile, the high, chiseled cheek-bones, that lush slash of sexy mouth.

He turned to her and smiled, and she felt that now-familiar melting sensation. "I hope you like champagne."

She took the glass he held out to her. "I love it, actually. And I think I need it today. It's strange, being away from Exotica, out of that fantasy environment. It makes me see you a little differently. Perhaps that was your intention. But it all seems too real."

He just smiled at her, sipped his champagne.

"So, are you going to tell me where you're taking me?" she asked him.

He gestured with his glass. "Out. Out in the world."

"You enjoy being mysterious, don't you?"

"Every bit as much as you enjoy the sense of mystery I provide." He leaned in and brushed his lips across her cheek, making her shiver. "I think you need that. Your life is too organized, Caroline. Your mind is too organized. I'm here to add an element of the unknown."

"Sometimes I think you know too much about me." She turned to gaze out the window once more. Scenery whizzed by in a blur of color: blues, greens, browns.

"Is that a bad thing?"

"Just . . . scary sometimes."

His tone sobered. "I want to know you, Caroline."

"Why? Why do you want to know me?" She turned back to face him, frustration swarming hot in her veins. "In a few days we'll be nothing more than employer and employee."

"You know that's not true."

"Do I? How do I know that? We've known each other for four days, Kian. And you . . . you're going to be

working at Exotica. Working for me. And your job..."
She shook her head, unable to continue. Did she even
have a right to talk to him about these things?

"Perhaps it doesn't have to be like that."

His eyes were dark and hot. She couldn't quite read
what was going on in there. But she was too worked up
to question it.

"This has been lovely, Kian. More than that. But we
have only a few days before things change. I can't afford
to be unrealistic about that."

"Why not?" He sounded angry now.

She shook her head. Did she really want to tell him
that he'd come to mean something to her? She couldn't
even face it herself. "Please, can't we just enjoy each
other for as long as we have? Can we do that without
looking at it too closely? I'm sorry for starting this discussion. I didn't mean for it to go in this direction."

His features softened, relaxed. "Of course."

He reached out and smoothed his palm over her
cheek. Why did that make her want to cry? He dropped
his hand and she sipped from her champagne, cooling
her aching throat.

They were silent for several moments, then he raised
her hand to his lips and laid a gentle kiss there.

"Let's not be angry with each other, Caroline."

"No, I don't want to be. I don't mean to be."

He smiled, kissed her hand again, sending tremors of
heat racing through her system. How was it this man
could arouse her so easily?

He leaned in and kissed her mouth, a gentle brush of
his lips. Her body ached for him. And deep inside, a tender ache started, as well. It wasn't about sex. She refused
to ask herself what it *was* about.

When he pulled her into his arms she didn't protest. She loved the strength of him, the heat of him, his clean, masculine scent. Pure sex to her, his scent, the touch of his hands, his lips.

He started kissing her again. God, the way this man could kiss! As though nothing else mattered. The rest of the world just went away and all she could think of was his lips on hers, his tongue in her mouth, the sweet taste of him.

Her body heated, every nerve lighting up with need.

He pulled away to whisper to her. "Have you ever had an orgasm in a limousine, Caroline?"

"No."

"You are about to."

He pushed her skirt up and delved beneath it, his fingers quickly slipping into her lace panties. She parted her thighs for him.

"Ah, you're wet for me already. I knew you would be."

He teased her lips with his fingertips, slipping over her slick folds, then in between them. Pleasure burned hot and pure. Within moments she was trembling with it.

She sighed when he moved his hand away, taking her panties with him, sliding them down over her legs. But in a moment he was moving between her thighs again. This time, he held the open champagne bottle to her body.

"Kian? What are you doing?"

"Shh. Lean back. Yes, that's it. And move closer to the edge of the seat."

She turned her face into his shoulder as he pressed the cold green glass to her throbbing clit. Strange, but it felt wonderful. He rubbed it over her cleft, circled her clitoris with the cool bottle. Sensation pounded through her like a series of small, exquisite hammer blows.

In moments she was panting, writhing. He shifted the bottle, spread her legs wider with his free hand, and pushed the tip of it inside her.

"God, Kian..."

"Let it happen, Caroline." He pinched at her clitoris with his fingers, massaged in circles as he moved the bottle inside her. It was cold, different. Devastating.

"Come for me," he whispered. "Come for me, my beauty."

And she did. She shook with the force of it, pleasure moving through her in undulating waves. Her sex clenched hard around the glass as he moved it gently in and out of her. Her fingers dug into his arm, she bit into his shoulder through the fabric of his shirt.

She shivered with the faint aftershocks for a long time. He kept his hand on her, between her thighs, his fingers massaging her gently. She was limp all over, warm, relaxed. And her body never let go of the desire, wanted him to keep touching her.

Finally, he moved his hand away. Her body still buzzed with need, but it was a banked fire now, rather than the blaze it had been earlier. And it felt good to lay against him, to feel the rhythm of his breathing with the rise and fall of his chest, along with the gentle rocking motion of the limousine. How long had it been since she'd lain like this with a man? Since she'd been with someone who made her pulse flutter with a simple look, from nothing more than the sound of his voice?

He was stroking her hair. She'd worn it down again today, without even thinking about it. She loved feeling his hands in it. But she understood it meant something more, as well. That it was about an internal loosening going on inside her, one caused directly by Kian.

Frightening, on some level. But exactly what she needed. She had to admit that to herself. God, how twisted up she'd been inside all this time! But she didn't want to think about the past now.

She didn't want to think about the future, either.

"We're almost there, Caroline. Yes, I can see the sign up ahead."

She sat up and looked through the window, saw the sign saying they were entering Santa Barbara.

"I haven't been here in years."

"They call this place the American Riviera, you know," Kian told her. "It does look a bit like the French Riviera. But more . . . American."

She turned to smile at him. His features seemed a bit softer than usual, his hair a little mussed. His eyes were glowing.

She looked back out the window. "The landscape here is so beautiful. Like something out of a painting. All these soft colors. And the mountains coming down to meet the sea."

"Yes, exactly. Even the boats on the water remind me of the Impressionists. That white against the blue, the way the sun lights the ocean with pink and gold."

She'd never met another man who talked to her in terms of art, someone who understood her on that level. Perhaps she hadn't been open to it until now. Yes, that was certainly true. She'd had too many secrets, locked away. And big pieces of herself locked away with them. But she also understood Kian was unique. She wanted to know more about him, but it seemed that whenever the discussion became too personal, he shifted away. Perhaps he had his secrets, as well?

They spent the rest of the ride in companionable

silence. Finally, the car pulled to a stop and the driver came to open the door. Kian handed her from the car, then climbed out himself. They stood in a wide circular drive in front of a low-built mission-style structure made of stacked gray stone. An enormous pair of wooden doors stood open, and they walked through, Kian's hand warm on the small of her back, and entered an enclosed, stone-paved courtyard. Grapevines in large pots twisted up the tall wood columns that held up a porch-like roof, which ran the circumference of the courtyard. The air was clean, cooler than in the desert, but still warm enough that Caroline didn't need her sweater. She could smell the rosemary that grew in wild profusion in large terra cotta pots.

Kian guided her across the courtyard and through a pair of iron gates, onto a wide stone terrace dotted with tables, overlooking a small canyon with a stream running through the bottom. Overhead, they were shaded by ancient, twisting oak trees.

"This is beautiful, Kian."

"I knew you'd like it."

A waiter came and led them down a short flight of stone stairs. There, they found themselves on a smaller patio, with only a few of the white linen–covered tables. He took them to one in the far corner that was nestled beneath the arms of one of the old oaks.

Kian held her chair for her, then moved his so that he could sit next to her, rather than across from her. She loved these small gestures from him.

Don't take it to mean too much.

No, this was all a bit romantic, wasn't it? She'd do well not to invest too much into that particular fantasy.

The waiter handed them menus, then left.

Kian leaned in, his head next to hers. "The duck looks very good. But I think the citrus-seared sea scallops will do nicely."

She couldn't think of a reason not to let him order for her, even though it seemed as though she should. It seemed to be easier and easier to simply let him handle everything, to hand herself over to him. She was changing. And it was because of him.

The sun was growing warmer as it filtered through the trees, and while Kian ordered their lunch and a bottle of wine, she closed her eyes and let the gentle rays fall on her face.

When she felt his fingertips on her cheek she opened them.

"You look happy, Caroline."

"I suppose I am. It's good to get away from work for a while. It's been far too long since I've done that. Actually, that's a lie. I haven't taken a vacation since I started at Exotica. I rarely take a day off. And when I do, I'll do a little shopping sometimes, but mostly I stay at home and just sort of hole up. God, I don't even know what I do there. But it's rare."

"And where is home?"

"Not far from Exotica." Why did his question feel intrusive suddenly?

He was quiet a moment. Then he said, "Home is a private place for you, isn't it?"

She nodded. "It's the only sanctuary I have." Why had she said that? It was true, but it was a little too honest. She felt a small chill race up her spine.

"We should all have such a place, a sanctuary. Some place we can feel safe when we need to."

"And where is your sanctuary?"

"I find myself currently without one."

"Well, perhaps your apartment at the staff lodge at Exotica will be a refuge for you. It's very comfortable."

She hated even saying it. But it was reality. A reality she was going to have to face very soon. She was really going to have to stop this constant ping-ponging of her emotions.

She looked at Kian and watched in surprise as his features sort of shut down, his eyes going dark, hooded.

Startled, she covered his hand with hers. "Is everything alright, Kian?"

"Yes, of course." He gave her a half smile, squeezed her hand, the darkness leaving his face as quickly as it had come.

The waiter arrived with a bottle of white wine, then shortly after, their salads. Kian was glad for the distraction of eating, drinking.

He'd almost blown it. Too close. That one moment about being without a sanctuary, a home. Why the hell had that gotten to him? He had almost come out and told her everything. Too late now, really. She was going to be mad as hell when she found out who he really was, what he was doing at Exotica. He didn't know why that bothered him so damn much. She was just another woman. There had been many in the past. There would be more in the future.

Even if he didn't want there to be.

He knew what his mother would say if he told her, she was such a romantic. But of course, his mother was French, and she always claimed the French had invented romance, invented sex. Perhaps she was right about the sex. But he'd missed the romance entirely. Not just flowers and champagne, but true romance. Love.

His parents had always been madly in love with each other. Such a powerful love, a force of nature. It was something which had always seemed far beyond his reach. No, his life was about other things, the simple pursuit of pleasure.

He'd told Caroline at least that one truth: his parents had indulged him, spoiled him. He'd always appreciated it. But he was beginning to think there were things on which he'd missed out, living so selfishly. Why had his family let him get away with it? Of course, all of that was soon to change.

Why was he thinking of his parents now? Was it that sense of permanence they'd always seemed to have, up until the day his father had died ten years ago?

But he couldn't even consider anything permanent with Caroline. Because once she discovered that Collette was his mother, that she had sent him to Exotica to play at being a companion for six months before her retirement, before he took over management of their U.S. resorts and hotels, becoming Caroline's boss, she would never let him near her again.

8.

CAROLINE WOKE in his arms. Such a lovely feeling. One she knew better than to get used to. There was something a little forbidden about it, which only made it better somehow. That seemed to be a theme with her, with the things she and Kian did together.

Forbidden, yes, but incredibly intimate, too, if she let herself think about it in those terms. But how could she do that, allow herself to experience that level of intense intimacy with him, only to give it up in a few days? Because there was no question that she would have to do that. There was no doubt in her mind that him working as a companion at Exotica would drive her crazy, if she allowed herself to get any closer to him.

Hell, the thought was driving her crazy even now.

She burrowed down in the covers, breathed in the sleepy scent of him, her eyes closed against the pale morning light.

Kian.

He was too...too much of everything she needed, craved. Funny, she hadn't even known she'd wanted this, to be close to someone, to be touched in the way he touched her. She had no idea she would respond this way to such a dominant man, to the roughness and the raw-ness of the sex. She was only beginning now to under-stand how the whole sexual dynamic between them was part of why she felt she *knew* him, that he knew her, in a way which should be impossible in such a short time. That because of the way he treated her in bed, she *had* to trust him.

Her relationship with Jeff had never been like this. She'd never felt this close to him, even though they'd been together for three years, had known each other even longer. Suddenly she realized she'd been a bit shut down even before that night she'd discovered Jeff and Sarah together, that it had prevented her from ever being truly intimate with anyone.

She was so much her mother's daughter, in ways she didn't very much like about herself. Closed off, never needing anyone—or, telling herself she didn't, anyway.

Now she knew better. And it was going to hurt to give it up. But this thing with Kian was temporary. She'd known that going in and she certainly wasn't going to kid herself about it now.

Dangerous.

Yes, he was dangerous. Her feelings for him were dangerous. She didn't want to think about these things.

Not now, when he was still here beside her. It seemed almost as though she were treading on sacred ground, to waste one moment with these desperate thoughts.

Don't do it.

Easy enough to tell herself that. But she was falling for him already. Too late to turn back. Oh yes, far too late. Too late after that very first day, if she was going to be honest with herself.

It was about damn time she was honest with herself.

She sighed, softly so she wouldn't wake him, opened her eyes to look at him. That beautiful face. She could only ever manage to think of him as beautiful. Handsome simply didn't do the job. He was so achingly beautiful it made her heart hurt to look at him. A lovely kind of pain. She preferred it to what would come later.

His lashes rested against his golden cheeks. She wanted to touch them, to run her fingers over those silky, fragile tips. She took a breath, waited, watching him breathe. Then she reached out and did it, just brushed one fingertip across his eyelashes.

He woke smiling.

"What was that, my beauty?"

He pulled her on top of him. Her breasts were pressed against the hard planes of his chest. The stubble of his morning beard was a dark shadow across his jaw. His eyes were lit with gold and silver, his cock hardening against her belly.

"I just wanted to."

His smile grew wider. "I could wake up like this every morning."

She shook her head, her throat closing up. "Don't."

"Don't what?"

"Don't say it, don't tell me things that are . . . impossible."

"Caroline . . ."

"No, Kian. We're running out of time. And I can't stand it."

She was immediately horrified that the words had come out of her mouth. Tears sprang to her eyes. She ducked her head, wanting to hide.

"Shh, Caroline. Don't."

"I'm sorry. I don't mean to."

"I know. But don't cry. There's no need. We're together at this moment."

"And tomorrow? And the next day? We'll be here together then, too. But by next week this will all be over."

He was quiet. Too quiet. Then he murmured, "I wish it weren't so."

She had a moment of pure panic. He hadn't argued the point. But then, neither had she. She had presented this as some sort of irreconcilable situation. Why would he think about it any differently? She hadn't given him reason to. But even if she did, even if she asked him for something more, would he be willing to give it?

There was no way to know.

She couldn't take that chance. Which left her with nothing more than today.

She rolled a bit, until she could take him in her hand. He had softened a little, but came alive quickly in her stroking grasp.

She whispered to him, "Then let's enjoy the time we have."

* * *

Kian lay in the big bed, Caroline curled against him. They'd spent the day there, had called for food, fed it to each other among the pillows and the silk sheets. They'd napped in between the sex. He'd fucked her three times, made her come even more, with his cock, with his hands, with his tongue. He'd slid into her ass again, that slick little hole, so tight he'd had to clench his teeth to hold his climax back. But what had really gotten to him was the way she responded to it all. She had opened herself to him, let him do anything he wanted. He hadn't been entirely certain at first if she would ever really allow him to take over, but it had happened more quickly than he'd imagined. More quickly, he was certain, than she had ever imagined.

She trusted him, he realized. Just when he'd gotten to the point when he came to understand exactly how he was going to hurt her.

No, don't think about that now.

He could still see it in her eyes sometimes, Caroline questioning herself. Her need for control was fierce. He understood it, so was his own. But he felt it was more natural for a man. Old-fashioned of him, probably. But he felt it was his duty to take over when it came to sex. That he owed that to whatever woman he was with.

He couldn't even think of another woman now.

But *this* woman, this incredible, lovely woman who lay against his chest, was miles away when he considered what they could have together. Only a few more days, and he was going to ruin it. But meanwhile, he had her, here with him.

He reached out and touched a strand of her long silky hair with his fingers, heard her soft sigh. His gut tightened up.

He really could not stand that he'd lied to her, continued to lie to her. But it was too late. The lie had already been told, had grown more toxic every day they spent together that he hadn't told her the truth.

He was fucked.

It was going to kill him if he didn't get things in perspective.

Time enough tomorrow to do that, though.

He looked down at her and she turned her head, her blue eyes half-lidded, sleepy. So vulnerable at moments like this. Her mouth was all soft and pink, naked looking. Irresistible.

He stopped thinking the moment he pressed his lips to hers. Then they were kissing like two teenagers, her mouth opening up under his, tongues twining, breath panting. Heat raced through his system. His cock hardened, and he pulled her in closer. He wanted her. Nothing else mattered.

She pressed her body hard into his. The heat was coming off her in waves. He wanted to growl out loud, to bite into her soft skin, to possess her completely.

His heart hammering, he pulled his mouth from hers.

"No. Just kiss me, Kian."

She pulled him back to her with her hands on his face, her lovely lips locking onto his, her sweet tongue pushing into his mouth. His body was hard all over, his mind going empty.

She sighed into his mouth. Almost too much, that delicate sigh from her.

Something in him shifted, something desperate and maybe even a little angry. He picked her up, his hands circling her waist, and flipped her over onto her stomach. He grabbed a pillow and shoved it under her hips, spread her legs apart and held her pussy lips wide so he could shove his cock inside her.

She gasped. He knew he was hurting her. He needed to. But she was soaking wet already, was pushing back against him to take more of him in.

Fisting a hand in her hair, he pulled hard, heard her moan. It went through him like a shock of pure lust: demanding this absolute acquiescence from her, and her giving it without even a struggle.

He pulled back, drove his cock into her, hard, harder. Pleasure rumbled through him like thunder, his cock swollen, hungry, as he plunged again and again. She was panting beneath him. He drew her body closer with his free hand, his fingers biting into her hip. She cried out. He didn't stop. Couldn't stop.

"God damn it, Caroline."

"Yes, Kian . . ."

She didn't understand. Didn't know anything but the pleasure. Didn't know about the seething anger burning through him, making him fuck her so hard his thighs strained with the effort. Better that way. Yet still he drove into her, trying to drive the emotion from his body, his mind.

If he couldn't truly have her, he would have her now. In the only way he could.

Pumping, pleasure coursing through him with every hard stroke, he bent over her and bit into the soft flesh at the back of her neck. She cried out once more. She was beginning to shiver all over, her hot pussy clasping around him as her climax took her.

"Kian!"

It was too much for him, her cries, her velvet sheath

clutching his cock, even the taste of her skin on his lips. He came, hard. Shattered, trembled, and fell.

It was late. Caroline could tell by the absence of incense in the air; it had been long enough that it had burned down, unattended, hours ago. A few candles still burned, illuminating the room in a soft golden glow.

She was still on her stomach on the bed, the pillow beneath her hips. Kian lay beside her, one arm and one leg still thrown over her. She was stiff all over, achy, needing to stretch. She shifted, trying not to wake him. But as soon as she moved, he did, too.

He rolled off her, onto his back, and she felt the sudden loss of his warmth like a small void.

Something had happened between them tonight. She wasn't quite sure what it was. The sex had been amazing. Hot, a little dark and dirty. She'd loved it. But looking back, she understood something had changed.

"Kian? Tell me..."

"What?"

She paused, feeling foolish. "I was going to ask you to tell me what you're thinking, like some teenage girl."

He was silent for a few long moments, while her pulse raced in her veins. What was wrong with her?

"Fuck," he muttered finally. He rolled back onto his side, his hazel gaze locked on hers, glowing hot in the last remnants of the candlelight. And in his face was an impossible softness she'd never seen there before. He had never appeared so raw, so completely vulnerable. "I'm sorry, Caroline."

"For what?"

"For being so rough with you."

She shook her head. "Don't be sorry. I ... I needed it. Needed it to hurt. Needed you to mark me in that way." She pushed her hair from her face with a rough hand. "I don't know why. I don't want to ask myself why, to be honest. But I think I understand why you did it. Why it happened that way. Please, Kian. We don't need to talk about it."

He paused, watching her face, then nodded once before he pulled her into his arms. Arms she trusted. She'd never trusted anyone this much. She didn't understand it. But she didn't need to.

"Kian."

"Yes?"

"I want to tell you ..."

"Tell me what?"

Her throat constricted, and as though he sensed it, he held her closer, his fingers twining with hers.

"I want to tell you what happened."

He was quiet a moment, then, "Yes, tell me, Caroline."

Just say it. Get it over with.

It came out on a whisper. "She died."

"Who died?"

She closed her eyes, images of flashing lights, the white sheet, Sarah's reddened cheek, harsh against her eyelids. "Sarah. My best friend." She paused to draw in a deep breath, blew it out. "I caught her with my fiancé. I told you that. We argued. I slapped her in the face, Kian. I told her to leave. And she did. And on her way to ... wherever she was going, she wrapped her car around a telephone pole. And she died."

"Lord, what you've been through, Caroline." He squeezed her hand in his, stroked her hair.

"No, don't feel sorry for me. It was my fault."

"How could it have been? Caroline. She chose to sleep with your fiancé. And you had every right to be angry. Furious. How could it have been your fault, unless you drove the car yourself? Surely you can't believe that?"

Did she? She'd lived with the guilt for so long, she couldn't remember feeling any other way. But Kian sounded so certain. And maybe he was right. She wasn't ready to give up her culpability. But she would think about it. Maybe there was some truth in what he said.

She still felt hard and choked up inside, only a little relieved at having told him. Maybe more relief would come later, after she'd had a chance to let it all soak in. Kian held her tight, so that she could barely breathe. But she didn't want him to let go. Ever.

They slept the rest of the night wrapped around each other. Caroline dreamed of Kian, of those gold and silver eyes watching her in silence. There was meaning there. She was supposed to understand, but realized she didn't know that silent language. The language of secrets which she spoke herself, unknowingly. And which held her back from him.

Kian glanced at the gates of Exotica in his rearview mirror. He'd just dropped Caroline off at her office, where she had to work for the next few hours. He'd hardly been able to let her go. But as soon as he'd watched her walk into the building, he'd known exactly what he had to do. But he needed to drive a little energy off first.

He shifted, stepped on the gas, and the little sports car flew down the long, wide roadway.

He loved the roads in Plam Springs. They were always so empty, so straight and flat. He loved the way the car slid over the black pavement, waves of heat already shimmering along the surface. He headed toward the distant mountains, those stark, jagged peaks, and felt the rumble of the engine in his chest, in his head. The speed helped to clear his mind, to calm him as it always did. Finally, he pulled onto the shoulder, in a spot where he could still see the mountains through the front window, looming closer now.

He pulled his cell phone from his pocket and dialed the series of numbers which would connect him to France. He waited, drumming his fingers against the steering wheel, as the tone rang in his ear.

" 'allo?" His mother's lilting tone came over the line.

"*Maman.*"

"Kian. You received my messages?"

"No, but I'm glad I reached you. Are you well?"

"A little tired, perhaps. But tell me, why are you calling if you did not get my messages?"

"I'm . . . having a bit of a problem."

"You are in Palm Springs, yes? At Exotica?"

"Yes, but it's not the resort. It's me."

"Are you unwell?"

"No, I'm fine. Healthy, anyway." He paused. Where to begin? He concentrated on the road for a moment, those rippling waves of heat coming up off the pavement even this early in the day.

Heat. Lord, Caroline had been all heat last night. The reality of it was a hundred times better than anything he'd imagined. "It's Caroline Winter, your manager." He paused. "We have become . . . involved."

"Ah..." His mother paused, and he heard her light up one of her dark French cigarettes.

"*Maman,* I've lied to her. You know I haven't told her who I am. That I came here to observe the business, to enjoy my role here, before taking over for you. She has no idea I'm your son."

"And now? How serious are you about her, Kian?"

"I would like to be. For the first time. If I haven't already destroyed any chance of a future with her by keeping the truth from her. Understand, *Maman,* I don't blame you. That's not why I'm telling you this. Perhaps if I'd told you sooner..."

"Ah... Kian, my darling, I am afraid I have done something which may have made this situation even worse."

"What do you mean?"

"I tried to reach you by telephone, but you have not answered for several days."

"Yes, I've been with Caroline. I haven't used my phone at all."

"I tried to tell you, but you see, my doctor insisted..."

"What are you saying? Are you alright?"

"I haven't been feeling well. Only a little tired, but my doctor believes it is my heart. He has asked me to rest, to take my retirement now, rather than to wait six months as planned."

"And you're still smoking?"

"I am French, my darling," she said, as though that settled the matter.

"Are you quite sure you're alright? Do you need me to come?"

"No, no. I am fine. But you see, I had to send out a

note to the management at all of our properties. To let them know I am retiring. To let the ones in the U.S. know you will be taking over for me. This message went out by e-mail just this morning."

The impact of what his mother was saying jarred him, going through him like a shock.

"I am so sorry, my darling," she went on. "I am very much afraid this presents a problem for you."

Kian sighed, rubbed a hand over his face, the stubble on his jaw scratching his palm, his fingers. His stomach tied itself up into a hard knot. "It presents a disaster. She'll never forgive me for keeping this from her. For not telling her myself."

He heard the whisper of his mother dragging in smoke, exhaling it on a long sigh. "Love is a very precious, magical thing, Kian."

"I know. Which makes me very much aware of how horribly I've blown this."

"Kian, what I am telling you is, if it is meant to be, you will find a way to work this out. Does she love you?"

"I don't know. I would like to believe she does, especially after last night."

"What happened last night?"

"Surely you don't want to hear details."

"I am French, my darling. But you are very much your father's son, as much as I know you'd like not to believe that. So, no details. Just tell me the important part."

"I fell in love with her last night."

The truth of it hit him like a hammer blow. He had to pause, to draw in a breath. "It started the moment I saw her. But last night...that's when I realized exactly what it was I've been feeling. When I could finally put it into words. In my head, at least. I should have told her last night. Before..." He stopped, the knot in his stomach aching. "It's too late now."

"Kian, I am so sorry."

"So am I. But it's not your fault, *Maman*. It's my own. I should have told her the moment I became involved with her. But I never expected this, to love this woman."

No, he'd never expected to fall in love at all. And now that he had, how the hell was he going to salvage any chance with her?

At this moment, his future seemed utterly dismal. He had no future without Caroline. Without the woman he loved.

He'd spent his life going from one woman to the next, never caring for more than the moment's pleasure. How ironic that the very carelessness which had brought him so much pleasure was going to destroy the one chance he had at true happiness.

Caroline sipped a cup of fragrant Darjeeling tea as she tapped in the password to her e-mail. Not that she was really in the mood to read it, but she did have a job to do. She wanted to catch up on enough work to free her for the next few days, so that all she had to concentrate on was Kian.

A delightful shiver ran through her just letting his name run through her mind. She smiled. Foolishly. Girlishly.

Focus!

She scanned through the dozens of messages, trying to prioritize, but it was hard to keep her mind on the task at hand. It was difficult to stay focused on anything, with images of her night with Kian flashing through her mind's eye.

A beautiful night. A night of passion beyond any she had ever dreamed of. Oh, she knew she sounded romantic, even in her own head. Knew it was dangerous to allow herself to revel in it. But she couldn't help herself.

Kian had played her body so expertly, and yet, there was nothing of his usual smoothness. No, it had been all raw animal passion last night. He had been every bit as lost in it as she had. She'd sensed him falling apart as he came, had gloried in that sensation of her own feminine power. And later, when they'd talked, she'd seen it in his face.

And had lost her heart to him entirely.

But she'd woken this morning promising herself not to think about the nearing end. Not until they were done, and it was over. Then she would hide herself away somewhere to lick her wounds. For now, she still had three more days and nights with him. She planned to savor every moment. She smiled just thinking about being with him again in only a few hours. Thinking about his strong golden body poised above hers. The sheer power of his kisses that melted her in mere seconds. Her yearning for him was sharp, nearly painful. Yet how luxurious to know that he waited for her in the Arabian Nights suite just after lunch. That she would be with him, know his touch, the safety of his arms around her.

She forced her eyes back to the screen in front of her, forced herself to concentrate.

An e-mail from Collette. She was glad she'd checked. Her boss rarely communicated, and when she did, it was always important. Caroline clicked the message open.

From: Collette Fournier, Fournier Enterprises
To: Caroline Winter, Management, Exotica

Dear Caroline,

I am writing to inform you that due to ongoing health issues, I am being forced into an early retirement. Although I have personally overseen all of my hotels and resorts in the U.S. in the past, I am now turning over management of my West Coast properties to my son, Kian Fournier-Razin.

Kian Fournier-Razin? Her pulse racing, she reread the first paragraph. And then again, and again, her heart thumping, her mind spinning. Dread and fear and a creeping sense of betrayal flooded her.

Kian was Collette's son?

That explained his smooth manners, the obvious wealth behind him. It explained his speaking six languages, his Old-World manners. What it didn't explain was what he was doing at Exotica posing as a companion. And it certainly didn't explain why he had kept this crucial bit of information from her.

Pain lanced into her chest, as though she'd been stabbed with a knife, as though she'd been beaten. She had. She'd been brutalized by his lies.

She had opened herself up to this man! And he had been lying to her all along. She wanted to cry. She would have, if she hadn't been so angry. Furious, really. Why had he done this to her?

And God, he'd known all along she'd made that up about auditioning all of the companions herself, even before she'd admitted it to him. What must he have thought of her? Why had he pretended not to know? But it didn't matter now. Nothing mattered.

She forced herself to read the rest of Collette's message.

> *My hope is that you will show my son the same loyalty you have always shown to me. I very much appreciate the fine job you do in running Exotica.*
>
> *You should receive a number of documents shortly, in which Exotica will officially be turned over to my son. Please do not hesitate to contact me should you have any questions.*
>
> *I look forward to your continuing association.*
>
> > *Sincerely,*
> > *Collette Fournier*

A continuing association? No, it stopped now.

Tears burned behind her eyes, but she clenched her jaw and held them back as she quickly drew up her resignation letter, sent it to Collette, sent copies to her assistant, and to her attorney by e-mail, printed out hard copies and left them on her desk with a note to her secretary to mail out immediately. Then she wrote a note to Kian, grinding her teeth against the wrenching pain it caused to put those words on paper. Even worse that *he* was now her boss. But she was leaving before the transfer would take place. Unbearable to even think about it.

Her heart was pounding, her stomach churning. She would not let the tears fall. And in her mind, one question played over and over: how could he have done this to her?

Have to get the hell out of here.

Her legs were shaky as she pulled personal items from her desk drawers and threw them into an empty box she'd found in the supply closet. She just had to stay focused on getting out of there before she fell apart. But she had to get everything together now. She was never coming back.

She opened her closet, moving as quickly as possible, fueled by a sense of desperation. She pulled out the change of clothes she always kept there, a sweater, two pairs of shoes. She tossed her key ring onto the desk, her pager. Picking up the box, the small pile of clothing, her purse, she pulled out her sunglasses to hide her damp eyes. And then, clenching her jaw hard against the pain, she walked with every ounce of dignity she could muster through her office door, down the long hallway, and into the bright sunlight of another lovely desert day.

But there was nothing lovely about it for her. She waited while the valet brought her car, nodded at him as though everything were perfectly normal. She would never be normal again, whatever that was.

She gunned the engine, her tires spinning on the hot pavement, holding her in place for a moment before her car shot down the long driveway.

Just go!

She clenched her teeth as a wave of pain threatened to overtake her. She had to get home, to her sanctuary, as quickly as possible.

Kian had no sanctuary. She remembered that conversation. She'd come to think of *him* as her sanctuary in the last few days. How foolish could she be?

The tears almost started then. She choked them back.

Down to the end of the driveway, then a left turn onto the wide, empty street. And as she made the turn, she caught sight of Kian's black Alfa Romeo from the corner of her eye, making the turn into Exotica's driveway.

God. Too hard to see him, even to see his car. Her throat tightened until she could barely breathe.

Just go!

She gunned the engine, raced over the streets, past the sand dunes, the palm trees, the big housing developments that seemed to pop up all over the desert these days. Her house wasn't far, but every block felt like an eternity. In the distance, the San Jacinto mountains loomed, a little misty against the sky. Or was that simply the tears gathering in her eyes?

Finally, she reached her house, pressed a button on her key ring, and waited while the iron gates pulled back, gripping the steering wheel, her pulse hammering so hard she felt almost as though it gnawed at her insides.

Almost home.

Somehow she got into the garage, remembered to grab her purse and got through the side door before the tears came. She crumpled on the floor of her kitchen, her head in her hands, pain ripping through her like a jagged blade.

How had she let this happen? How had she failed so miserably to protect herself? She, of all people, knew better. And yet she'd allowed this man to break her heart.

She curled into a ball, wrapping her arms around herself, and let out the ocean of tears, some of which had waited for years to be shed.

Her entire body shook with the sobs that welled up in her throat, poured from her mouth despite her resistance. She had no idea how long she was there. But when the tears finally stopped, she ached all over, her body stiff and sore.

She stood, thoroughly disgusted with herself. She hadn't known how much she'd held on to all this time, but it was clear now. And this had to stop. Jeff had been an idiot for doing what he'd done to her. It was wrong. And it was foolish. He'd thrown her away. Well, she wasn't having it again. No, this time, *she* walked away. And she would walk away intact.

She wiped her face with a paper towel, wanting the roughness of it on her tender skin. Needed to feel that physical pain to make the emotional pain stop. God, she couldn't go through this again. She would not. She was so much stronger now than she'd been after things with Jeff had ended so horribly. She'd grown up. And now, she knew herself better than she ever had. Yes, some of that was due to Kian. She couldn't deny it. But that was something she could take away from this whole disaster, something which was, in the end, entirely hers.

She would never speak to Kian Razin again, of that much she was certain. As for the rest of her future, she had no idea. Didn't really matter right now. She knew she had to simply survive this day, this night.

She moved through the kitchen and into the large airy living room, done all in white and neutral shades of sand and stone. So soothing, normally. But nothing would soothe her now.

Her eyes ached, her head hurt, her whole face felt tender. She went to curl up on the long white sofa, pulled a pillow to her chest, and stared out at the million dollar view. Oh yes, she had paid a million dollars for this place. Her job at Exotica had paid for it. These windows looked out at the mountains. They were so enormous, majestic. So solid and permanent. The only permanence in her life. The tears wanted to start again but she bit them back.

She would cry no more. She had allowed a man to destroy her before. It was not going to happen this time.

She realized that for once, she didn't hear her mother's condemning voice in her head. Fairly amazing, considering that was something she'd lived with her entire life, before and after her mother's death. But now, there was only her own voice in her head. And a trace of Kian's, if she let herself think about it.

She didn't.

She wouldn't.

Not now. Not ever.

She took a deep, sighing breath, let the air flow into her lungs. She would never see or speak to Kian again. She knew it was the right thing, even if the thought cut like a knife, that sharply, that bone deep.

It was over.

9.

KIAN BURST into Exotica's reception area, strode across the tiled floor to the desk. "I need to see Caroline."

"She's left for the day," the receptionist told him. "Would you like to leave her a message?"

Fury burned through him, bright and clean. "Do you know who I am?"

"You're one of our companions. Kian Razin." The girl looked flustered, perhaps a little afraid of him, of his anger.

"I am Kian *Fournier*-Razin."

"Kian Fournier...oh. My apologies, sir. Caroline didn't tell me."

"I must speak to her right away."

"I have her cell number and her pager."

"I have already tried them both. I need access to her office. Does she keep it locked?"

"No, sir."

He nodded, moved past her and through the double doors of Caroline's office.

He could see immediately that a number of things were missing. Her closet doors stood open. Totally unlike her, he was certain, to leave her office—or anyplace—in a mess. She'd been in a hurry to leave. And he knew exactly why.

He was too late.

Damn it! How had he let this happen?

This was his fault. And now he'd hurt her. Hurt her irrevocably, he was sure. Deception was her worst enemy. And now, so was he.

He paced the length of her office, his mind churning over arguments, rejecting them just as quickly. There was simply no good excuse for what he'd done. Why the hell hadn't he told her? The moment he and Caroline had become intimate, he should have told her everything. Or he should have refused to do it.

He moved behind the desk, wishing her there, sitting in her chair where he could see her, talk to her. But it was empty. He sat down, ran his fingers along the cool glass edge of the desk. Clean and smooth, like the perfect surface of her skin. Just like glass. Like water.

Impossible. He could never have turned her down. He was only human. He was a man. And she was a lovely, fascinating woman. Oh yes, he'd wanted her from the first moment he'd seen her. But that wanting had quickly changed to something more. So quickly, it had left his head spinning. That was his only excuse for why he'd failed to admit to her who he was. But the excuse was not good enough.

Despair flooded him, something he'd never experienced before in his life, making him feel as though his body were weighed down with lead. Despair and anxiety, making his muscles draw taut, making his nerves buzz. He had to get out of there, drive it off, maybe. What else could he do? He could barely think straight. He had to talk to her. But would she agree to talk to him, to see him? He didn't think so.

What could he possibly say to her that would allow her to forgive him? He felt so utterly humbled. A new sensation, and one he didn't care for. But he deserved this. And he would get down on his knees before her if it would help. Whatever he had to do, he'd do it. If only she would see him.

Yes, he had to go to her! He stood, strode from the office, and found the receptionist on the telephone. He put a hand on her arm, interrupting her call, demanded, "I need her home address. Caroline's." The girl looked startled. He didn't care. He just needed to get to Caroline. "Please. I need it right away."

"Yes, sir." She turned and tapped out something on her computer screen, wrote a note on a message pad, and handed it to him. He glanced at it and thanked her briefly before moving quickly out the door. Back in his car, he gunned the engine as he swung onto the long driveway. Everything moved past him in a blur of heat and emotion.

Just get to her. Talk to her. Fucking impossible, but do it.

He had to find a way. Because frankly, he didn't think he could live without her.

*　*　*

Caroline was still sitting on the couch contemplating the mountains when she heard a noise outside: the squealing of brakes, the slam of a car door. Then yelling at her front gate.

"Caroline!"

Kian.

She wanted to bury her face in the pillow she still held clasped to her chest, over her aching heart. She wanted to cover her ears, to shut him out. But just hearing his voice made her heart beat faster with need for him, a sharp, yearning need that cut deep.

Even after what he'd done to her! How ridiculous she was! No, she would not talk to him.

"Caroline!" His voice was muffled, but she could hear the edge of desperation in it. "I must speak with you. Caroline!"

God, please go away.

She couldn't take this. The tears started again. She pressed the back of her hand to her mouth, willing them to stop.

No, no, no!

She was not going to cry! And she would not see him, talk to him.

He was shaking the gate now, she could hear the grinding of metal on metal. She pulled more tightly into herself, dropped her head into her hands.

Please stop.

Her chest ached with a deep, wrenching pain, her eyes burning with unshed tears.

"Caroline, please. I must talk to you. I must!"

She sat, frozen, while he shook the gates, yelled for

her. Every muscle in her body hurt with the effort to keep herself there, to sit still, not to go to him. Her breath was coming in ragged pants, her skin hot and damp.

When her cell phone started to ring she forced herself to hold perfectly still, her jaw clenched. It stopped, then rang again.

I will not talk to him.

Again the ringing stopped for a few moments, only to begin once more.

Please stop.

She wasn't sure how much longer she could hold out.

He started shaking the gate again, the grinding sound of the metal spearing into her head, making it ache.

"Caroline!" Then, more quietly, "Caroline, please."

She shook her head, as though he could see it.

Then he was yelling again, "Caroline! Open the gate!"

She sank into the sofa, buried her head in the pillows, holding her breath.

Finally, silence. The yelling stopped, and she heard his engine start up, heard the car take off. She wanted to pull in a deep breath, but she couldn't do it. Agony even to breathe. He'd cut her so deeply. And it hurt that he'd been right there and she hadn't talked to him. It hurt that she never wanted to see him again. She had no idea how she was supposed to survive this.

She stayed on the sofa, trembling, weeping, until it grew dark outside. And still, she didn't dare move. Through tear-blurred eyes she watched the course of the moon as it traveled across the night sky, the shining points of a thousand stars a glittering backdrop. And she felt her smallness in the world in a way she'd never thought about before. So small, so cold. So alone.

She had never felt so completely alone. But she was

going to have to get used to it, wasn't she? The emptiness inside her seemed to be growing by the hour, threatening to swallow her up. She fought against it as long as she could, until finally, exhausted, she slept.

Kian woke in the dark, his heart pounding, trying to remember where he was. Oh yes, the hotel. He'd checked into a hotel yesterday. He couldn't bear to go back to Exotica after...

He rubbed a hand over his jaw, the stubble biting into his skin. He glanced at the clock. Almost four A.M. But his pulse was racing, his mind whirling. He'd never get back to sleep, was shocked he'd fallen asleep at all.

Lord, how was he ever going to fix this mess he'd made? He couldn't stand it. Couldn't stand to want her so badly, when he couldn't have her.

It struck him, then, that he didn't *want* her. He *needed* her.

Is this what love was? To need another person this way? Despite his lifelong independence, despite the notion buried deep in his brain that love and romance were not meant for him. He needed her. Needed to be with her.

He had to tell her. Had to have the chance to prove himself to her. To show her that he could be the man she needed him to be. The man she deserved. The man he should have been all this time, and was now, only because of her.

He'd already thrown his clothes on and was searching for his shoes before he realized it was the middle of the night. Didn't matter. He had to see her.

The streets seemed wider than ever in the dark. He didn't pass another car on the road as the Alfa Romeo moved smoothly through the night. He found her house quickly enough. There was one small light on inside the garden courtyard; he could see the amber glow of it through the gate.

He pulled over, turned the car off, and got out, went to the gate. He shook it, as he'd done earlier. It stood as solidly closed against him as it had before.

Damn it!

He dug his cell phone out of his pocket, dialed her number. It rang and rang, as he ran an impatient hand through his hair.

Pick up, Caroline.

Finally, a sleepy "Hello?"

"Caroline. Thank God."

"Kian." A long pause in which he heard her gulp in air. "I don't want to talk to you. Why are you calling me?"

"Because I have to tell you...I have to tell you so many things."

"Now?"

"Yes, now. Right now. Caroline, you must come to the gate and let me in."

"What? Where are you?"

"I'm here. Outside. Please don't make me yell for you again."

"God, Kian, it's the middle of the night. You can't do that. Someone will call the police."

"Then come out. Talk to me."

He heard the muffled sound of movement over the phone, then her front door swung open. She came down the steps in a creamy silk nightgown that barely grazed the tops of her thighs, a matching robe that fluttered as she moved.

She stopped just on the other side of the gate. "What are you doing here?" She sounded angry, tired. Her hair was mussed, all that glorious hair, like strands of silk in the golden glow from the garden lights.

He said quietly, "Please let me in, Caroline."

"I can't."

He drew in a deep breath. "I understand. I understand perfectly why you feel you can't do that. And I am so sorry. You must believe me. Caroline, I never meant for any of this to happen."

"For what to happen? For you to get caught in your deception?"

He shook his head. "No, that's not what I mean at all. I know I should have told you who I was—"

"Yes, you should have. Right from the start! But certainly after we . . . became involved." Her eyes were huge, burning.

"You have every right to be angry. It was wrong of me."

"Tell me why. Was this some sort of game to you?"

"Would I be here now if it were?"

Her shoulders slumped. "No."

"Let me in, Caroline," he said again.

She shook her head. "I can't do it. This place is . . . this is my safety. My refuge."

"Your sanctuary," he said quietly.

"Yes."

He gazed into her eyes. They'd softened a little. "I need refuge, Caroline." Was that really his voice, so strangled? So weak?

"You can't come to me for that. You gave up that right when you lied to me."

"I know. I need it, anyway."

"You've never struck me as a man who needs anything."

"I'm not. I never have needed anything, or anyone. Until now."

She stared at him, and he thought she might open the gate. Then she shook her head once more.

"Not good enough, Kian." He could hear the tears gathering in her voice.

Desperation surged through him now, hot, frantic. He hated it, hated that he had no control. Over her, over his own emotions. "Don't you see what's happened? This was never meant to be anything more than sport between us! I came here to watch how Exotica operated, under my mother's instructions, yes, but I wanted to do it. To spend the last six months of my self-indulgent life—and I will admit to that fully—before taking over the business. It was to be my grand good-bye to my former life. And then, you changed everything."

"How can you say that? You still lied to me."

"Yes. My mother insisted I keep my identity from you. She meant no harm. She wanted me to see the place from the inside, to see exactly how it operated. Businesses do this sort of thing all the time. But she didn't know what would happen between us. I had no idea what would happen. How I would feel about you—"

"Please don't! Don't say that to me."

"I must. I have to tell you, to explain. Caroline, you changed everything for me! It took me a few days." He paused, ran a hand through his hair, his fingers gripping his scalp as though it would help him to think, to put the words together in the right way. "No, that's not the truth, either. I knew right away something was different with you. But you see, I had no experience to draw on. I had no way of knowing I was falling in love with you."

"God, Kian, please." She was crying now. And all he wanted was to take her in his arms.

"Caroline," he said, almost whispering. "Open the gate."

"No. No." Her head was in her hands, and she was shaking it.

"What do you want me to do? Do you want me to beg you? Because I will. I will get down on my knees and beg you to hear what I'm saying to you." And he did it, hardly believing it in some small corner of his mind, but he went down all the same. Gravel bit into his knees, and he wrapped his hands around the filigree ironwork of the gate. "I have never kowtowed to another human being. But I will do this for you. I will do whatever I must. Because I love you, Caroline. And I believe you love me."

She let out a small sob as she stepped forward. "Kian..." But whatever she was going to say trailed off into tears.

He reached through the bars, wrapped his fingers around her wrist. Her bones felt so fragile in his hand. He could feel her racing pulse. And she sank to her knees, crying, her face coming to rest between the bars.

"God help me, I love you, Kian."

A flood of relief and love rushed through him. But he knew full well that even so, she might not let him in. Into her house. Into her life.

"Caroline?" He waited. She knew what he was asking. She looked at him, watching his face, an expression of puzzlement on hers. Her elegant brows were drawn together. And he held his breath, waiting.

He heard the small metallic click as she opened the gate. Rising to his feet, he pushed through and took her into his arms.

Caroline couldn't stop crying. Even though he was here. He was here and he loved her. They would figure the rest out later.

He felt so good to her, his arms strong and solid around her. And he smelled like Kian, that earthy, masculine scent. She didn't care that it was the middle of the night, that she stood in the cold air in her garden. All that mattered was him.

He pulled back to look into her eyes. His were dark, intense, filled with emotion. He touched her cheek with one finger, as though he couldn't believe they were together. Well, neither could she.

His hands moved over her face, his features concentrating on her, his gaze going from her eyes to her mouth and back again. And then he kissed her, and the rest of the world fell away.

When he stopped they were both breathless.

"I love you," he told her again. "And I need you, Caroline. I understand now how much I need you, that I can't do everything alone. That I'm not meant to, as I'd always assumed. And that needing you doesn't weaken me. That it's right."

All at once, she knew exactly what he meant. Understanding flooded her in a warm rush. But he was kissing her again, and her heart and her body were responding. She was heating up, everywhere at once.

He pulled back long enough to tell her, "Take me inside."

Wordlessly, she took his hand and led him into her house, through the front door. And as they crossed the threshold, she had some sense of the significance of that moment. But then Kian closed the door behind them, and nothing else mattered except that they were there together.

She led him to her bedroom, that clean, open space no man had ever entered before, with the vaulted windows looking out at the desert sky and her big white bed. Everything white and simple, so it wouldn't compete with the stunning desert view she loved so much.

She stood before him in the pale moonlight and let her robe slip from her shoulders, then her nightgown followed, falling to the soft white carpet on the floor. She was naked and unashamed, in every way. Open to him physically, emotionally. And for once, there was no fear.

He watched her with dark, glittering eyes as he stripped his clothes off. She loved seeing his naked flesh as it was revealed to her, bit by bit. The strong planes of his chest, his taut abdomen, his hard and beautiful cock. She loved seeing how he wanted her. Needed her. But tonight, she would show him how much she wanted him. Needed him.

She moved toward him, her hand outstretched. He took it, just a tangle of fingers, and let her lead him to the bed. She paused there, ran her hands over his shoulders, his chest, over the hard male nipples. Felt him shiver beneath her touch. And felt her power, and the power of them together.

"You missed a night, Kian," she told him quietly.

He nodded. "Yes, I did. I'm sorry."

"And so tonight, I'm in charge."

With her hands on his shoulders, she pushed him onto

the bed, and he went down onto his back, let her stretch his arms over his head without questioning her.

She watched him for a moment, her body shivering with desire, with that profound sense of having him under her hands. She understood what it meant for a man like Kian to give himself over to anyone. And he was so beautiful, his naked body on her bed, in that attitude of want and surrender. She was wet already.

"Tell me what you need, Kian."

"I need you to touch me," he said, his voice low, full of heat and smoke.

She nodded. "I need to. To touch you. To have you at my mercy, for once. Not to pay you back. I just... need it."

"Yes..."

She stretched out over him, straddling his thigh, and his cock twitched, grazing her skin. But right now she wanted his mouth. She leaned in and took it, brushing his lips with hers. Smiled when she heard his soft moan. She flicked her tongue at his lower lip. He lifted his chin, but she pulled back, just that fraction of an inch which told them both that she was in control.

When he moved his hands she grabbed them, pinned them above his head, held them there. Again, that shock of desire at the knowledge that she was the one in command. Of *this* man. Moving down, she ran her tongue along the sweet skin of his neck. So silky, yet his scent was all male. All sex. Lower still, and she took one of his hard, dusky nipples between her teeth, heard his gasp when she bit down. Desire flooded her. Desire and a deep satisfaction at his pleasure, at her own, at the knowledge that she could do this again and again. That he would be there. And so would she.

Kian arced his hips, the tip of his cock brushing her stomach, but she pulled back. Then, suddenly impatient, she ground down onto him, her slick cleft spreading over his rigid flesh. She sighed as heat shimmered through her system in a long warm coil. She rocked against him, his cock sliding between the lips of her sex, over her hard clitoris. Shock waves rippled through her, stunning her. She could almost come already.

Tilting her hips, she guided his cock and fit it inside her. In one hard thrust, she impaled herself on his flesh.

They both groaned. She caught his gaze. His was all dark fire and aching need. For her.

Her hands on his wrists tightened, her nails biting into him as she began to move, pleasure suffusing her, overwhelming her. His gaze stayed locked on hers, as dark and endless as the night sky. And she sank into them, as he sank into her.

Her body tensed. She hovered at that lovely, wicked edge. She wanted to draw it out, to hold on to it as long as she could.

"Caroline," he gasped. "Please..."

Oh yes, to hear him beg...

She pulled back, let him slip out of her. Hovering over him, she watched his face, watched that lovely expression of agony, his struggle with the need to come. Again, that fierce sense of power flooded her, heady and intense. And she realized it truly didn't matter which one of them was in charge. It was the fact that they gave themselves over to each other in that way. It was the trust implicit in the act. And she understood there was just as much power in letting go as there was in being in control.

"Tell me, Kian," she demanded.

"Caroline..." His voice was a rasping pant.

"Tell me."

"I love you. I need you. I need your body. I need... you."

She smiled as she found his cock once more, lowered her slick heat over that heavy, pulsing flesh. Their moans drifted into the dark.

One more thrust, and she shattered, pleasure coursing through her in blinding flashes. And behind all that fire was his beautiful face, twisting in pleasure as he came, arcing hard into her body, helpless beneath her.

They shuddered together for long moments. His gaze was locked on hers, his dark eyes glossy, hazed, but the intensity was still there, even now.

"I would never have submitted to anyone but you," he whispered to her.

"That's why it means so much."

"It does. I love you, Caroline."

She still could barely believe it. But she trusted it. Trusted him.

"Thank you," he said. "For letting me in."

She looked down at him, at the tenderness in his face. She had never seen anything so beautiful in her life.

"Thank you for making me want to."

They spent an entire week in bed. They left it only long enough to eat on occasion. Some meals they ate in bed, feeding each other, talking quietly. They left the windows open, where they could see the mountains and the desert sky they both loved. They talked about the future, made plans, made love.

They lay in Caroline's big bed on their last night

before they both had to return to work, face-to-face, limbs twined, sated yet still hungry for each other, as always. The white sheets were a tangled pile on the floor. Kian would have to travel soon, to visit his family's resorts on the California coast, in Sedona, in Vail. To begin his new life. Caroline didn't mind, as long as she was a part of it. As long as he came home to her.

"I've realized my house is going to seem awfully small to you, Kian, now that I know how you've lived, in your grand apartments in Europe."

"I was thinking of building a house, an Arabian palace in the desert. What do you think?"

She laughed. She suspected he was serious. "Are you sure, Kian? Are you sure you'll be happy staying in one place, after the kind of life you've led?"

He turned her in his arms, leaned in, and brushed a kiss across her lips. She shivered, as she did whenever he touched her.

"I've been everywhere already. Now the only place I want to be is with you. Except that someday I must show you Paris. We can stay at the George V, explore the city. I know where the best pastries are, better than any in the world. And we must go to see Sacré-Coeur in Montmartre. It's the most beautiful church anywhere. I want to show you everything. We can do anything now, you know."

It was true. Now that she'd found him, had broken through the barriers of her past, anything was possible. She knew he was the only man who could have helped her through it. He was the only man strong enough. Stronger than she was. Strong enough to show her that love allowed her to forgive and trust again. To trust him, to trust herself.

She was finally, truly, on her way to putting the trauma of her past behind her, as she should have done a long time ago. But sometimes things happened as they were meant to. And she was meant to be with him. Perhaps it couldn't have happened any other way.

Things had moved impossibly fast, but that wasn't the important thing. He had taught her how to love. To open herself, physically and emotionally. It still felt risky, loving him. Needing him, allowing him to need her. But she couldn't stop it now. She didn't even want to try.

He loved her. That in itself was a revelation. And it gave her the strength to love him back.

The sun was beginning to set behind the mountains, to touch the sky with streaks of pink and amber light that reflected in the silver and gold of his eyes.

They were supposed to have had only nine days together. Far too short a time to fall in love, to experience the intensity they had together. For her to heal herself. But again, sometimes things were meant to happen a certain way, and there was simply no use fighting it.

She was done fighting. And now, they had all the time in the world.

About the Author

EDEN BRADLEY lives in southern California with a small menagerie and the love of her life. She can be contacted at www.edenbradley.com.

Read on for a sneak peek of

Eden Bradley's

steamy story "The Art of Desire" to be published in

HOT NIGHTS, DARK DESIRES

Coming in summer 2008

HOT
Nights,
DARK
Desires

EDEN   SYDNEY   STEPHANIE
BRADLEY, CROFT & TYLER

Hot Nights, Dark Desires
On sale summer 2008

1.

"DID YOU HEAR ME, Sophie? I'm getting my new tattoo today and I want you to come with me."

Sophie pulled in a breath, trying to concentrate on her friend's words over the sharp buzz of desire running through her system. *Tattoo.* That word, the mere idea, had always had this effect on her. And once more, she hated that she wasn't ever brave enough to indulge her secret yearning.

She shifted her weight, the old wood floor of Crystal's apartment creaking beneath her. "Sorry, Crystal. I was . . . thinking about something. Why isn't Boone going with you?"

"He had a last-minute gig come up, a studio job, so he packed his drumsticks and took off. Anyway, he spent the night last night, and if he came with me he'd want to stay again. If I let him stay too often, he'll begin to think he owns me. You know how I hate that."

Sophie rolled her eyes and laughed.

"I don't want to go alone, Sophie; say you'll come with me." Crystal turned around on the old, wobbly piano bench that sat in front of her baby grand, where she'd been playing and singing when Sophie had knocked at her door. "Hey, you're not afraid, are you? I know the whole tattoo thing freaks some people out."

"No, I'm not afraid. I mean, I guess I am, but it's because..."

Sophie stopped herself. How much to tell? She'd known Crystal for only three months, since she'd moved into the apartment upstairs. She certainly couldn't tell her new friend that she had such an intense attraction to the idea of tattoos, of being tattooed, that it bordered on obsession. That even thinking about it caused her entire body to surge with an unexplainable, searing lust.

She looked out through the French doors behind Crystal's piano, through the paned glass with its peeling white paint, to the small enclosed courtyard with its overgrown greenery, the profusion of flowers whose perfume fought against the smell of mold and decaying plaster in the air.

This place was like something out of a dingy, perverse dream: old pink stucco that was literally falling down at the corners, every window graced with the intricate black ironwork New Orleans French Quarter architecture was famous for, the wide-plank wood floors countless generations had walked over before her. Sophie had loved the place immediately. And she and Crystal had taken to each other right away, too. But she had to pay attention to what Crystal was saying.

"Because why, Sophie?" Her friend's exotic turquoise eyes were trained on her.

Sophie shrugged, trying to dispel the knot forming in her stomach. Trying to make this all less important. "I've always had a sort of fascination with tattoos," she admitted. "I've always wanted to get one. You have no idea how badly."

"Then why don't you? I don't get it."

"God, Crystal, I can't!"

"Why not? You're a writer, Sophie. It's not like you have to clock in at an office, wear a suit every day. Or, God forbid, panty hose. And with the stuff you write, all those ghosts and vampires, people probably expect you to be a little eccentric, anyway. So, why not?"

Yes, why not, indeed? She tugged on the end of her dark, waist-length brown hair, twisting a strand around her fingers. Maybe because the rules her strict Italian-Catholic parents had ingrained into her ran far too deeply for her to ever completely escape from? Maybe because, despite the fact that she'd escaped their house, she could never quite get away from what they'd taught her about who she was, and what she should be?

She hated that no matter how far she'd run—and she'd spent most of her life since the age of eighteen running, all over the country—they still had a hold on her. She'd never managed to shake the sound of their voices in her head.

"Why can't you be more like your brother?"

Maybe because her brother, that uptight, sanctimonious snob, was a priest.

Crystal snapped her fingers in front of Sophie's face. "Hey, where are you?"

"Sorry." Sophie shook her head. "This tattoo thing

is... an issue for me. A huge issue, if you want to know the truth."

"Yeah, I can see that." Crystal flipped one of her thick, dark braids over her shoulder and leaned back, resting her elbow on the keys of the piano, and a small clash of chords sounded. "I think you should do it. You obviously want to. And if something is holding you back, then maybe the only way to ever face down that issue is just to go for it."

"You're probably right."

Just the idea was sending tremors over her skin, making her warm all over. She could never tell Crystal the real reason that she was so afraid of being tattooed. She was afraid she would love it too much.

Crystal leaned forward and put a hand on Sophie's arm. "Look, why don't you just come with me and see? This artist is a friend of Boone's. I've seen some of his work and he's really good. It can't hurt to sit and watch me, right?"

"I suppose not." She took in another breath as her pulse fluttered with excitement. Crystal was right; there was no harm in watching. And to be that close to the process, to see it happen...irresistible. "When is your appointment?"

Crystal glanced at her watch. "In about twenty minutes. The shop is just down on Canal Street, but we should get going. I let Boone take my car, so we'll have to walk."

Her heart skittered in her chest. "Now?"

"Yes, now." Crystal laughed as she stood up. "Come on, Sophie. I don't want to be late."

* * *

They walked down their little street that was really nothing more than a cobblestone alley, onto Dauphine and turned right, headed toward Canal Street. The air was damp and close around them, but Sophie liked it, enjoyed the feel of it, soft on her skin.

They passed the crumbling buildings, the lovely old architecture a beautiful combination of French, Spanish, and Caribbean influences. Sophie loved the look of the French Quarter: the colors, even the decay caused by the constant heaviness of the tropical air. Many of these places were literally falling apart at the seams. Small piles of plaster lay at the corners of the buildings, the red brick underneath showing through. No one bothered to clean it up. And everywhere vines clung to the walls, climbed the iron balconies, trailed across the tiled roofs, in brilliant shades of green in between the flowers. New Orleans was pure magic to her. Dark magic, to be sure. The first place she'd found that felt like home.

Crystal took her hand as they walked, humming a tune.

"Is that a new song?" Sophie asked her.

"Yeah, Boone and I were working on it late last night. Sex always inspires me."

"Crystal!"

"What?" Crystal turned to her, smiling, a wicked gleam in the tilt of her blue eyes. The sooty black eyeliner she always wore made them stand out against her pale complexion. "What could possibly be more inspirational than sex? That feel of skin against skin, that buildup, and then..."

"Okay! That's more than I need to know about your sex life." Sophie shook her head. "Tell me about the tattoo you want to get."

"Well, you've seen the little Cheshire cat on my ankle. He's cute, and I love him, but I wanted something more meaningful this time. So, I went to talk to Tristan Batiste—he's the artist—and he helped me figure out the design. It'll be two koi fish, arched around each other like a Yin Yang symbol, with their fins sort of fanning out. And they'll be all in black and white, which is Tristan's specialty. I love the idea of the image being all about contrast. It seems symbolic of the Yin Yang. Opposites, you know?"

"Yes, light and dark. Balance."

"Exactly."

Crystal swung their clasped hands as they walked, turning left down Canal Street. They passed colorful cafés, funky used-clothing stores, antiques shops. And everywhere, people lined the sidewalks. It was mostly locals here, the wealthy old New Orleans gentry as well as the more bohemian younger crowd.

"Here it is." Crystal stopped in front of a storefront with a blue neon sign in the window that spelled out "Beneath the Skin." The glass was painted in classic Japanese style: tsunami waves, cranes flying against a backdrop of snow-capped mountains, warrior gods with frightening faces, brandishing swords.

"Wow. This is beautiful." Sophie reached out to lay her fingertips against the cool glass. "Did he do all this?"

"Tristan? Yeah. He owns the shop. Come on, wait until you see what he can do on skin."

On skin. Yes...

Just thinking about it made her shiver with anticipation. She followed Crystal into the shop.

Inside, the cool air washed over her, raising gooseflesh on her skin for a moment before her body adjusted. Music played, a hard-driving rock song. Godsmack, she thought. She looked around curiously. She'd never actually been inside a tattoo parlor before. The first thing she noticed was the enormous carved desk to her right, a beautiful Asian piece. A tall, skinny man with fully tattooed arms stood behind it, bent over an appointment book.

Crystal approached him. "Hi. I'm here to see Tristan."

"Sure, I'll get him."

He came around the desk and disappeared through a heavy gold velvet curtain. Sophie and Crystal sat on a wooden bench against one wall to wait.

Sophie's heart was pounding as though she were the one about to be tattooed. She glanced at Crystal, who was humming her new song again, as calm as though she were there to get a massage.

"Aren't you nervous, Crys?"

"Why should I be? I've done this before. It doesn't really hurt much, you know. God, you're pale, Sophie." Crystal laughed, taking her hand and giving it a squeeze. "Maybe you'll relax when you see how hot Tristan is."

"Hey, Crystal."

Sophie looked up to find a man coming through the curtain. He was tall and broad; a football player's physique outlined by his fitted black T-shirt and worn jeans. His head was nearly shaved, just a layer of dark stubble showing against his skin. Square features, partially covered by a dark, close-cut goatee. But the most striking thing about him was his eyes. They were a dark shade of gray, like smoke. Striking. Intense.

Sophie blinked, letting her gaze fall to the dragons tattooed in coils of black, red, and gold around both arms. The work was exquisite, she saw right away. But that wasn't the only reason why her entire body was lighting up with need.

Calm down.

She had to tear her gaze away, to look instead at the samurai swords that decorated the wall behind the desk. To catch her thready breath.

But then Crystal was standing up, pulling Sophie with her. "Hi Tristan. This is my friend, Sophie Fiore. She's going to sit with me today."

"No problem. Hey there, Sophie."

Deep voice, with a beautiful accent; a little of the South mixed in with that exotic European inflection so many people in New Orleans spoke with. And oh God, he was holding his hand out to her. She couldn't very well refuse to take it. His fingers wrapped around hers, warm and strong. Her knees went weak.

Pull yourself together!

But he was still hanging on to her hand, making it hard to think. And he was looking at her, a small smile on his strong mouth. Too beautiful, this man. She tried to smile back, to behave normally.

"It's nice to meet you, Tristan."

"Very," he murmured, staring at her a moment too long. Then, "Let's get started."

He released her hand and she had to pull in a deep breath of the air-conditioned air to cool her system, to clear her head. She felt as though she'd just been slammed in the chest by a wall of heat.

And pure desire.

Was it this man? Was it being here, in this place? Was it the sheer ecstasy and fright of being so close to her most secret and powerful fantasy?

But she had to follow Crystal through the curtain, which Tristan held aside for them. As she passed, she caught a faint whiff of his scent, something dark and fresh at the same time. Like the deepest part of a forest.

God, she must be losing her mind.

Behind the curtain were six workstations; some with leather chairs, some with long padded tables, all of the furniture covered in black, making a strong contrast to the red-painted walls. Two of the stations were in use. To her left, a short, stocky woman with a shock of spiky white-blond hair was bent over a man lying on one of the tables, a humming tattoo gun in one gloved hand, a white cloth in the other. To her right, the tall man they'd first seen out front was talking with a female client, showing her drawings of what she assumed were tattoo designs.

Her pulse was racing.

Tristan led them to the largest workstation, one which spanned the width of the back of the room. There was another padded table, and one of the big chairs. It reminded her of a dentist's chair, everything adjustable. And, she noticed, everything was spotlessly clean.

"Climb on up, Crystal." Tristan patted the table and Crystal sat down on the edge while he pulled out a drawer in a metal cabinet built into one wall. "I have your design here. Take one last look and make sure it's right."

Crystal took a translucent piece of paper from him, smiled, then passed it to Sophie. "It's perfect. What do you think?"

Sophie nodded, and handed the paper back to her friend. "Yes, it's beautiful." But she'd hardly glanced at it. She was too shaken up inside. Trying too hard not to look at Tristan.

"Sophie, why don't you take a seat here?" Tristan laid a hand on the back of the big chair.

Too good, to sit in that chair. Too close to her fantasy. She trembled a little as she slipped into the seat.

Crystal was unbuttoning her army-green cargo pants and pulling her white tank top up around her waist, settling onto her stomach on the table. Tristan leaned over her, wiped the skin at the small of her back with a white cloth. Sophie watched as he took the transfer paper and laid it at the base of Crystal's spine, then smoothed his hand over it. Then he carefully pulled the paper away, leaving an imprint of the design on Crystal's skin.

All Sophie could think was, *it's going to start now.*

Her heart was hammering harder and harder as she watched Tristan pull on a pair of latex gloves, check his equipment. The intensity of his expression as he bent over her friend, the tattoo gun buzzing in his big hand, was almost too much for her, but she couldn't look away. And when he touched the needle to Crystal's skin, Sophie jumped inside as though it were her own. Shock filtered through her in waves. And lust stabbed through her like a lovely, hot knife.

God.

She never knew she would respond this way to simply watching this. She shifted in her seat, trying to ease the ache that had started between her thighs.

It only got worse—or better, depending on how one looked at it—as she watched Tristan work. The muscles in his forearms flexed as he worked the ink into Crystal's flesh, and she saw the dusky golden tone of his skin beneath the tattoos.

She took the opportunity to really look at him, letting her gaze wander over his features. He really did have an incredible face. Beautiful, yet thoroughly male at the same time. An aquiline nose, a strong jaw. And his voice was deep and husky, rolling over her like whiskey each time he spoke.

"I'm done with the outline, Crystal. Now for the shading. How are you doing?"

"I'm a little sore, but it's fine."

"We'll take a break for a minute." Tristan looked up at Sophie, his gun poised. "And what about you?"

His dark gray gaze on her was too intense, too piercing. She didn't know what to say.

Crystal spoke up. "Sophie's always wanted to get a tattoo."

"Really?" His brows rose a fraction of an inch, making his eyes seem even more penetrating.

"Yes." Her voice was barely a whisper. She swallowed, hard.

"Do you know what you'd want, Sophie? What sort of design?"

She nodded. This was something she'd thought about for years. "I like . . . the Kanji symbol for 'create.'"

"She's a writer," Crystal interjected. "She's just sold her first book. She'll be published soon."

"An artist, then." Tristan nodded. "What do you write?"

"Paranormal. Ghost stories, vampires. Dark stuff."

"Ah, you're in the perfect place, then, New Orleans."

"Yes, it is. I've been going to the old cemeteries. They're so beautiful." She let out a nervous laugh. "That must sound strange to you."

"Not at all." He smiled, his teeth a strong flash of white that sent a warm chill down her spine. "A true artist can find beauty in anything. Everything. But some things are, by nature, more beautiful than others."

He paused, his eyes locked on hers. What was he saying, implying? She was going hot all over.

He went on. "I've done a lot of sketches at the cemeteries myself, the Cities of the Dead, we call them. Some headstone tracings. Saint Roch is my favorite. I love the starkness there, the statuary, the gray and white stones. It's a shadow place."

"I haven't been there yet. I've only been in New Orleans for a few months."

"Ah, well, it's not to be missed."

Still hard to talk, with him looking at her like that, with her pulse racing at a thousand miles an hour. Why did his gaze on her feel like a caress? And that he understood her fascination with the graveyards! Was she imagining this sense of connection?

He glanced back at Crystal, lying quietly on the table still. "Are you ready to begin again?"

"Yep. Let's finish it. I can't wait to see how it looks."

He dipped his tattoo gun in a small pot of ink, leaned over Crystal, and began once more. The electric hum of the equipment seemed to resonate deep in Sophie's body, in her breasts, between her thighs. She couldn't look away as he moved over Crystal's skin, the needle pushing the ink into her flesh.

She wanted to do it. She'd wanted to for as long as she could remember. And to have Tristan be the one to do this to her for the first time...the idea of it was too good. But could she really do it?

Hell, she was never going to be what her family wanted her to be. That had been perfectly clear for a long time. She hadn't even talked to any of them in months. She'd gotten tired of the constant recriminations. Why did she still allow herself to be manipulated by them? This was her body, her life. They didn't like that she was a common fiction writer, either. Useless, they called her career. And her mother was convinced she'd been influenced by the devil, simply because of her subject matter.

Sophie knew it was ridiculous. So why did she let what they wanted hold her back from what she wanted for herself?

As she watched Tristan fill in the shading on the gorgeously drawn koi fish, she became more and more convinced that if she were ever going to do it, to get tattooed, he *must* be the one. And frankly, the idea of this man putting his hands on her was irresistible. Almost frightening how overwhelming her attraction to him was.

"Okay, you're all done," Tristan announced, giving Crystal's skin one final wipe with his white cloth. "Go take a look in the mirror."

He helped Crystal to sit up, steadied her with a hand on her arm as she stood. A gentleman, Sophie thought vaguely. Nice.

Crystal stood before the full-length mirror on one wall, looking over her shoulder. "Oh, I love it. It's exactly what I wanted! Sophie, you really should get one."

Tristan turned his penetrating gaze on her once more. Yes, exactly like smoke, those eyes. "Well? What do you think, Sophie? Are you ready?"

"What? Now?"

"I have an open schedule today. It could be now. Or another day. It's up to you. But I'd be honored to work on you. To be your first."

He grinned down at her and she felt her cheeks go hot. The question was not whether she wanted to do this, but could she? She wanted to, with her entire being. All but that censorious voice in her head that was becoming more and more faint by the minute.

Crystal was still admiring her new tattoo in front of the mirror. "You should go for it, Sophie. You know you want to. And Tristan's the best."

Oh, she wanted to. Her heart skipped a beat as certainty washed through her, making her go weak all over. Yet strong on the inside, somehow. There was strength in choosing her own path. She'd come to understand that in the last few years. Or, she'd thought she had. Maybe this was that last step she had to take before she was truly free?

She looked at Tristan, right into those impossibly dark eyes of his that seemed to see through her.

She nodded her head, beginning to shake inside with nerves and heat and yearning. "I'm ready."